LINSENBIGLER

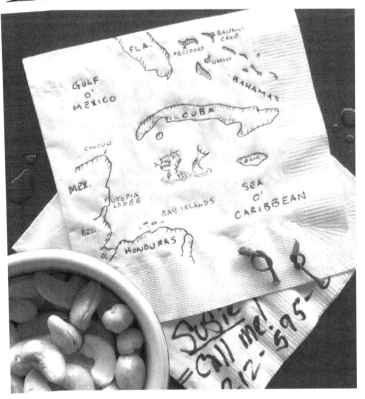

BRIAN M. WIPRUD

ISBN: 154649409X
ISBN-13:9781546494096

DEDICATION

For Joanne, as always.

ACKNOWLEDGMENTS

Many thanks to my friend C.J. Box
for providing the preface.

PREFACE

I **DON'T** think I'll ever forget meeting Boone Linsenbigler, but there is a substantial period of it I can't actually remember.

Fly Fishing for trout on Rocky Mountain rivers is my passion. The problem with this kind of fishing is winter. I can't fish for at least five months a year because to do so means dodging huge chunks of floating ice and getting stuck in the snow going to the river as well as coming back home. So when a fishing buddy of mine suggested a sun-splashed holiday bonefishing in the Bahamas in February I was all over it. I'd never fished for bonefish or been to the Bahamas before. But it was February in Wyoming and I was tired of clearing snowdrifts with my tractor.

My buddy booked a week at a tropical resort he was familiar with. It was exotic, right on the beach, and with a view of the ocean. There were several other serious fishermen there but it was a sleepy place and all anyone talked about was fishing. My kind of place. However, I was nervous about going after the legendary bonefish in the flats. It required a larger rod than I usually use and heavy flies that looked like crabs instead of the tiny insects. Luckily, my buddy had been bonefishing many times and I drafted in his wake. He was on a first-name basis with the guides and the owner of the lodge. They called him "Cowboy" since he was from Wyoming and I was a little embarrassed how much he played it up.

On Day One our captain poled us out near the mangroves and he spotted several bonefish under the surface. Before I could even strip line from my reel to cast, "Cowboy" threw a beautiful crab-fly at the fish and hooked one. The fish made a wild run but threw the hook. The crab fly slingshotted back across the top of the water and hit Cowboy in the groin with a solid "*thwack!*"

Cowboy dropped his rod, doubled over, and fell into the bottom of the boat. An ambulance greeted us at the dock and drove him away. He called me that night in a drugged stupor and said the tip of his penis looked like "a purple light bulb." He repeated that description several times. I knew we wouldn't be fishing the next day and probably not at all.

SO, ALONE and a little depressed, I made my way from my bungalow toward the bar. Even before I got there I could tell something was very different. There was loud music and raised voices. I hadn't heard *Herb Alpert and the Tijuana Brass* for, oh, forty years.

Something was seriously different.

When I poked my head inside the bar the din got louder. New fishermen had apparently arrived and they'd taken the place by storm.

Thomas, the jet-black petulant bartender, was no longer behind the bar but spinning around on a stool in

LINSENBIGLER

front of it with a drink in his hand.   The serious fly fishermen from the night before were crooning *A Taste of Honey* out of tune and hoisting cocktail glasses. A sultry woman in a short skirt leaned an elbow on the bar and took a long seductive drag from a brown cigarette in a gold-plated holder. In the corner, two dark men wearing sunglasses kept their own counsel in a way that suggested to me they were up to no good.

And greeting me from behind the bar was a gleeful fop with a serious mustache who motioned to me to have a seat.

Despite my misgivings and my dislike of frivolity, I sat.

For some reason, I thought I'd met the man behind the bar before. He looked familiar and I wracked my brain to try to figure out where we'd met. Whoever he was, he'd somehow convinced the surly Thomas to switch places.

"The sports are swilling my special Pineapple Dragon," he said as he grinned toward the singing anglers, "May I whip one up for you?"

"No thank you. I'd like a bourbon on the rocks."

The man looked at me like I'd just ordered a plain hamburger at In-N-Out.

"I'll pour whatever you'd like me to pour," he said with a wink. "But do you trust me to make the best Bourbon drink you've ever had in your life?"

I thought about it for a moment and said sure.

The man grinned his approval.

"I know you…" I said.

He nodded. But that wasn't helpful.

Then it dawned on me. I'd seen the name and the face on a product but I'd never actually met the man before. I'd also seen him on commercials, and heard about him on the news. He was a *brand*. It was like meeting Orville Redenbacher, the popcorn guy. Right there in front of me.

"You're Linsenbigler."

He took a moment while assembling my drink and thrust out his hand. "Call me Boone," he said.

"*Boone* Linsenbigler?"

"The same," he said while he slid an amber drink toward me in a martini glass, garnished with a long coil of orange peel and a coffee bean in the bottom. "And this is the Linsenbigler Manhattan."

He paused while I took a sip. I wanted not to like it for some reason. But it was the best drink I'd ever had and it filled me with ... joy.

"Crafted with my own special cocktail bitters," he said.

I didn't know what bitters were. They sounded bitter, but weren't, and I downed the drink more quickly than I intended.

"Another?" he asked.

"Another."

WHEN I AWOKE we were on a skiff with the captain poling us toward the mangroves. Linsenbigler was in the front holding his fly rod as if it were a Samurai sword. My head pounded in pain.

"You're up!" he said with too much cheer. "That's good because the bonefish are ripe for the taking!"

"How did I get here?"

"You insisted on sleeping on the boat to not miss our outing," he said. "Last night you told me you've never caught a bonefish, and I agreed to accompany you to show you the ropes. So here I am to assist! Now let me see your fly."

I was confused at first but I handed him the rod and fly I'd been using the day before. Linsenbigler studied the crab fly for a moment, scoffed aloud, and glared at our captain for recommending it. The captain looked away.

"Here," he said. "You must use one of mine."

He dug into a fly box and produced something that looked like a small glittery rodent that had been run over by a fleet of semi-trailers. It looked nothing like the flies I'd been using.

He tied it on.

"What is it?"

"My own invention. I call it the Ginger-Tongued Pizzle."

WE CLOSED in on the bonefish. Linsenbigler insisted I make the first cast.

"Remember," he said. "It's not about casting. It's about catching fish. Throw it out there and strip it back like a madman."

I did and I caught my first bonefish. And then my second, third, and fourth. I was on the fifth when I heard Linsenbigler rattling a cocktail shaker over his shoulder to make what he called a "Bonefish Wahoo."

ON THE way back to the lodge, he said, "So you don't remember anything last night?"

"No."

"You don't remember those two men in the corner?"

"No."

"You don't recall the knife fight?"

"The *knife fight?*"

"It's all for the best," he assured me. "Better you can enjoy a good day fishing without guilt or remorse."

"Remorse for what?"

"Never mind," he laughed. "Forget it. It happens to me all the time. It happens everywhere I go, it seems. I'm like a Ginger-Tongued Pizzle. Trouble is inexplicably drawn to me."

LINSENBIGLER WAS the best angler I've ever encountered. He was also the best cocktail maker. Yet his real talent seemed to be finding himself in the wrong place at the wrong time, like the previous night.

"My life has become a series of misadventures," he said.

"Have you ever thought about writing it all down?" I asked as we cut the engine and glided in toward the dock. "It might make a great book."

"That takes time I would rather spend on fishing, cocktails, and the ladies," he lamented. "But if you buy me a drink I'll tell you the story of how my exploits began..."

C.J. Box, 2017, Saratoga, Wyoming

CHAPTER 1

I WAS THRUST into moderate fame when a brand of cocktail bitters bearing my bewhiskered likeness – and name – went viral.

In my basement apartment, the kitchen was the factory where the bitters were made. Bottling occurred in the living room, where I applied labels by hand. Through some drinksology blogs I distributed a few bottles to fellow cocktail enthusiasts. Wild and unexpected acclaim followed as cocktail-savvy social media latched onto my bitters as a 'find.' Rarity made the bitters even more popular – bartenders were stalking me in an attempt to 'score' a bottle. Before you knew it, I had a long waiting list, and I was struggling to maintain my freelance writing career.

As luck would have it, the popularity of my bitters came to the attention of executives at Conglomerated Beverages, a multinational corporation that owns many famous distilleries and brands. Several greying men in suits took me to dinner and told me Conglomerated liked the cut of my jib: the name, the rakishly curled mustache, the mane of wavy brown hair, the athletic build, the hype

– and lastly – the bitters. Others had come before me: Captain Morgan, The World's Most Interesting Man, Spuds MacKenzie. Conglomerated wanted to brand me and sell the living daylights out of my bitters in association with their other brands. They wanted Everyman to feel that he, too, could make fancy cocktails if only he subscribed to the full line of expensive bitters, tinctures, tonics and sugar cubes bearing the name and dashing likeness of Boone Linsenbigler.

I was only too happy to oblige, selling the secret recipe and contracting to be their promotional totem for a fat annual salary.

Not much past my fortieth birthday, the S.S. Fortune had finally sailed into port, surfacing like a giant sleek submarine from beneath the waves.

I was a well-known fly angler and free-lance writer at the time, but marginally successful if were you to inspect my 1040. A choice salaried position at an established fly fishing magazine eluded me. My existence was pretty much hand to mouth, and month to month. I never had any money to travel and fish exotic locations that beckoned me from the colorful pages of the magazines. However, as a 'brand' with a thick wallet, I *did* have money, enough so that I did not have to write, which meant I had time *and* money. So to the devil with scratching out articles about crease flies, rubber hackle, back casts, trailing loops, furled leaders and Bimini twists – I was just going to travel and fish and keep my mustache in shape for the commercials. And keep an eye out for the ladies. How utterly improbable that a second-tier freelance fishing writer and bar fly could fall into so much clover?

As a way of embracing my brand, I was sent by my publicist to a coach who enhanced my vocabulary and mannerisms accordingly. This intensive course lasted several months and upon matriculation, I dare say that my Jersey accent and f-bomb vocabulary had been entirely supplanted. They taught me how to move more gracefully, improved my posture, and enhanced my public speaking acumen. If I was going to play the Master Cocktailer, I had to be *grand*.

Which was how I blundered into a different kind of fame about a year into my contract with Conglomerated.

I had been a figurehead for a little over a year when I journeyed to yet another flats fishing destination, one on the northern Mayan Coast. Flats fishing is pretty much what it sounds like – angling huge mud or sand flats flooded by tides. In turn, fish swim into these shallow waters seeking food, like crustaceans buried in the bottom. For the angler, the attraction of flats fishing is principally that the water is so shallow that you can see the fish and cast to them. Seeing the quarry can be challenging in and unto itself because you have to have an aptitude for picking out their shapes moving through water rippling with wave shadows. Fly fishing makes the sport livelier because you are flinging the line at a distance and using your hands in large part to manage the line. The reel is only used once the fish is hooked and running. Usually, the "flats" fishing destinations are not relegated entirely to the flats, but also to fishing nearby channels and mangroves for snook and tarpon.

After a hard day of fishing in the blazing sun, and after an equally hard evening of swilling Pineapple Dragons and arguing the dubious merits of switch rods, my bladder roused me from slumber. I was in a spacious second floor suite at the Boca Boca Tarpon Lodge, curtains billowing with sea breeze, moonlight and the scent of bougainvillea. Toilets at some of these far-flung tropical fishing lodges have more difficulties than those back in New Jersey. Significantly more difficulties, either due to the brackish water eroding the plumbing or the lack of plumbers experienced in the nuances of a porcelain crapper. This is a long way around saying that my toilet was broken. I had no wish to contribute further to the sad state of affairs in the commode, and so having a penchant for the great outdoors, I picked up the remainder of the Pineapple Dragon on the bed stand and stumbled toward the balcony.

Crude? Vulgar? Yes, I suppose so, and micturating off the balcony at the Boca Boca Tarpon Lodge was likely frowned upon. Alas, who would suspect the Grand Cocktailer, the one whose flowing whiskers endignified the label of *Boone Linsenbigler's Plain and Fancy Cocktail Bitters*, of such a boorish act? Which was exactly the point and why I elected to do it – out of perversity and mischief.

And likely as not because I was still a little snookered.

Mug of booze in hand, buck naked, I stepped onto the moonlit porch.

Swaying palm trees bracketed the black ocean check-marked by white caps, a dusting of stars beyond. Tomorrow, I mused, would not be a good day of fishing: windy. Damn.

I set my drink on the railing and prepared to get down to the business at hand, so to speak.

As fate would have it, the railing before me was not flat on top, but round, and the mug slipped off the railing toward the ground below. I hoped it would miss the steps to the lower unit below and land with a gentle thud on the sand.

Fate was certainly in the air, even if my whiz was not – a person suddenly emerged from the porch below onto the steps, intercepting the heavy glass mug on its journey.

The sound of mug on skull was a loud 'THOK' and the poor soul below reeled from the impact, stumbled and fell back onto porch below with a deafening crash of collapsing deck furniture.

Well, it was clear at that juncture of the proceedings that I would have to go back inside and tinkle in the sink. People would soon appear. Bereft of my buckskins, I didn't fancy an audience or blame for the injury to the unfortunate night owl who intercepted the mug.

Let's get something straight: I appear dignified and noble. The key word being 'appear.' Clearly, the fact that I was set to urinate off a balcony in the middle of the night – that I resumed drinking in the middle of the night – that I skulked back into my lodgings in the middle of the night after seriously (albeit mistakenly) injuring someone – indicates otherwise. This does not mean I am not a nice person. I like animals and even some people. However, my submarine had surfaced and by God I intended to sail that ship for all it was worth. Damn the torpedoes and all that.

Having made use of the sink, I slid back into bed but heard considerable commotion downstairs. More and more of the other guests and the staff were arriving to see what was going on. There was no way I would have been able to sleep through the hubbub – it would have looked suspicious had I not made an appearance and inquired innocently what was going on.

I put on a robe, unquivered a cigar from my travel humidor, and stepped out onto the porch, flaming the cheroot as I approached the rail, the very picture of nonchalance. Below, now lit by porch lights, I saw six guests, the bar tender and the lodge manager encircling the stricken man who'd been tossed on a chaise longue in front of the lower porch. The man was Mexican, and he was dressed all in black. Before I could say anything – and thankfully, I did not – the lodge manager turned his portly visage up at me and said: "It's the burglar!" In his hand was a pile of jewelry no doubt liberated from the stricken man's pockets. "He cut the screen into Bungalow One!"

There had been a series of nighttime burglaries at the local fishing lodges, and in one case, the criminal attempted to rape a sleeping guest in addition to stealing her jewelry. Despite added security measures, the fiend had persisted.

One of the guests, named Bob – the one with whom I had been drinking that evening and discussing fishing tackle – picked up my Pineapple Dragon mug from the sand. He inspected it, and looked up at me. Bob knew I had been drinking from a similar if not identical mug earlier. He looked at the mug, the stricken man and then at me again. Two and two had come together in Bob's mind.

Cunning was required on my part. I could have said it was an accident. I could have said that I came naked to pee off my balcony and put my drink on the railing and it slipped off.

I chose to avert embarrassment.

Without really committing to it, I floated a yarn out there to see if it would stick, thinking I could easily retract it as a joke, but thought it funny that people might actually believe it. Lest we forget, I was still a little drunk.

From his perch on high, Boone Linsenbigler tweaked his mustache:

"As you see, I have subdued the burglar." I waved my cigar in the air in a grand gesture. "I had decided that it was my duty to watch and protect Boca Boca from villainy. And so I stood sentry on my balcony, keeping a sharp eye. He came from the side onto the lower porch, so I did not see him approach, rather I heard porch boards creaking and the screen being cut. Had I sounded the alarm, the burglar surely would have escaped. Instead, I laid in wait for his eventual emergence, and when he appeared, I used my cocktail mug as a projectile, disabling the scoundrel."

They all gasped, looking at the mug in Bob's hand, at the unconscious burglar in the chaise longue, and at me. Everybody but Bob swallowed the yarn hook, line, sinker, rod and reel. Bob didn't say anything. Could he be a hundred percent sure I was a liar? Though he knew that I had consumed six Pineapple Dragons, rendering my tale borderline ridiculous.

The local police arrived and took the groggy burglar away. After a round or two of free drinks at the bar and much back slapping for my heroics, I made my way majestically back to my lodging, proud of being the successful liar that I was.

When I returned to New Jersey the following week, I found that the story of this singular exploit had made the rounds of the fishing discussion boards, but more ominously, all the way back to Terry Orbach, my publicist at Conglomerated. He invited me to lunch, so I took a train to New York and met him at a famous cocktail bar. Terry would never meet me anywhere other than famous cocktail bars in Manhattan because he wanted to parade the one, the only Boone Linsenbigler before the cocktail-savvy public. Most fancy bartenders did not like me as they knew this was all sort of a sham. But only because they play the game as well. They have the smart vests and whiskers and bow ties; they are selling an image just the same as I. Perhaps they dislike being upstaged, or the notion that Everyman can make his own damn cocktails just as well as a bartender can, if not better, with or without my products. Indeed, I invented a new kind of bitters but I don't actually like many of the vogue cocktails they make these days. Yet I'm obliged to indulge in them when I am out in public view, and of course insist that my own products be part of the recipe. So I ordered a Pimm's Cup, a vile concoction of lemonade (Boon Linsenbigler's Citrus Fizz, I've been directed to push that product), cucumbers and gin. It was all I could do to look at it. Give me a Pineapple Dragon any day.

To me, Terry looks like a weevil: short, squat, with long hooked nose – and he scuttles when he moves from place to place. He is indelibly sly, and manipulative, which I suppose is the mark of a good publicist. He sat at the adjoining barstool looking pleased with himself.

"Boone!" Terry gripped my shoulder. "This story about the burglar in Boca Boca is just fantastic. Super stuff, just the kind of thing that Conglomerated needs to concretize your brand. How would you like to go to the Bahamas?"

I pushed my Pimm's cup aside. "My next trip is to Louisiana for redfish."

"What I mean is that Conglomerated is sending you to the Bahamas. I know I asked if you'd *like* to go, but we *need* you to go."

"You want to send me fishing in the Bahamas? Your dime?" I smoothed my mustache. "Really?"

He gripped my shoulder harder. "Yes! That's it in a nutshell."

"Why?"

"Because it's super stuff, these trips. The team is working on a commercial campaign centered on your exploits. The first one will be about how you subdued the burglar with a cocktail. I mean, it just doesn't get any more super than that."

This was going somewhere, and I wasn't sure entirely where – yet.

"Well, Terry, I can't guarantee that anything as *super* as dropping a cocktail on the head of a burglar will happen in the Bahamas. I mean, it was a fluke, really. More like an accident."

"That was no accident!" Terry recoiled. "Boone Linsenbigler is not only the pre-eminent man about town and cocktail genius, but he is also a crime solver!"

"I went out onto the balcony that night to pee."

"That's a lie!" he thundered. "Conglomerated will sue anybody who says so for defamation! Libel!"

I chuckled, incredulous. "So what exactly do you propose I do in the Bahamas – manufacture some sort of crime and then solve it? That's absurd."

He shook his head vigorously, the long hooked nose wobbling. "Not the plan. There's already a crime, and we're sending you down there to solve it."

I held up a hand to silence Terry and waved over the bartender. "Give me a double Old Forester, on the rocks, twist of lemon." I grimaced at the Pimm's Cup. "And you can take that away." I turned back to Terry. "I am not a policeman. I am not a detective. I am an angler and a boozehound who just happens to be your front man. The last time I did any acting was when I worked as a kid at Medieval Knights dinner theater in Ho-Ho-Kus."

"Acting?" He shook his head patronizingly. "Boone, *you're a brand!* You're what we say you are."

More to the point, I was contractually obligated to promote my line of products wherever they told me to go.

A week later, I was on a flight to Nassau.

CHAPTER 2

BY THE TIME THE AIRLINER tires scrunched onto the tropical tarmac of Lynden Pindling International Airport, my anxiety over the task at hand was largely dispelled. And not because of the eight vodka miniatures I had tippled at cruising altitude. My angst had been quelled by the simple fact that failure was as inevitable as it was desirable. It was one thing to strut around cocktail events tweaking my mustache and charming the ladies. Tangling with bad guys and derring-do was not in my wheelhouse.

From my first-class perch near the airplane's hatchway, I was on the gangway into the terminal in a jiffy. A representative from the lodge was to meet me and shuttle me to a hotel for an overnight. The next morning he would pick me up again and bring me back for a propeller flight to the actual lodge located on a far-flung scrap of sand and palms. I imagined myself dining that evening in Nassau by lamplight at the lush and leafy Café Picasso, as usual, curried prawns and champagne my only companions.

It was a surprise when – after scanning the arrival gate for the usual ragamuffin that would be my valet –

that I was approached by a busty tanned gem in her thirties. She wore a snug white halter top, white shorts and espadrilles on her feet. A wild streak of blonde sliced across her chestnut mane. Her violet eyes fixed on mine, the kind of startling eyes that men fear but likewise can't resist: they were the eyes of trouble. Yet it is the sad fate of men that they are rarely able to repel trouble incarnate in a halter top.

She sashayed up to where I stood and hooked her arm through mine – she smelled of coconut, perhaps suntan lotion. Turning me toward the baggage claim, she purred:

"What's your favorite position, Mr. Linsenbigler?"

As we began our walk toward baggage claim, I considered the question carefully. I was not sure what she meant: could this be a political position, or a position on some greater social issue, like gun control? And just when I suspected that I did know what she meant I felt that I must be mistaken. She clarified before I could respond:

"I like doggie style. I feel a person's favorite position says a lot about a person. Missionary is fine, of course, but that's what most persons do, and so is kind of boring. I'm down with reverse cowgirl, too, but the penetration isn't quite as boss. Hay stacking is groovy but it's hard on my neck. My name is Tabatha."

I finished a rapid series of blinks, smiled politely, and said. "You can call me Boone." I made a mental note to look up *hay stacking* at my earliest opportunity.

"So what's your favorite position, Boone?"

She was not going to go unanswered, so I parried:

"That depends on whom I'm with, Tabatha."

"Slick answer, Boone."

I decided to steer a course to a more conventional line of conversation. "So how long have you worked for Banana Cay Lodge?"

"Long enough, too long. How long are you?"

I could see that inimitable tact on my part would be required with this girl.

"Long enough, but not too long."

"Another slick answer, Boone. I'm pitching it out there, and you swing, and you connect. Are you really here to solve a murder?"

I suddenly preferred the previous line of inquiry. "I'm here to fish. If someone wants my help solving a murder, I'm happy to do what I can, though I am not qualified in any manner."

"I heard you threw a cocktail glass, like, a hundred feet across the beach at a crook in total darkness and took him out."

"That is exactly what happened," I fibbed. "But I don't imagine long-distance mug throwing is going to solve any murders."

She pointed a turquoise fingernail straight ahead. "Grab your bags, I'll bring the van around." She veered away from me, her behind swinging delightfully.

Steady, old man.

When I emerged through the airport entrance, my bag and rod cases wheeled behind me, humid tropical air and cab drivers besieged me. I waded through both to the curb where a Banana Cay white van and Tabatha were waiting. Through the van's side door, I loaded my luggage and snaked my way into the front passenger seat. We lurched away at a rather alarming speed, palm trees zipping past my window as Tabatha weaved through traffic that looked like it was standing still.

I gripped the dashboard. "Are we in a hurry?"

"Pfft. I'm always in a hurry."

The rest of the roller coaster to Paradise Island was blessedly quiet except for the squealing of tire and brakes, and of course, the plastic dash buckling under my finger nails.

She swayed ahead of me through a grandiose lobby surrounded by tall potted palms. We passed the front desk and went immediately to the elevators.

I asked: "Shouldn't I check in, at the desk?"

Those turquoise fingernails dipped into her halter top and retrieved a key card. "I already checked us in," she purred.

Weigh anchor, old man. This ship is under full sail.

I dare say that Tabatha was the last thing I imagined happening to me my first day in Nassau, and surely it brought new meaning to the words "fishing trip" as it seemed I had lucked into fair weather and a falling tide in the pursuit of a mermaid. Was she genuinely attracted to me, or was she attracted to my fame? Perhaps she was simply a nymphomaniac in need of servicing. It did not occur to me that there might be some other, darker purpose.

No sooner were we in the door of the plush cream room with floral curtains than her halter top was on the floor. Her back to me, she marched up to the curtains and threw them open, the expanse of sea rewarded with a view of her naked torso.

Then she turned toward me and I was rewarded with a view of her resplendent torso.

"How do you like them?"

I kicked my luggage into a corner and picked up the phone, both without looking away from Tabatha. "Exquisite," I said with a slight bow at the waist. Into the phone, I said: "Yes, please send up two bottles of your coldest champagne, glasses and…Tabatha is there anything else you'd like them to bring?"

She smiled. "A box of their best condoms."

Into the phone: "…and a box of your best condoms. Yes, and please make it snappy."

I wondered, looking at what surely were tits sculpted by the skilled hands of a plastic surgeon, whether Tabatha was a professional, and thus there would be an invoice associated with the proceedings. Yet in my limited experience, professionals were exactly that, and they did not sell what was not pre-arranged in dollars, neither client nor provider wanted the awkward situation whereby funds were lacking.

Either way, I was chips all in. If she'd said this was going to cost me a thousand, I would not have batted an eye. Venerable on the outside, that's me.

The tits approached me and then slid past on my left and into the bathroom. The shower came on, and she said: "I'm going to rinse off so I'm all clean. Join me? Let me wash you."

I admit that this invitation was the culmination of a rather thrilling prospect, and for a moment, I was dizzy as my circulatory system furiously pumped blood in the opposite direction from my brain.

As I was pulling my shirt over my head, buttons popping off onto the floor, there was a knock at the door. Thank God, the champagne, I feared that it would arrive at an indelicate moment and interrupt the proceedings. And frankly, I needed to slow things down and enjoy this. Here I was in a hotel room with a bombshell and no obligations for the rest of the day, so I could afford to take my time and work my way though that box of rubbers at my leisure.

"Is someone at the door?" Tabatha hollered.

The person on the other side of the door answered her:

"Police."

Even as a mighty wave crashes the shore, it retreats in a great surge back to the abyss – and so did my corpuscles.

Tabatha stuck her head around the corner of the bathroom door, her insane eyes locked on mine. "My brother is Superintendent Phillips!" she hissed. "Don't tell them I'm here! Tell them you were about to take a shower!"

A cold one, so it would seem.

She vanished back into the bathroom.

I kicked her halter top under the bed and went to the door bare chested.

Outside the door, there were two black men in khaki tunics and police caps, both with hands clasped behind their backs. The one on the right was older with a fancy mustache and a red band around his cap – he said: "I'm sorry to bother you, but you are Boone Linsenbigler, yes?" His accent was clipped, his smile courteous.

I nodded, and he continued: "I am Superintendent Phillips."

I returned his courteous smile. "A pleasure."

"We were wondering if you might indulge the Royal Bahamian Police by having tea and a discussion down at headquarters."

I cocked my head. "A discussion? I was about to take a shower – what is this about?"

From behind his back, Superintendent Phillips produced a folded newspaper, his fingers clasped next to an article with the headline:

"BOONE LINSENBIGLER TO SOLVE LUNDY MURDER."

I rolled my eyes in disgust: *That weevil Orbach placed an item in the local paper to drum up publicity! Damn him!*

"I had no idea my arrival was going to be publicized in this way, Superintendent. I hardly know what to say except that my ability to help with this investigation is greatly exaggerated."

He nodded, his smile becoming sly. "We look forward to hearing a full explanation, Mr. Linsenbigler. Shall we?"

"Now? Can't this wait a few hours, I just arrived and…"

"Now would be most convenient. Obliging the Royal Bahamian Police will only act in your favor, I assure you."

First rule of dealing with the police: never argue.

I spread my hands, palms out, the very picture of accommodation. "Let me put on a shirt, turn off the shower."

I chose to do the latter first, and was flabbergasted by a full frontal of Tabatha coiled in the shower, her fold neatly clipped into a tiny tidy V. She turned off the shower, pulled me close at the belt line and gave me a tonsil cleaning that almost made me faint again. She whispered: "Don't go to Banana Cay, stay here, I'll call you and we'll have fun."

I tweaked my mustache and whispered back: "I'll drink to that."

Exiting the bathroom – a little unsteadily – I turned out the light on Tabatha, the police still standing in my open doorway. As I was putting on a new tropical shirt, room service arrived, and the police eyed the tray, complete with a box of a dozen A+ condoms. I tipped the waiter, and he set the tray on a table and left. I picked up Tabatha's card key from a dresser and went to the door. As we walked down the hall, Superintendent

Phillips cleared his throat and said: "We certainly do appreciate this. I hope that we, um, did not terribly interrupt your plans?"

Second rule of dealing with the police: never let them see you sweat.

I smiled weakly at him, and took a deep breath. "Not at all."

CHAPTER 3

AT THE RISK of branding myself racist, I noted that Superintendent Phillips was black and that Tabatha was merely tanned, so for him to be her brother seemed genetically a little far-fetched. What that implied I wasn't sure.

Phillips was across his desk from me, pushed back, one leg crossed over the other, a cup of tea on his khaki knee. Behind him was a large bright window that had been retrofitted with an air conditioning unit. The grey plaster walls were hung with photos of Phillips handing commendations to officers and photos of dignitaries handing Phillips citations. His adjutant stood by the door, hands behind his back, at parade rest.

My cup of tea was on the opposite edge of his desk, untouched except for a polite first sip. I didn't suppose he had a bottle of bourbon in his bottom drawer, but that's what I was really more attuned to given the circumstance. The preliminaries and niceties of my visit dispatched, I launched into my defense.

"Superintendent, you have nothing to worry about, I have no intention of involving myself in this murder.

That newspaper article was a publicity stunt. In no way, shape or form am I a detective, but the publicity team at Conglomerated Beverages want to give the impression that I am. I intend on going fishing at Banana Cay and that's it."

He nodded at his tea, but looked up with a sly smile. "And the prophylactics?"

I tweaked my mustache. "Are we not both men of the world, sir?"

Phillips tweaked his mustache as well, and cleared his throat, as if to signify: *Next Topic.* He placed his cup and saucer on the desk next to his cap and directed his attention to the ceiling fan's lazy rotations. "Mr. Linsenbigler, you are right that our first concern was that you might actually insert yourself into this matter. As you can imagine, the Royal Bahamian Police are probing this matter fully, and don't need anybody complicating our efforts."

"You have my word, sir, that I will do what is best for the Royal Bahamian Police and not involve myself in this matter even one iota." I stood, reflecting on the possibility that Tabatha might still be naked at my hotel. "May I go?"

"Not as yet, Mr. Linsenbigler." He continued to examine the ceiling fan. "Were we intending to impress upon you not to get involved, we could have conducted that business in your hotel room and you would be drinking that champagne this very instant. No. We have thought carefully about this, and in point of fact we want your help."

I sank slowly into my chair. "You're joking, surely."

"Not a bit of it." He uncrossed his legs and leaned forward on his desk, eyes locked on mine. "As it happens, our investigation has stalled, and we feel your insertion into this case has the very real possibility of worrying Lundy's murderer to the extent that he will make some sort of misstep."

"A misstep?" I squinted. "What kind of misstep?"

"We are hoping that if we sanction your trip to Banana Cay that the perpetrator will believe you are a threat to him and show himself either by making a break for it or possibly...making some sort of attempt to divert you."

I was still squinting. "Divert me? Divert me how?"

He leaned back and rolled his hands casually in the air.

"Well, you know, perhaps plant false evidence."

"Or try to kill me, is that it?"

Phillips: "Tut, tut, tut! We have planted one of our detectives undercover at the lodge to ferret out the murderer, and to watch the other staff and locals to see who behaves differently upon your arrival. It's all very routine, Mr. Linsenbigler, and I dare say that we may be able to arrange it so that it appears you solved the case on our behalf. I took the liberty of discussing this arrangement with Mr. Orbach at Conglomerated Beverages and they were quite taken with the scheme."

"They were, were they?" My intonation was – as you might expect – verging on indignant. "Don't I have any say in this matter?"

He shrugged. "Or we can send you packing back to the States, and you can tell Mr. Orbach and your employers that you refused. Your choice. Either you're in or you're out, we can't have you here unless you are actively involved, for your own safety, and for the sake of the investigation."

"Do I have any time to think about this?"

His smile was withering. "I'm afraid not, old man, either Mathers takes you back to the hotel or to the airport."

The hotel. Tabatha.

"And I do get to go fishing?"

"Of course, all you have to do is go there, be there, and we will take care of the rest."

"Throw in the bar tab?"

He stood and extended a hand. "Agreed."

We shook, and as Mathers drove me back to the hotel, I felt Superintendent Phillips' scheme seemed reasonable.

What was the worst that could happen?

CHAPTER 4

TABATHA WAS NOT in my hotel room, blast it. There was a note that said "C U L8tr – stay in Nassau" next to a Moët bottle with one drink missing from it

I slumped into a chair by the window and drank the Moët straight from the bottle. Stays colder that way.

` Tabatha did not call, and I dined at Café Picasso alone.

When she had not called by the next morning, I had little incentive to stay in Nassau as she requested. The front desk called to tell me my ride to the airport was waiting, and it was with some disappointment that it was not a bombshell but a frantic little Cuban with a severe comb-over that had come to collect me. He was falling all over himself, apologizing for not picking me up the previous morning. Apparently, he had fallen mysteriously ill after drinking a soda and someone stole his van – but that it had been returned. I told him that Tabatha had picked me up.

His mouth drooped, eyes went wide: "Who?"

It seemed there was no woman named Tabatha who worked for Banana Cay Lodge.

On the noisy, cramped propeller-driven flight to Banana Cay, I was understandably pensive. I should have guessed that any bombshell that threw herself at me would have been up to no good. *If it's too good to be true it's bad,* Dad used to say. Then again, there must actually be attractive nymphomaniacs out there – I just hadn't run into them yet. Tabatha, though, was clearly an imposter, and the ruse must have had some purpose. Lacking any other compelling circumstance, I had to assume she had something to do with this Lundy murder investigation – that she either was sent to try to influence me, or – what was it Phillips said? – Oh, yes – 'divert' me. She made it plain that she didn't want me to go to Banana Cay. Why? I could only wonder.

Orbach sure knew how to put me in a pickle. That newspaper article likely had the murderer thumbing the blade of his carving knife. *C U L8tr.* I hoped not. Well, sort of. I'd packed the condoms and second bottle of champagne just in case. Men are pathological optimists when it comes to sex.

We landed bumpily at one island and then had to be transferred by boat another half-hour to Banana Cay.

Tropical fishing lodges are usually arranged in a similar fashion, and Banana Cay did not disappoint. There's a central bar restaurant building, an administration hut, and a scattering of cabanas, all tastefully arranged amid a grove of palm trees cheek by jowl with a white sandy beach. Architecture of the buildings vary from thatched huts to mortar and brick. Banana Cay buildings were mint green clapboard cottages on stilts with sheet metal roofs.

The lodge was ocean-side, and the docks for the boats were bayside, accessible via a trail through the scrub. At this lodge, the cabanas were single story, so there would be no peeing off balconies or falling mugs, but I think I would have preferred a second story room just the same. If thugs came creeping around trying to silence the Great Detective, I'd rather they had to climb a flight of stairs. I could put some hundred-pound monofilament fishing line across it as a trip wire.

A typical day at a flats lodge usually starts about sunrise for breakfast. Afterward, you rig up your rods and join your guide in a skiff for the day. Lunch is on the boat, and you arrive back at the lodge late afternoon. Cocktails – of course – are followed by dinner and possibly more drinks and then sleep: repeat for however many days you are staying.

Flights to Banana Cay arrive early, so the boat from the airstrip put me at the lodge's ocean-side docks late morning. At the steps to the mint green main building, the owner Carlos was waiting for me, a swarthy Hispanic man in his late 40's with aviator sunglasses perched atop his shaved head. He was in tan shorts and white guayabera, a gold chain around his neck and a number of matching baubles on his hands. I exited the van and shook his muscular hand. He greeted me and said:

"If you like, our most excellent guide Elvis can take you out for a half day of fishing. You can just grab your rods and gear and go. We will put your luggage in your room."

I grinned. "That would be *most excellent*, just what I need." By the way, if you think some of these guide names like Elvis and Ferdinand are unusual, the Bahamas is where all the retired first names go to die. Know anyone named Delbert? Humphrey? You might down there.

Carlos bobbed his head, and snapped his fingers. The minions spirited my luggage away while I hefted the rod cases and gear bag.

Carlos added: "Would you like a refreshment, Mr. Linsenbigler?"

"Is there beer in the boat?"

"Yes, as well as water and sodas."

"That should suffice."

"Follow me. Elvis is waiting at the boat, a short walk from here. Let me take your gear bag."

We walked past the administration hut on the dirt road and traversed a spikey jungle path, presumably toward the island's lagoon.

Carlos smiled at me and said: "We're honored to have a man of your caliber here at Banana Cay, Mr. Linsenbigler."

"You can call be Boone, Carlos. Linsenbigler is kind of a mouthful."

"As you wish. Did you enjoy your night in Nassau?"

"I did. I always eat at Café Picasso."

"That is a nice place, not too many tourists - the prices frighten them. Elvis can show you where Ferdinand's body was found. Terrible. And to think it is likely someone I know who killed him. This Cay is a small place where everybody knows everybody."

"I'll look at it, but I will be honest with you: I'm not a detective, that's all a publicity stunt, and it is unlikely that I will be any help whatsoever." Superintendent Phillips would have been disappointed in me, but beans to him and everybody else who was trying to dangle me out there as bait for the murderer. My charter was to fish and drink, and by thunder I was going to stay on course.

"Perhaps you are being too modest, Boone. It was in the newspapers that you were coming here to solve the crime! It was Elvis who found him, so he can provide any details."

My protestations were wasted on Carlos, so I abandoned further denials.

We arrived at the edge of the crescent-shaped lagoon, the mangrove shores arcing away for miles left and right. Before us was a rickety, narrow dock. Parked at the dock was a flats skiff, which is a midsized speedboat designed to drift shallow water. There's a platform in stern above the outboard for the guide to push the boat along quietly with a long pole as he looks for fish to which the angler can present a fly. The bow has a triangular deck on which the angler stands and takes direction from the guide as to where to cast and how far. Sometimes, because of his vantage on the poling platform, the guide is the only one who can actually see the fish – he's certainly the one who spots them first.

From the brush on the left, a large black man in ultra-light khaki clothing approached. He extended a hand and we shook.

For a large man he spoke gently: "Elvis."

"I'm Boone – shall we?" I gestured to the boat.

Carlos retreated toward the path back to the lodge: "Good fishing, Boone!"

I waved, clambering into the white boat and sitting on the center console seat, my view forward unobstructed. Closing my eyes and heaving a big sigh, I filled my lungs with the crisp salt air. I heard a beer bottle open behind me, and opened my eyes to see a bottle of Kalik Beer in Elvis's enormous hand. He said quietly: "They said you like to drink."

I took the beer and replied: "Not usually while fishing, but I'll make an exception this time."

"I'll join you, if you don't mind."

"By all means."

In short order, the boat, Elvis and I were zipping across the lagoon, blue skies above dotted with midsized clouds. Wind flailed my hair, mustache curls bouncing. There's something liberating about heading out in a boat like that, battered by wind, low horizons and sparkling blue water 360 degrees around you. Makes me feel completely transported from my previous reality. It was like there was no murder investigation, like there had been no Tabatha or Superintendent Phillips, as if everything was going to be hunky dory.

Before long, Elvis throttled back and approached a creek flowing out of the mangroves, the deep water of the channel sticking into the lagoon like a giant green thumb.

"You like jacks?" Elvis mumbled.

I gave him a thumbs up, and began assembling my eight weight rod. For the uninitiated, fly rods come in 'weights' from one to eighteen. By 'weight', I mean different rod thickness that translates into the ability to turn and subdue a fish of a certain size.

One weight rod = goldfish.

Eighteen weight rod = marlin.

Eight weight rod = between a one-ounce goldfish and a five-hundred-pound marlin.

I used the eight-weight rod for most flats and backcountry fish to include bonefish, permit, snook, redfish, medium tarpon and just about any fish in the one to two-foot range. Jacks I think of as reef fish, but they school and feed eagerly in other deep spots, especially creek mouths on an outgoing tide. They school in channels waiting for baitfish and shrimp to be drawn into their lair by the tide.

On my palm, I showed Elvis the sardine pattern I planned to tie on and he nodded his approval, killed the motor, and clambered onto his platform. We were about two hundred feet from the creek mouth, and he used the pole against the sandy lagoon's bottom to get us into casting distance – my outer range is about ninety feet with the eight-weight rod, but sixty or seventy-foot casts are more the norm.

Fly cinched to my leader, I kicked off my sandals and stepped up onto the bow and began false casting. By 'false', I mean that a fly caster needs to sling the fly in the air a few times in increasingly longer back-and-fourths to add distance. If you've seen fly casting, false casting looks like the angler is whipping the air with his fly before letting it go and land in the water. Once the fly is in the water, the angler pulls on the line in strips to bring the lure through the water in a way that looks like swimming bait.

I let the fly soar and plop onto the deep green water.

I let it sink for three seconds.

I began to strip, moving the fly toward me in the water in short bursts.

Line snapped tight and I raised my rod, the tip pulsing one moment, my drag squealing the next. Fish on!

When I tell the uninitiated that I fish, they most often ask if I eat my catch, as though that's the object of the game. For some it may be so, but many anglers – such as I – do it only for sport. It requires a level of athleticism to put the fly where you want it and to battle the fish, pressuring the quarry as much as you can without breaking the line. It requires strategy and skill to know where to go and when and how. Finally, it requires an appreciation of wild things, of the dark water, of the unknowns and of the special kind of surprises that nature conjures. A quiet aqua pool, a fly, a pause, and a startling eruption of primal might and fight. If I could bottle *that*, my friends, I could buy Conglomerated Beverages lock, stock and barrel.

We boated a horse eye jack a few minutes later. They are roughly teardrop shaped, bright silver body, black tinged fins and stunning yellow tail. The eye, as the name suggests, is larger than a quarter. It was almost two feet long and had bent the rod double. As anglers often understate when pleased with their catch: *Nice Fish*.

I caught three more jacks out of the pool before the rest panicked and fled into the mangroves. I sat back and gulped the remainder of my beer, which was warm, but satisfying just the same. "Thanks, Elvis."

He climbed down from his perch, stowed his pole, and smiled. I'd have liked to see his eyes, but they were behind polarized sunglasses, as were mine, better to see into the water. Sometimes you never see a guide's eyes the entire trip. I imagined Elvis had knowing eyes.

The sun was high, so I pulled on a ball cap, rolled down my sleeves and hit my neck and ears with sunblock before we shot off again across the lagoon.

Next, we came to a bay of dark spots. That is, in the middle of white sand bottom in about two feet of water there were a series of almost black circular areas of dead vegetation.

Motor off, Elvis said: "Cuda." From experience, I already knew this. Barracuda like to hide on dark spots. Yet they are difficult to see, so you have to cast blindly at dark spots until one jumps your fly.

I changed my leader to braided steel, and chose a fly that resembled a short length of yellow nylon rope with two large eyes up by the front hook. I had tied this one myself but added a rear hook. Cuda often hit a fly short, just at the back, to maim their prey, so a hook in the tail helps an angler connect with them. Typically, you cast just to the side of the dark spots to draw the fish out. If you toss the fly directly into the spot you risk dropping it on the fish's head and spooking it.

We fished four spots before – in the wink of an eye – a big cuda exploded from his hiding place and inhaled my fly. Rod up and line tight, that silver monster shot straight up out of the water and pin wheeled back into the lagoon with a gigantic splash. Then he headed for the horizon, my drag singing, my line flying past the primary casting line and into the thin nylon backing.

Elvis scrambled down excitedly from this platform, uttering: "Big fucking cuda, Boone, we go after him."

He started the motor as that leviathan burst from the water five hundred feet away. With the eight weight rod, there was no way for me to put the wood to a fish that big and turn him, Elvis knew, and so he elected to follow the fish until we could wear him down.

Which we did, after eleven jumps and thirty minutes. Once in the boat, a tape measure indicated the cuda was pushing five feet long. Got some great pictures: *Nice fish.*

Elvis shook his head in disbelief. "Don't usually see cuda that big off the reef. You fish good, Boone." We high fived and popped some more beers.

It was turning into a spanking good day of fishing.

Our next stop was an unremarkable bay that was very shallow, so shallow that Elvis jumped out of the boat and guided it toward shore by hand.

I asked: "Are we going to wade fish?" I was prepared to put on neoprene boots specifically made for wading flats, likely for bonefish.

He shook his head and towed the boat all the way to the shore.

There was a coral-strewn clearing cupped by mangroves on all sides.

In the center of the clearing was a cross and some plastic flowers.

Damn: this was where Lundy was murdered.

Time to go through the motions.

"So tell me what happened, Elvis."

He shrugged, and told me softly, flatly and without much emotion.

"Ferd was late coming back from other side of island where he lived with his sister. We find his boat out there, anchor down, the tide was out so he could not get his boat here and so was on foot. Why he come here I don't know, nobody knows. But when we find his boat we see him on shore, laid down, bullet hole right here." He pointed to his chest. "A lot of blood on the ground. He dead for maybe eight hours. Gulls had eaten his eyes."

"What time of day would that have beendesert, when he was killed?"

"Early morning, when he coming to work."

"So why do you suppose he came ashore here? To meet someone?"

He frowned and shook his head. "Nobody live here, Boone."

"But somebody could have come by boat. Think maybe he met someone here to buy drugs or something?"

"Heh. He not even a drinker, mon."

"But he came to shore here for a reason. Any reason you can think of?"

He shrugged slowly. "Maybe he see a boat here, thinking maybe people stranded, but they here for another reason."

"And that reason?"

"Drugs, mon. Smugglers sometime come through at night in fast boats, maybe they stop here and when he come they kill him."

"The smugglers: would they be local?"

He wagged his head. "Mexicans. They just passing through, they go island to island, then to Florida."

"So you don't think whoever did this was local?"

He wagged his head. "There no guns around here, Boone, and nobody kill anybody."

That was reassuring news. If it were transient smugglers, they would no longer be around and not be a threat to Ol' Boonie. They could be reading the newspaper about my arrival back in Nassau or Mexico City and laughing that I was snooping around fruitlessly for them.

"Sounds plausible, Elvis. Why don't the police believe this?"

"They don't live here. They don't know. Or they don't want to know about the smugglers. Or don't want people to know about the smugglers. Even Carlos, he thinks it is a local, he the one telling the police what he thinks, they don't ask me."

I cocked my head and he continued: "Sometimes, the police, they not always honest people. This is the Bahamas, mon, not a lot of money around. It doesn't take much to make RBP look the other way."

Curious. Did Phillips really want to find the murderer or was I just some sort of patsy sent here to make it look like he did his best to find them? Didn't matter. If I didn't find them, I didn't find them and I was determined I would not even try to find the guilty party. Things looked peachy.

Elvis hung his head, and I saw a tear roll out from under his sunglasses. "Time to go back now, sun is low."

I felt bad for Ferd and those who missed him, but I had just caught the biggest cuda I was likely ever to catch on a fly rod.

We downed another beer as we ripped across the lagoon, back to the dock. All I could think to myself was *nice fish.*

CHAPTER 5

BACK AT MY CABANA, I awoke from a nap a half hour before dinner. Making haste to salvage what was left of any day's most cherished hour, I did a bird bath in the sink, coiffed my hair with a few deft strokes, twisted my whiskers just so, and threw on a Hawaiian shirt. Bring on the Mai Tai!

I strode into the barroom adjoining the dining room – it was a suitably long, curved bar hung with wicker lamps shaped like monkeys holding bananas. Nobody was cocktailing; the place was empty. The barman was a chubby little islander with a pug nose and freckles, his black eyes sad. He stood behind the bar resolute and ready.

I surveyed the offerings. Mostly rums, vodka and of course Jack and Walker. "My name is Boone," I said to the barman.

"I am Cecil." He spoke with a lisp, so he pronounced his name *Theethal*. "Can I get you something?" *Thumthing*. This unfortunate disability did nothing to improve his overall bearing – that of a cartoon pig.

When ordering a drink in a strange bar, I try to size up an establishment and the bartender: what cocktail might be made well here? If I am outside a metropolitan area, I never order a dry vodka martini, because likely as not the barman will reach for the white vermouth (dry means DRY as in probably no vermouth whatsoever.) He is also likely to over-shake the martini with blown ice and dilute it to the point that it tastes like hydrogen peroxide. If I suspect a bar is not up to the vagaries of cocktails that require stirring or shaking I will demur and order a drink on the rocks. Also, you don't go to Kentucky, bourbon capital of the world, and order a vodka martini. Thus, I was not going to the Bahamas to order a cosmo or – god forbid – a Pimm's Cup. In the tropics, I order rum, it's in their wheelhouse, and they never ever have any lemons, so you have to go with lime. "Muddle pineapple and two cherries in the bottom of glass, and then top with Myers and lime squeeze, with a splash of Cointreau and white wine, and a splash of soda, and a drop of bitters, please." That's my version of a Planter's Punch.

His brow wrinkled at the mention of adding white wine, but he did as I asked. I have found that just as with vodka, many liquors are leavened by adding red or white wine, and not just vermouth. Likewise, I've found that just a splash of soda 'brightens' a drink, that the bubbles increase the surface area of booze on the tongue and send flavor vapors to the nose.

I'm sure some drinksologists would disapprove of my Planter's Punch. Contradict cocktail authority Boone Linsenbigler at your own peril! *En garde!*

I took my first sip, and the cold molasses and lime flavors rolled over my tongue, the aromas filling my sinuses. Delightful. A good day of fishing is made great by an exemplary cocktail.

The screen door opened and slammed behind me. I turned to behold a man and a woman. I could tell they were guests because he was wearing zip off fishing pants and vented blue fishing shirt. He had a reddish complexion, and not necessarily from the sun. I guessed him to be Mexican, close-crop hair, 40's, with a hatchet nose and sharp eyes, not overly tall. He approached.

"I am Miguel."

I shook his wide hand. "Boone, happy to make your acquaintance. Have good fishing today?"

"We just arrived."

"I was only out for half a day myself, but landed some nice jacks and a really nice barracuda. I'll show you the photos later."

"And this is my wife, Tamara."

She came around from behind him and extended her hand.

Violet eyes met mine.

Ay yi yi.

It was Tabatha.

Her hair was cut shorter into a swirl and dyed blonde, large sunglasses atop her head. Her nails were no longer blue but clear. There was no halter top and shorts, but a blue floral shift, the kind a girl might drape over a bathing suit.

As I shook her hand, she said: "So you're Boone Linsenbigler, the one on the commercials." There was absolutely no recognition in her eyes; she betrayed nothing. One cool cucumber.

I took a gulp of my drink while trying to find my voice, and said hoarsely: "One in the same, *Tamara.*"

"How did you get the first name *Boone?* I've never heard it before."

"My father was a fan of frontiersmen, and taught American History." This was a common question so I had a perfectly canned answer. "Can you guess my sister's name?"

They both drew blanks, so I helped them out: "Crocket. If we had had another sibling the name would have been Bowie."

"Those are fun names!" she said, trying to be light and happy.

While my mouth was working on autopilot, my mind was racing as I tried not to betray any alarm over this blatant subterfuge. Possibly Miguel did not know that Tamara had been with me yesterday – otherwise why parade her before me? No, it must be that Tamara was putting one over on him but clearly not afraid that I would recognize her. Gadzooks, why in the dickens was she following me around, in disguise? Was she really Miguel's wife? Or just arm candy, a companion for the trip, or a beard perhaps to disguise Miguel's actual intent? Maybe he was just *saying* she was his wife. However, you cut the deck it came up jokers. I felt like asking for the check and securing the first flight black to Nassau and beyond.

Tamara saddled a stool next to me and I could smell coconuts. To this day I can't drink a piña colada without adjusting my shorts. She ordered a bottle of añejo, two glasses and chopped limes. Miguel sat on the other side of her, and they both did a couple quick shots to begin the proceedings. Personally, I am not a fan of tequila, if for no other reason than people who drink it seem to have a predilection for drinking it as fast as they can, seemingly to get it over with, or merely to get hammered.

I find the flavor acceptable, just not the fashion and trappings.

If she could play it cool, I could play it cool. At the very least, it was up to me at that point to be a moving target, and by that I mean if her intent was to play me somehow, I had better make myself slippery and hard to predict.

"So where are you folks from?" I asked.

They exchanged a glance and she said: "San Diego."

"I hear the weather is nice in San Diego. I'm from New Jersey, the Garden State. We have a lot of gardens."

"Really?" she said sipping a shot of tequila.

He said: "How's the fishing in New Jersey?"

I smiled. "Almost as good as the gardening. Where do you fish around San Diego, Miguel?"

"In the sea," he blurted.

"Do you see submarines?"

He looked confused, and I continued. "I fished in the bay there once and we saw submarines. There's a submarine base in San Diego. Funny where you find submarine bases."

She just stared at her drink.

"Oh, of course!" He laughed. "The submarines."

Luckily for Miguel and Tamara, four male anglers came into the bar, and I forgot their names almost as soon as I shook their hands. You could have picked them out of a crowd as anglers: the zip off pants and vented shirts are a dead giveaway. As it happens, when actual anglers (as opposed to Miguel) meet, the fishing stories immediately begin to tumble out. The supper bell rang, and we headed to the dinner table. I was separated from Miguel and Tamara by the new companions – but not from a refill on that cocktail. I felt a twinge of triumph for tweaking them about San Diego submarines

– they clearly had no idea there were submarines there. I thought that perhaps hinting that I knew they were imposters afforded me the upper hand and that it might steer them clear of me and whatever game they had afoot.

Carlos the lodge manager joined us for dinner at the head of a long table lit by lanterns on the porch. I sat at his right, and he asked me again about my meal at Café Picasso, but I spent much of the meal consumed with a discussion with the man on my right who had spent the day chasing a fish called *permit*. It is a perfectly idiotic name for a fish and confuses those who are not anglers. For the uninitiated, permit are likely the most annoying, but most highly prized fish in the ocean. You need to make long casts to prevent from spooking them. If they do turn on your fly, often as not they simply follow it – they won't inhale the blasted thing. My theory is that the permit cannot smell the crab fly and so won't eat what it cannot smell. Having been frustrated in the past by these persnickety fish, I had taken the precaution of equipping myself with some crab scent in a discreet tube from which I could secretly apply it to my fly.

You may ask why I would have to do this secretly – *is not the object of fishing to catch fish?* Precisely! However, my fellow anglers are akin to my fellow cocktail enthusiasts, and believe that there are right ways to fish/drink, and wrong ways to fish/drink. Scenting your fly is not cricket for a gentleman angler. Were anyone in the fishing community to discover that I had done such a thing, shame would be heaped upon my reputation as if I had spit in a Pimm's Cup. I'm sure Terry Orbach would be mortified to know I was contemplating such a maneuver, given the potential downfall. Anyway, I was keen on this trip to Banana Cay to cast to some permit and see if the scent worked. The man next to me had been frustrated by three permit that very morning and I wanted all the details.

Bottles of wine circulated the table as the chicken entrée was devoured.

In the pause after the plates were cleared and before dessert, I went for a refill of my rum drink. When I returned, Carlos had the entire table in rapt attention. He was solemnly recounting Ferdinand Lundy's sad demise. Carlos focused on me as I retook my seat. "Mr. Linsenbigler was kind enough today to take it upon himself to investigate the scene of the crime and tell us his thoughts. In case you did not know, Boone has a reputation for solving crimes."

I was reasonably sober. Yet I had – as they say – one foot in the bag after all the wine and rum.

I squared my drink in front of me, smoothing my mustache. "I'm afraid, Carlos, you exaggerate. My reputation for solving crimes is in fact founded on a single instance last month in Mexico whereupon I subdued a burglar with a cocktail mug in the middle of the night."

He looked a little deflated, but I continued.

"This does not mean that I have not solved other crimes at other times." Orbach would have been proud of me, and I traced my gaze across those assembled, including Tamara, who eyed me suspiciously. "I really know very little thus far about Mr. Lundy, his family and friends, his habits and acquaintances, so it is really quite premature to make any suppositions at this time. That said, at face value it seems to me the most likely culprit are drug traffickers." The most original theories, my friends, are usually those you steal.

Miguel looked tense.

Tamara went blank.

Carlos looked confused. "Drug trafficking? Here?"

I folded my arms. "Well, it is no secret that the Mexican cartels use the Bahamas as a way station with fast boats to Florida. If they were beached here somewhere for some reason and Lundy stumbled upon them, would they not have killed him? Given the remote location here, and the paucity of firearms, and the closeness of the community, it seems highly unlikely that anybody here could be responsible without everybody suspecting. Anybody in the community who had a dispute with Lundy would be well known."

"That certainly is an original theory!" Carlos said, but with laughter in his voice as if to dismiss it.

Miguel spoke up. "Florida would take two days and lots of fuel to reach from here. How would the fast boats not be spotted by U.S. Coast Guard?"

One of the other anglers spoke up – a red haired gentleman that I believe was called Red. "I just read about this. The fast boats travel only at night, and during the day they stop and put up camouflage to prevent being spotted."

I waved a hand at Red. "There you have it."

Red continued. "Did you know that in Columbia the cartels actually have submarines? They make their own submarines out of fiberglass."

I thumped the edge of the table. "Perhaps there is a submarine base close by to Banana Cay?"

Tamara reached for her wine glass and knocked an almost full bottle of Pinot Noir crashing to the floor. Hubbub ensued as she stood and the men around her came to assist cleaning up the glass and wine. Which was good timing, because it was my chance to slip out with my drink and smoke a cigar, give myself a pat on the back for having been Conglomerated Beverages' good little mascot. I'd supplied my detective's theory, and I was done. It couldn't be proved one way or the other. On to doping flies for permit!

As to whatever Tamara and Miguel were up to, that was their problem.

I returned to the dark porch of my cabana, kicked back, fired up a cheroot and enjoyed the night breeze and sizzle of palm fronds.

Surprisingly, there was no further subterfuge that evening. Tamara did not come by to explain what the hell was going on or pass me a cyphered message. Miguel did not signal me with a pen light from his porch. Superintendent Phillips' inside man did not make himself known through Morse code tapped out on the plumbing.

I went to bed with the peace of mind of a man with the world on a string.

CHAPTER 6

THE NEXT MORNING the sun rose gloriously and framed by palms over a mild, sparkling ocean.

I arrived at the restaurant early and ran into Elvis hauling our cooler for the day toward the door.

"How's it look for permit today, Elvis?"

He gave me thumbs up. "Let's leave early, Boone. Tides are right for tailing permit in the bights. Wind will come up in the afternoon, but it's good now."

"Capital. I'll just gobble something down and be with you at the dock in fifteen minutes, how's that?"

He grunted in the affirmative and stomped his way toward the path to the docks.

There was a buffet, which helped expedite breakfast: I slapped eggs and bacon on a couple slices of toast and made myself a big cup of coffee to go. This was the day I would catch a permit, I could feel it, and I didn't want my mood changed by any weird encounters with the other guests.

I ate my sandwich and drank my coffee on my porch bathed in orange tropical sun, terns pinwheeling in the sky, and magpies whistling in the fronds.

In short order, I hefted my gear bag and strode directly from my cabana to the path, catching a glimpse of Tamara and Miguel ascending the sun-dappled steps to the restaurant. She had fine legs, to be sure, but good riddance to them both, I was on to conquer a fish named permit.

The sun was still low and orange as Elvis and I raced across the lagoon, our shadows cast long and inky on the water portside. My guide veered the boat between some mangroves, up a narrow channel, and then burst from a creek into an expanse of blue water, before us a batch of small mangrove islands that looked like giant ragged muffin tops.

I fingered the lip balm container in my pant pocket – that's where I had cleverly concealed the crab scent, and compulsively checked to make sure I had it where it would be easy to access.

Elvis cut the engine well short of the first green muffin tops, and poled us the rest of the way in so as not to spread wake across the leeward side of the island. He was breaking a fair sweat by the time we slid into the calm side of the small cay, and climbed down from the platform to dispatch some sports drink. "Let me see your permit flies, Boone."

I handed him the box, which mostly contained kooky-looking crabs made from felt discs and rubber bands. He poked an index finger slowly through the flat plastic box, sorting out a few he liked along the way. He had selected several large tan crabs as well as a few smaller green ones. All but one of those he selected went into his top shirt pocket. "Tie this one on, Boone. I put the rest in my shirt in case we need to switch flies in a hurry."

Once the fly was on and I was on deck, Elvis climbed back onto the platform and began slowly poling the boat across the gentle ripple of the shallows. We were looking for fins of a permit, which stick out of the water when they are feeding on a flat. The fish are more or less disc shaped, with sickle-like fins on their back and tail. When they move through skinny water both dorsal and tail fin stick out of the water, and when they duck down to eat a crab their entire tail sticks out of the water.

Elvis pointed into the shallows around the knees of the mangroves. "Tails!"

He began to pole in earnest toward where he had pointed.

I stared at the flickering sunlit ripples and didn't see any tails. They are silver and can be very hard to see against the glint of the water – in effect, camouflaged.

Wait. I saw a glint that wasn't the water. *Then again.* I saw ripples that weren't from the breeze, and then I discerned the signature twin sickle-shaped fins of a permit cruising between clumps of mangroves, contrasted in front of a white expanse of sand. The single fish was about a hundred and fifty feet out, and the permit was just going about his business looking for crabs among the brush, unaware of our approach.

With the sun at our backs, I was afraid my air-borne fly line would cast a shadow and spook it unless Elvis poled us into position to the side. That would make my cast more difficult across the breeze, but I would compensate and lay the fly out in front of the fish some twenty feet and wait for him to come across it. When sight fishing for permit or bonefish, many anglers prefer to put the fly right where the fish can see the offering, but I often prefer to err on the side of not spooking the fish and taking my chances that the fish will stay on course.

When the fish is a few feet away from my fake crab, I gently move the fly across the bottom, all very natural.

I pretended to apply balm to my lips but actually put some between thumb and forefinger, massaging the crab scent into my felt crab fly.

The set up was exactly as I suspected, Elvis quietly moving the boat up and to the side, both of us saying nothing, but knowing what to do. We were within sixty feet of the permit, its tail to us, and I glanced back at my guide. He gave me a deep nod: *Now.*

I hesitated: a puff of breeze kicked up, and I waited another ten seconds for it to die so as not to have to over compensate. The fish's tail wagged lazily in the air as the head poked around the mangrove knees trying to scare up a crab. I dropped my fly from my sticky fingers and began to false cast, conscious of remaining calm and letting the cast develop nice big loops before pushing the cast out and letting the fly drop *gently.*

It landed to the side of the fish, and closer than I wanted. Fins jerked above the water when the fish heard my fly touch water ten feet away. He turned toward where my fly landed, paused and then swam casually toward it.

Elvis and I both crouched; the fish's eye was turned toward us. We needed to have a low profile to prevent being seen.

Usually a permit hovers over the fly, staring at it until you give it a little motion, and then it either picks it up or it continues to stare at it, wondering why this crab doesn't smell like a crab.

The permit accelerated as he approached the fly – he could already smell it.

That bastard raced up and just gulped it down.

I set the hook.

Water exploded as the permit felt the hook's sting, racing in a few tight circles before he shot off toward deep water, my rod high and drag screaming.

Elvis cheered: "Haroo! That fish like that fly!"

We boated that fish. He was about twelve pounds, and we boated two more, one a little smaller, one a little larger, all in similar fashion. Snapped some great pictures. *Nice fish.*

Elvis released the third fish, and as he wiped his hands on a rag, he laughed and cocked his head at me. "I see you fish permit Bahamas style!"

I raised my eyebrows. "Bahamas style?"

"You dope the fly, Boone." He smiled with all his teeth. "That's what we do when we fish permit, without customers."

I began to protest and he held up a hand. "Dats OK Boone, it stupid to come here and just cast and no catch fish. Don't even try to say you not doping that fly, a permit never take like that unless the fly is doped."

I shrugged. "Exactly. Stupid not to dope."

"But here's what we gotta do. You get back to Banana Cay, you tell everybody you caught one permit, not however many we gonna catch. You say we caught three and Carlos gonna think that Elvis doped your fly and I get fired, mon. Boone can't tell anyone ever that you doped that fly or it's a world of shit for both of us, trust me."

I laughed. "OK, partners in crime." We shook hands and both laughed.

"Boone, now we try something really fun." He fished through his own box of flies and came up with a crab fly that was made of foam. "Tie this on."

I snipped off my fly and began to tie on the new one, eyeing it curiously. "The fly looks like it floats."

He nodded deeply. "Yes sir, we gonna dope that fly and you see a permit take a fly from the top of the water! Nobody see dat who don't dope."

I laughed a diabolical laugh, mostly to myself. This was great. Imagine, a guide as unscrupulous as myself?

In short order we were polling toward the next clump of mangroves, and Elvis said: "I see two!"

The sun was much higher, and the hour was probably approaching noon, so I didn't have to worry so much about the shadow of my line on the water. I snugged my cap low so the brim would cut the glare better. I saw the two permit, and they were coming toward us steadily.

Elvis whispered "Now, Boone!"

I cast in a hurry and so didn't make the best presentation, a little too close to the fish, and they spooked, splitting left and right, my fly floating between them.

Both turned back toward the fly.

Both charged it like heat seeking missiles.

They smashed into each other, my fly thrown into the air. Permit actually fighting for the privilege of eating my fly!

One of them whipped around and saw the fly plop back into the water. He launched himself at it, the entire fish right out of the water and onto the fly. Fish on!

"Haroo!" Elvis cheered.

Over the scream of my reel, I heard what sounded like a tennis ball hitting a brick wall. I looked away from where my permit was charging to deep water.

At the mangrove.

At my feet.

At Elvis up on the platform behind me.

He had is sunglasses off, and was looking at a growing red spot on his chest.

The red spot sputtered from his punctured lungs, and blood drooled from Elvis' mouth.

The sound of a gunshot finally reached us from the direction of the mangroves.

I couldn't take my eyes off Elvis, I was thunderstruck, and his eyes looked up to mine.

The eyes I had never seen...he had hazel eyes!

I gasped, and made some sounds that were not words but the guttural articulation of anguish and terror.

Elvis slumped and rolled off the platform into the water.

The fly rod dropped from my hand; the permit pulled it off the deck and into the water.

I lunged from the bow toward where Elvis had fallen into the ocean, a plume of blood staining the water and making it hard to see him as the boat drifted over him. I lunged to the other side, and saw him sinking to the bottom, about four feet down, bloody bubbles coming from his open mouth like empty red words, the hazel eyes staring right at me.

My crab flies, the ones he'd put in his top pocket, were drifting around his head.

Again, I made some sort of unintelligible grunt of incomprehension and disbelief, my brain aflame with panic.

PANG!

The steel support for the polling platform sang from the impact of another bullet, just over my head.

I dropped to the bottom of the boat, breathing hard, eyes wild.

They're trying to kill me and I don't think there's anything I can do to stop them.

Feverishly I scanned the bottom of the boat for something with which to protect myself.

I heard a motor start in the direction of the mangroves.

Blast! They're coming to finish me off.

I scrambled across the deck to the skiff's center console, which had a compartment underneath: rags, tool kit, safety whistle, broken pair of sunglasses, a stray nob of some sort, fish cleaning board, folding filet knife, large screwdriver, flare gun.

I wrenched open the flare gun case and there was a single cartridge left. The slim gun itself was a little bigger than palm-sized and made mostly of bright orange plastic. I loaded the gun, snapped it closed, and shoved it and the folding filet knife deep into the pockets of my baggy zip off pants.

I heard the boat approach and voices.

"Do you think I got him?" It sounded like Tamara.

"I'm not sure if your shot hit him." Miguel replied. "I should not have given the rifle to you after I took out the guide, then we'd know both of them were dead, I do not miss."

I reached over to where Elvis' blood had trickled from the platform onto the deck, scooped some up and slapped it to the side of my head. I rolled face down, splayed, playing possum. I was hyperventilating so it made it hard to lie still as I felt the approaching boat nudge mine.

Shadows were cast over me.

"You got him." Miguel sounded surprised.

There was a pause, and Tamara said: "No, I didn't get him. See, he wiped the blood from over there, you can see his fingerprints. Get up, Linsenbigler."

I rolled to my back, palms up in surrender. My voice cracked: "Don't shoot."

All I could see were their silhouettes above me, the sun between their heads, and a rifle in Tamara's hands pointed loosely in my direction.

She had the other hand on a shapely hip. "Look at the mighty detective now. See what happens when you stick your nose in other people's business?"

Miguel took the weapon from her and shouldered it at me. "I'll finish him."

My vision swam, and all I could think in that moment was: *Fucking Terry Orbach!*

"No." Tamara put a hand on the rifle, pushing it down. "Don't you think Enrique would want Conglomerated Beverages to pay a big ransom on this one? And he'll give us no trouble, will you, Boone? He's just a drunken little boy."

I shook my head "no" very rapidly, *no ma'am*, still on my back trembling, palms up.

Miguel said: "*Excellente* idea. OK, you drive this boat, I'll drive that one, back to base. Get up, Linsenbigler, and sit in the bow where I can keep an eye on you. You know I will kill you without a second thought, don't you? She may miss, but I never do."

I nodded and scrambled up onto the bow, blinking hard, trying to catch my breath. *If I survived this, would I ever be able to sleep again? Would I ever be able to forget Elvis' eyes as he sank to the bottom, crab flies floating around his head?*

Nothing would ever be the same.

Nothing could undo Elvis' murder or make it right.

Not unless I could kill Miguel —retribution. Killing him might set things right for having survived. I was scared, but also intensely angry, so vengeance seemed cleansing.

Yet I wasn't sure I could kill Miguel. I didn't think I was ruthless enough to outsmart him, to catch him unawares.

Perhaps the best I could honestly hope for was to escape with my life.

CHAPTER 7

AS THE TWO BOATS ZIPPED across the bay, wind racing through my hair and mustache, I was careful to take note of where we were headed and had been. It was not easy – all the little mangrove islands looked the same to me. The one feature that helped keep my bearing was a cellular tower that was just south of Banana Cay Lodge. My cell phone might have come in handy were it not on my nightstand in the cabana recharging. Just the same, the tower was tall enough that I could see where we were in relation to the lodge. We were headed north around the tip of the main cay out of the lagoon side and to the ocean side of the archipelago, toward an outlaying island that was unusually tall and rocky. The open ocean water was noticeably different from the protected lagoon – it had large rolling undulations that sent the flats boat airborne every once and a while, and we'd slam down hard, practically knocking me off my perch.

The journey gave me a little time to collect myself, wipe Elvis' blood off my face and assess the mettle of my character. Was I a drunken little boy, or did I have the ability to try to escape? Did I have the capacity to risk my life? Did I really have a choice? Might they be going to use me for ransom and then just kill me anyway? I could not see how, at this stage, they would risk letting me go with what little I knew, which was that a cartel was running drugs to Florida through Banana Cay. I couldn't imagine that I could be wrong about that. Considering the location, it wasn't diamond smuggling. I wondered, however, about Miguel's calculus. Killing people, having boats and major beverage brands go missing would only draw attention to this area and along with it likely the police, possibly even the US Drug Enforcement Agency. The authorities seemed mystified by Lundy's murder, certain that it was someone local, not a cartel.

Upon reflection, I noted that the numerous news stories on the drug cartels. Someone crosses them, someone gets too close, and they just start killing, it is pretty much their proactive default maneuver. I recalled that many killings were as much a warning to others as a way to stem information leaks about their operations. Still, if they operated a fast boat fleet through Banana Cay it would soon have to fold, as I had to imagine there would be all manner of police and military boats patrolling here once Elvis and I were found missing.

Tamara was standing at the transom of the boat ahead of us as it surged over the waves, her beautiful legs bowing and her tits bouncing as the craft topped each swell. Damn, what a missed opportunity.

As we drew near to the cliff side of the island, we motored around a rocky point where the blue swells crashed, water raining down into the boats as we passed through. Steering hard into a cove, there was a slight lee area and mangroves. Folded into the face of the mangroves was a tunnel through the branches – we throttled back passed into the channel leading back into the mangroves. The water was light green, with a sandy bottom littered with blackened mangrove twigs. Schools of black-banded minnows zigzagged out of our way as we motored in further.

Yet I was not prepared for what came into view around the next bend.

Overhead, camouflage netting spanned the channel creating a canopy over a cozy, enclosed lagoon. In the dappled sunlight filtered through the netting were five drab green prefab cabins at the end of the lagoon, the kind that come in sectional walls and snap together. There was a porch in front of each with folding lawn chairs. On one porch five brown men in undershirts lounged, three drinking beer, two drinking coffee. Sub machine guns hung on the walls behind them. I could hear the steady hum of a generator.

In front of the cabins was a main dock, with five finger docks extending outward. Next to two of those finger docks were two mottled-blue crafts that at first I could not make out as to what sort they were. They seemed very small and elongated, sitting low in the water. There was a low cabin of sorts in the center, both enclosed, with windshields and some pipes extending from the rear. The shells of the craft betrayed the unmistakable resin strokes and strand mat of fiberglass.

As we drew closer, headed for the slips next to the nearest craft, I saw that much of the crafts were underwater.

I said absently, and aloud: "Submarines."

Miguel looked vexed. "Yes, and I'd like to know how you knew."

I blinked at him, instinctively holding my tongue. *The less you say, Linsenbigler, the better!*

He continued: "As soon as we met at the lodge you

are hinting about submarines, signaling that you knew. And then at dinner, speak of smuggling operations through here and narco subs! Now we must move all this. You must be with the DEA. She does not believe it, but we have sources that told us an agent was on the way to infiltrate us. Prepare yourself for some discussion about that later."

I wanted to say: *Why in blazes did you have to say you were from San Diego? I only mentioned submarines because of San Diego. And I never said anything about narco subs, it was that other angler Red who said that. I was talking about fast boats only because Elvis surmised that it was smugglers. But if you'd just kept your heads down and not over-reacted to the arrival of some puffed up beverage brand dunderhead named Boone Linsenbigler your operation would be safe and not have to move, and I'd be safe, we all wouldn't be in this mess. Lundy's murder simply would have gone unsolved, and you wouldn't have had to kill Elvis for no God damned good reason. And you call yourselves clever smugglers – well no amount of submarines and secret bases make up for stupid!*

But I didn't say that. If you ever find yourself effectively talking into the barrel of a gun, I think you'll find you don't make many self-righteous speeches.

Some of the men from the porches came down and helped tie up the flats boats while Miguel kept the rifle pointed in my direction.

I reaffixed the cap on my head at a jaunty angle and smoothed my mustache. Perhaps under the circumstances it was best to let Miguel think what he wanted to think, while I searched within myself to become the indomitable Boone Linsenbigler, world traveler, master cocktailer and adventurer. I needed to become Orbach's fiction, if even just a little bit, to save my whiskey-sodden skin. Blubbering and begging for mercy certainly would not get me anywhere. Besides, my mustache would get soggy.

Orbach. If he could only see me now he would be
beside himself with glee. When it comes to scoundrels, I
am a piker compared to that weevil. If I was drawn and
quartered, he'd no doubt arrange for some sort of Super
Bowl halftime funerary event in my honor, him dancing a
jig like a beetle on a skillet back stage the whole while.

Tamara led the way, Miguel behind me, toward the
nearest cabin. We went up the steps, and Tamara pointed
her cell phone at me. "Stand over here, back to the wall.
Miguel, why not put the gun barrel to his head, you stay
off camera."

I did as I was told and so did Miguel. She said:
"Boone, time to record your ransom note. We want one
million for your return. Make it brief."

I cleared my throat. "Is there any special drug cartel I
should mention by name? Or just refer to generic drug
smugglers?"

"Drug smugglers. Tell them to post their reply on
Twitter with a phone number we can text to for
arrangements. They have twelve hours to respond.
Ready?"

I nodded, and she said: "Start now."

Chin up, and defiance in my eyes, I began – in the full
knowledge that Orbach would likely run wild with it.
"This message is to the fine people at Conglomerated
Beverages, who manufacture and distribute my very own
Boone Linsenbigler's Cocktail Amenities." Tamara rolled
her eyes, and I continued. "As it happens, in the course
of my investigations in the tropics, I have been kidnapped
and am being held for one million dollars' ransom. Please
post a reply to these demands on the Conglomerated
Twitter feed with a phone number that can be texted with
instructions on where the ransom is to be paid and how.
Should you not respond in twelve hours of receipt of this

message, my captors will execute me by firing squad. That being the case, I only hope that a last request can be granted so that I might have one last cocktail containing Boone Linsenbigler's Plain and Fancy Cocktail bitters. Farewell."

"Firing squad?" Tamara lowered the phone in disgust. "That's more than enough, Linsenbigler."

I shrugged. "You want the million dollars don't you? They might just make a million dollars on that message alone once it's on every nightly newscast."

Miguel lowered his rifle. "The million is for Enrique, not for us."

Enrique. That was the second reference, but I dared not ask who exactly that was. My impression was that he was their boss.

"When does he arrive?" Tamara checked the time on her phone.

"He'll let us know five minutes before he gets here. He never lets anyone know where he'll be until five minutes in advance. He's not going to be happy."

Tamara sighed. "Well, a million dollars should help cheer him up."

Miguel wagged his head. "You don't know him."

"Can it be helped? Can it be helped we have to fold this up? We would have had to eventually and not have a million dollars." She looked at me. "And you. We can get that million and still kill you. Your best hope is to just sit down and wait and behave. There's no way off this island for you except if we drop you somewhere. We might do that, and let you go. But not if you piss us off."

"Understood. Am I going to be tied up or...?"

"You can wait in here, unrestrained, I'm not taking you to the bathroom every ten minutes." She shoved the door to the cabin open and when I entered, I was hit by a wave of air conditioning. This cabin was obviously an employee lounge, with a pool table and fully stocked bar. The walls were bare plywood and studs; the only windows flanked the front doors. Dangling bulbs with lampshades hung from the ceiling over the bar and pool table, and there was a wicker couch with floral cushions against one wall. I perched on one of the rattan bar stools and jerked a thumb at the bar.

"Is it acceptable if I prepare myself some sort of cocktail while I wait? It's the best way to make sure I behave."

Miguel shrugged, but held up a finger. "Empty out your pockets."

Pockets abound in fishing pants, some high, some low. When I went fishing, I had my wallet in my gear bag, and had very little in my pants except a bandana for wiping my hands or brow. The flare gun was in the pocket with the bandana. The knife was on the opposite side.

I handed over the knife, turning the pocket inside out, and Miguel eyed me sidelong as he examined the folding filet knife. "What plans did you have for this, Linsenbigler?"

"I didn't know that I was going to be kidnapped."

When I came to the flare gun pocket, I managed to wrap the gun in the crumpled red bandana. I held it out. "Do you want my handkerchief or can I hold onto it?"

Miguel wrinkled his nose, turned and walked out.

Tamara locked eyes with me. "You heard what I said, right? Behave, and you'll save your skin."

I gestured at the bar. "I'll behave, my word as a gentleman."

She closed the door, folded a hasp across the doorframe and padlocked me in.

Of course, I was no gentleman so my word meant nothing.

I strode behind the bar, surveying the selection. As one would expect, it was light on whiskeys and heavy on tequilas and rums, but they had vodka and gin. I noted they had absinthe for some reason. If only it was toxic as many people still believe, then I might be able to use it as a poison, maybe make an escape in one of the boats.

The bar fridge had ice, and I put some of that into a Boston shaker with some vodka and a slice of lime. They had no bitters, so I plopped in a dash of absinth instead and gave it a good shake, tracing my eyes around the room looking for cameras. Of course, they make cameras so small nowadays, but I thought I should at least see if there were any obvious ones. I didn't see any. I couldn't imagine why they would have cameras covering a lounge for their submarine crews, but...

I set the shaker down to let it rest. I'm a firm believer in letting a vodka martini – or equivalent – rest so that the ingredients have time to intermingle, chill and dilute ever so slightly. While I waited for my drink to chill, I made use of the bathroom that was over by the pool table. I thought it a tidy little bathroom for a smugglers' submarine base, with just a sink, medicine cabinet and flush toilet. Lounges and nice bathrooms – who would have thought? I would have imagined thatch huts, smoky fires, and trenching tools for crapping.

Zipped up and ready to go back to my cocktail, I paused and opened the medicine cabinet. Lots of adhesive bandages and first aid ointments, hydrogen peroxide, Pepto, aspirin, etc. Looked like an ordinary medicine cabinet. I closed it.

I opened it again.

There was a container of methanol – rubbing alcohol.

Methanol – as opposed to ethanol, which is the essence of liquor. I was told that they taste the same. What I was considering scared me. Should I even try to escape, really? On the other hand, did they really have any impetus to not take the million dollars and put a bullet in my noggin just the same? At the very least, as with the flare gun, I needed at least some sort of options, some card to play when the chips were down. My mouth was suddenly dry and sour as kale chip.

I put the white square plastic bottle into my baggy pants and returned to the bar. I strained my cocktail into a martini glass and took a deep sip. The icy fire and citrus tang rolled over my tongue and down my parched throat, while the piney absinthe pricked my sinuses. Bracing, just what the doctor ordered. I guessed it was about two in the afternoon, Elvis had bought the farm just two hours or so earlier. I was inspired to make a small eulogy. I raised my glass: "To you, Elvis. I can't say how sorry I am, I'll make it right if I can, somehow. Here's hoping you're up there doping flies, drinking beer and catching permit hand over fist." I took another gulp, and it went down hard with the lump in my throat, those hazel eyes sinking to the bottom.

Escape. Make it right. Did I have the guts? Was that the smart thing to do or just the foolhardy thing to do, some ill-advised assertion of a wounded ego, or misguided attempt to right a wrong?

Conscious that there might be cameras in the room, I removed the bottle of methanol under the bar and poured a smidge into the cocktail shaker. I put it up on the bar and pretended to pour some vodka in as well. Then I added lime and absinth as before. I gave it a good shake, and then strained the contents into another martini glass.

I gave it a sip, ducked my head under the bar as if I were reaching for something and spit the methanol cocktail into the sink.

It was not much different from a terrible vodka martini, and would likely make any man gag. I noted that there was a water pitcher under the bar, the type with a charcoal filter. Back before I was a brand, it was not beneath me to purchase low grade vodka in large plastic bottles and run it through a Brita filter to bring the spirit up to snuff. I poured the rubbing alcohol through the filter into the pitcher – I hoped that this would remove some of the ketones and other harsh impurities that are found in cheap booze.

I mixed another methanol martini, this time pretending to use other ingredients in case I was being watched. They would simply think I was getting inventive.

The methanol was less bitter filtered, but still blasted sharp.

In the bar fridge was a half-empty bottle of white zinfandel, and I mixed another filtered methanol cocktail with some of that as my vermouth.

By Jove, it was damned close to the vodka drink. Or maybe I was just getting accustomed to it.

I emptied a reserve bottle of vodka that was under the bar and filled it half way with the filtered rubbing alcohol. I then placed that bottle up with the others behind the bar, all very surreptitiously, like I was simply re-arranging things.

Now, I knew methanol was poison, but little else about the exact outcome of consumption. I had no idea exactly what the effects were or how long they took to take effect. Had I internet access, I could have found out, of course. Short of that, all I knew was that methanol had a very similar effect as ethanol short term.

It gets you drunk. The trouble comes later when the liver transforms it into formaldehyde and then from that into something else that quickly degrades the optic nerve – as you likely know methanol makes you blind. It also destroys your liver and can kill in relatively small quantities. Yes, but how much methanol kills? At the very least, perhaps I could convince Miguel to drink a martini of the stuff. Would one martini be enough? Would two or three ounces do the trick? He might not die in front of me, but he would have serious problems the next day even if he did not die. That might be the best I could do to avenge Elvis. Hand to hand combat with the filet knife was no longer an option – not that it really had been to begin with. The little flare gun with a single cartridge wasn't going to be a game changer, either.

And yet how fitting that Boone Linsenbigler, Master Cocktailer, would lay low a rogue by mixing him a deadly cocktail?

I dumped all the methanol cocktails in the sink and resumed with my vodka drink, swirling and spitting the first sip to clean out any residual methanol. All I needed was to poison myself!

I leaned on the bar, sipping my drink, my resolve to act solidifying.

But when?

Enrique. The Boss – or at the very least their supervisor and a go between with the headman. He was arriving at some juncture, and they had only five minutes to prepare for his arrival. As there was no helipad or landing strip that I could see, I had to imagine that he was arriving by boat through that narrow channel. Then again, there was always the possibility he would arrive by seaplane, and that they would go out and meet him. In some ways that made more sense – for the boss to come all the way there by boat would make him vulnerable to pursuit and capture by the authorities. I decided that air transport must be the case. Perhaps when they went out to fetch him and I was alone with the submarine crews I could implement an escape in one of the flats boats. Perhaps I could use the flare gun to create a distraction.

Yes, but if I went out through the channel while they were out in the bay they could give chase, possibly with the plane. I had to bottle them all up in here if I could.

I didn't see a way, and was mortified to think that I might have to act spontaneously and just wait for an opportunity. Worse, I might become paralyzed with fear and not act even if the opportunity came.

I finished my martini, and realized that if they were watching me on a monitor somewhere, it would look like I'd already had three concoctions. They would think I drank most of the methanol drinks, and that I was a smidge tanked.

Perhaps that was a good thing. Then they'd let their guard down a little and in the process give me some sort of opportunity. Then again, perhaps this was just an excuse for another limetini – and so I bellied up once more to the well. Might the mirror behind the bar conceal a camera? As such, I made sure to mix and pour my drink with a little bravado to make it look like I was on the bus to Snookerville.

Limetini in hand, I came around the bar, picked up a bar stool, and set it in front of one of the front windows flanking the door. Might as well watch what goes on out in the compound to draw a bead on the comings and goings of my captors.

Three brown men in white T-shirts were moving shrink-wrapped packages from one sub to the other. The two remaining men stood in the open cockpit of the second sub. They had put on hooded blue windbreakers that closely matched the color of their sub. It looked like they were preparing to leave. I would have thought they would have waited until dark but perhaps their handlers were happier having the goods underway rather than possibly bottled up at the base should the shinola hit the fan.

Interesting. I surmised this loading from one sub to the other meant that the one sub had come in the night before from the west or south with drugs so that the other sub could now complete the link to Florida. I had to bet that on the return trip from Florida the sub brought cash back to the base. Yet I didn't see packages of money going into the other sub. If I were running the operation, I wouldn't trust a huge sum of cash to a dinky sub on the open ocean. I'd come in at night and fly it out. Which was precisely why I imagined Enrique was flying in – to pick up his money. There could be a huge sum of money at the base.

Just as I thought that, Tamara and Miguel appeared from the far left hefting duffle bags down to their flats boat. *Aha, the money for Enrique.* I could see Elvis' blood on the platform of the other boat, but otherwise they were quite similar flats boats. With a chill up my spine, I wondered what Miguel and Tamara did with their fishing guide. I couldn't imagine Carlos would let them go out unguided. Banana Cay was soon going to run out of guides at this rate. At day's end Carlos would likely be beside himself – two boats, two guides and their clients all missing. I had to believe that once he sounded the alarm that Phillips would send the fleet – if the Bahamas had one. At the very least this base would have to be evacuated within a couple days, and either they took me with them or left me here in a watery grave.

I watched as Miguel and Tamara walked the docks from their boat to the sub that was being loaded with the last packages. They had a brief conversation with the pilot and first mate before the other three men untied the sub from the dock and gave it a shove toward the channel. The captain maneuvered the craft down the channel – I didn't hear a motor so guessed it must have an electric motor for silent running. It must have had a gas-powered motor as well or it would never make it to Florida.

I watched as the sub and the back of the pilot's head disappeared down the channel.

Tamara turned and glanced up at me. She and Miguel spoke in earnest for five minutes before walking toward my cabin.

Showtime.

By the time Tamara removed the padlock and entered with Miguel I was back behind the bar.

I smiled broadly and said: "Can I get you something?"

They shared a blank look, and she said: "We heard from Conglomerated already. They're going to pay."

I raised my glass. "And why wouldn't they? You just provided them with one hell of a publicity angle. Let me make you a drink. It's the least we can do to make the time pass. So how are you going to hand me back to them?" I reached for the methanol and began to mix a limetini with it.

They didn't look at each other again, but I could tell they wanted to, and he said: "We have to abandon this base tomorrow. You'll stay here. We'll send them the coordinates." He made every attempt to hold my gaze and not blink.

My jaw tightened as I realized he was lying, he had to be, why would they let me see all of this and them and

73

know about Enrique unless they knew I would never tell anybody anything? After all, their original intention was to kill me because I knew about the submarine base. Why even risk that I might provide inside information that could be valuable to their nemesis?

I waved my hand at the bar theatrically. "Excellent, I certainly can stay busy while waiting, unless you plan on packing all this up and taking it with you?"

"We leave everything," he said, eyes dark.

That ominous exchange convinced me I needed to try to escape or die trying. I had no choice. I strained the methanol into a martini glass and held it out to him. "Well, no hard feelings, Miguel, this one's on me." He stepped forward and took it, hesitantly. "And for the lady?"

"Same." She plunked on a bar stool, looking a little exhausted, strain showing around her eyes.

I reached for the methanol but passed it up in favor of the vodka. She didn't kill Elvis, after all. OK, so she tried to kill me, but she didn't, did she? Maybe she missed intentionally?

Miguel set his drink on the bar. "I have to go get my phone. He may call any minute."

As soon as he was out of the room, she whispered: "Hand me a napkin and a pen from back there."

I was shaking her drink, and feigned a sloshed response: "Ah, your phone number perhaps? I can look you up next time I'm in Columbia!"

She hung her head, "You're an idiot, you know that?"

I strained her cocktail into a glass and set it atop a bar napkin. "There's your napkin, I'll see if there's a pen. I don't see one. Nope. No pen. Not over here either."

She dipped her finger in her drink and wrote in vodka on the bar.

I ducked my head to try to get the right angle with the light from the front windows so that I could see what she wrote. There were other smudges on the bar so it was hard to make out. Best I could tell it read: *IM DEAF.*

I said: "Well, you read lips like a champ."

Grimacing at me she wiped the letters off the bar.

What in blazes was she trying to tell me?

Miguel strode back into the room, phone in hand. "Enrique's here, far side of the island out of the swells and wind. They couldn't get closer." Clearly nervous or anxious about Enrique's arrival, he glanced at his drink, reached for it, and downed half.

His eyes bugged out a little, but he swallowed, and he said hoarsely: "We need to go. Let's lock him back up."

She toasted her glass with his and downed the limetini is one slurp. He finished his and headed for the door.

She stood to follow. "You know, I don't like him in here alone, with us gone for two hours. Let's just put the boys in here with him, not lock him up. I want him watched. Besides, he's half drunk."

This made it clearer than ever that they had been keeping an eye on me.

He kept going. "OK, but let's hurry."

She eyed me and said: "The boys have been drinking already, so don't serve them too much rum."

She swayed from the room and called the boys over.

Two hours. Rum.

I turned from Tamara's retreating form to the bottle of 151 behind the bar, cracking my knuckles.

Belly up, boys!

CHAPTER 8

IN MY CONSIDERABLE EXPERIENCE, there is no more potent cocktail than those that contain 151 rum, brandy and champagne – or malt liquor if available. These are the foundation of the most lethal cocktails one might conceivably find at the local Tiki Bar. I recall one such night with these ingredients at a Polynesian restaurant in Lyndhurst many years ago. The drink was named "The ICBM." Under its listing on the cocktail menu was the admonition: "One Drink: Lift Off. Two Drinks: Supersonic. Three Drinks: Detonate on Target. Limit: Two Drinks Per Customer."

I tossed in some Jägermeister for good measure and had "the boys" passed out on the porch furniture in an hour, three empty glasses next to each.

With the hush of a cat walking on plush pile carpet, I crept to the other porch and unhooked the three sub machine guns hanging on the wall. I placed them gently into Elvis's flats boat. If the boys awoke during my escape, I didn't want them getting trigger-happy.

Yes, but how to leave quietly? I couldn't very well pole Elvis' boat out – that platform barely fit through the opening in the mangroves much less someone standing on top of it.

I tip toed over to the submarine. There was a hard canopy, like a lid with a windshield, which was folded back but could be folded forward and locked in place to make it water tight and submerge. With the canopy open, the cockpit was exposed, and it was large enough for a man to stand, with a fold-down seat. The pilot could sit in the cockpit, close the canopy at a height that would allow him to look out the windshield. Below the cockpit was dark, open cargo space front and back. I examined the controls. There was a joystick on one side, a steering wheel in the center, throttle on the other side, and various gauges around the steering wheel. To the side were a series of rubberized valve handles that I assumed worked the submersible mechanics of the thing, allowing water into ballast tanks as well as compressed gas to blow out water. There were no markings on the nobs like "up" or "down", you couldn't tell by looking at them what made the thing rise or sink.

Kneeling on the dock, I moved the joystick forward to see what would happen. Nothing. Then I noted a toggle switch to one side of it, and when I flicked it, a red light came on over the joystick. When I moved the joystick again, there was a hum and the craft slid forward, straining at the ropes. The joystick operated an electric motor for silent running.

I found a painter rope in the front hold of the flats boat and connected that boat to a cleat at the stern of the sub, laying the rope across the dock so it would slide off when the sub moved forward.

Slinking back to the lounge, I recharged the vodka tonic I'd been sipping, untied both boats, and slid into the small cockpit of the sub. Red light on, I gently angled the joystick forward. The sub hummed forward, the rope sliding across the dock until it plopped into the water, the flats boat in tow. There was no place to put my drink so I wedged it between two of the rubber-handled valves at my side. I mean, if you're going to enact an escape, there's no reason in the world not to do it with a cocktail. In hindsight, I'm not sure a vodka tonic was the best choice as it seemed a little twee. I would rather have had a solid tumbler of whiskey to embolden me. But all they had in that department was some generic blended 'American' whiskey, an abomination.

The flats boat bumped the mangroves here and there on the way out, but gently, I did not hear any of the boys stir. Light at the end of the tunnel was blue seas and late afternoon sky, puffy clouds and gulls soaring. I stopped just before exiting, checking for any boats or aircraft, but there were none that I could see from that vantage. So I glided forward a couple hundred feet into the small lee area, the surf pounding the rocks to my left. I kept my eyes right where the mangroves curved away and still saw no other craft.

My heart was thumping: by God, Linsenbigler, you've done it!

I pulled my cocktail from between the rubber handles and took a deep sip to congratulate myself.

A growling torrent of bubbles shot from the sides of the submarine – I had accidentally turned one of the valves with my drink but I wasn't sure which one. I grabbed the nearest handle to try to move it back into place, and the bubbles only grew larger. I wrenched it the other way and they were less, so I grabbed the other handle and even more bubbles erupted.

As I fiddled with the levers, I was rudely made aware that the craft was submerging and that water had begun to top the cockpit. I took another deep sip of the cocktail and bitterly sent the remainder to Davey Jones. Abandon ship!

By the time I had swum to the flats boat and pulled myself aboard, the sub was just that, sunk, and headed for the bottom fast, huge bubbles rising and bursting from the cockpit.

The flats boat started to move. The painter rope was still attached to the submarine, which was pulling my boat down with it!

I fell upon the painter rope, but as it was taut, it was the devil's business to get the loop of rope off the fore cleat. In no time, the sub was directly below, the rope groaning as it went tighter and tighter.

I hadn't imagined it was that deep where we were, but the bow of the flats boat began to be pulled down.

Bah! If only that filet knife was on board! The screwdriver!

I rummaged through the skiff's console, found the screwdriver, almost threw it overboard, and then hurriedly set to unscrewing the cleat from the bow, again almost letting it fall into the ocean.

The first screw popped out and flew fifty feet, the cleat jerking to one side.

The stern was coming out of the water; I could hear the water cascading off the motor.

The cleat was so tight to the screw that I couldn't turn it. I wedged the screwdriver under the cleat and pried up as hard as I could. There was a splintering sound from the fiberglass, but the screw wouldn't budge.

BANG.

All at once, the cleat shot off the bow and vanished, the back of the skiff slamming onto the chop.

I collapsed with a groan of relief, calamity averted.

One might suggest my near undoing was the product of bravado, that I should not have brought that cocktail into a submarine or on my escape.

I, on the other hand, blame the near catastrophe on those inept narco sub designers who did not install a cup holder. What on earth were they thinking?

Turning the ignition key, I fired up the flats boat. I could see the cell tower to the west, turned the wheel, and rammed the throttle forward, around the point through the crashing waves, and out across the swells back toward Banana Cay. I hoped I had enough gas, though I had to imagine that Elvis knew he had plenty to get home. I looked behind me at the rocky cay and saw no boats. I adjusted the trim and the flats boat went further on plane, and faster. I would have put in a distress call but there was no radio on the boat – cell phones in many places have replaced the need for radios.

Egad, through ingenuity and sneakiness I had affected my escape! Astounding. Though I had to admit, I was deuced lucky, it was a huge help that Tamara left me unrestrained while she was away. She did that of course only because she thought me jiggered, too drunk to pull off an adventure. Best not to underestimate the liver of Boone Linsenbigler, my lady!

Late day sun was orange like it had been that morning a million years ago when I was eating breakfast and thinking only of permit. My mind now was full of anything but permit. Damn, but it was awful what happened to Elvis. I had to get back and have Carlos sound the alarm. I kept checking my back for any pursuers, but there were none that I could see.

What the blazes had Tamara tried to write on the bar? *IM DEAF*. Thinking back on it, I had to assume she was trying to tell me something that she didn't want Miguel to hear, but at the time I was pretty wrapped up in being the happy drunkard. Hard to make out what she wrote what with it being clear liquid, I had to get the light on it at an angle. Suppose it could have been something sexy, like… or wait, could it have said 'I'M DEA?' She's with the Drug Enforcement Agency? Confound it, that would explain why she missed the shot at me and allowed me to roam about when they were gone, wouldn't it? She likely knew I was going to be shot the next morning, and rather than have interceded directly and blow her cover, she left the door open so I could fly the coop. But would that explain why she vamped me at the airport and hotel? Anyway, if she was DEA, I reckoned that she was in very deep cover and up to her pretty little neck about now. I may have made things a little complicated for her, but at least now I was out of her hair.

With the wind at my back, it took me something like forty minutes to round the outside corner of Banana Cay – Elvis had taken a short cut through narrow channels that I was afraid to retrace, not knowing if they were passable at a lower tide. Once on the lagoon side, I adjusted the boat's trim and shot as fast as I could toward the docks in the distance. As I drew near, I could see the shaved head of Carlos standing on the dock, no doubt wondering why we were late.

I throttled back as I drew near, and threw him a rope. I didn't give him a chance to ask any questions, just opened up full bore:

"It was drug smugglers, they have a submarine base on an out island, I was captive but escaped. Miguel and Tamara were not guests but smugglers looking to try to throw me off the track if they could. They killed Elvis but held me for ransom. They are packing up and moving out of that base tomorrow, so the RBP better muster and get down here on the double." I hopped on the dock as he tied off the front. "I stole three of their machine guns, they may come here looking for me, and so we'd better be prepared unless..." As I tied off the back, I looked up I saw Carlos had a black pistol in his hand.

"Perfect, Carlos, we may need that gun." I stood. "Kind of dangerous to point that at me. Do you mind, uh...Carlos?"

His face looked carved from stone. "Let's go, Linsenbigler. We're going for a little walk."

Oh, that didn't sound good. I gulped: "You're with them?"

He didn't respond; he didn't have to. Of course, Miguel and Tamara didn't have a fishing guide at all; they didn't need to pretend with him to be anglers because they were confederates in crime with Carlos

"Let's go." He backed down off the dock and waved me ahead of him and I started toward the path back to the lodge.

"Not that way," he said. "The other way." He nodded toward a less well-beaten path that led up the coast. I'd seen that coast, and there was nothing up there, no house or shacks or anything. He was taking me up there to put a bullet in my head. Possibly the reason nobody followed me on my escape was they knew I would come back to the lodge and they alerted Carlos to intercept me.

My mind raced. What to say? Did I have anything at all that I could offer him that could make him change his mind? I had only one last thing.

I reached into my pocket and pulled out my handkerchief, mopping my brow. "Where are we going, Carlos? You know they have a ransom out on me, a million dollars. They might not get the money if I'm dead."

He took a step forward, only five feet from me. "I said get moving."

"Look, this is crazy," I gestured at him with my handkerchief and pulled the trigger on the little flare gun.

The ball of fire burst from my hand and hit him in the neck – he yelped, jerking to the side as he pulled the trigger on his pistol, the shot zipping about a foot past my head. The flare seemed to have become caught in his shirt collar or something because Carlos clawed at it and thrashed and squealed, his shirt catching on fire at his neck.

A Porsche or Lamborghini may be fast, but I felt as if I went zero to sixty in three seconds flat as I dashed for the lodge. My mind was so intent on putting as much distance between me and that murdering bastard Carlos that I remember nothing of the hundred-yard dash only the moment I hit the restaurant steps. Where was I going? Was the bar the best place to hide? Or was it just Linsenbigler instinct to find safety in a barroom? I burst in: nobody there.

I charged into the kitchen: nobody there, either. It was like a nightmare, one of those horrid dreams where there's nobody around when there should be.

There were some pots and pans hanging by the stove, and I grabbed a cast iron skillet and killed the lights. I positioned myself by the kitchen door to the barroom, and I waited, my heart seemingly jumping a foot or two out of my chest.

So much for escaping!

I held my breath as I heard footsteps, growling, and cursing coming up the steps into the barroom.

He kicked open the swinging kitchen door, and in the backlight from the barroom I could see the smoke coming off of his burnt neck, the gun in his hand.

I swung with everything I had with that pan.

He heard the whoosh in time to dodge it.

The skillet slammed the doorframe; he lurched forward and caromed off a butcher block to the floor.

The kitchen door swung shut, the dark room lit only by the glow of the square door window. I dove to the floor away from Carlos, toward the back door.

Flash and *BANG*.

A ricochet *tinged-tanged-patueyed* around the metal surfaces of the kitchen. If you ever hear a gun go off in a small room like that, you will not be able to believe how loud it is. My ears rang as I scrambled on all fours for the back door, scuttling in the gloom headlong into the edge of the stove and falling to the side, but to a side that separated me from Carlos by a prep island. I gripped my head. *Youch.*

The back door next to me burst open, and the person fanned the light switches.

Blinding light filled the room, and I squinted at Cecil at the back door. *Thethal, the cartoon pig bartender.*

Cecil had a pistol in his hand, but he only glanced at me before charging to the other side of the room where Carlos was just scrambling to his feet. Both men fired – and both missed! Again, bullets *tinked-tanked-patueyed* around the room as the two of them were grappling in man-to-pig combat on the other side of the prep table, their guns swinging perilously in my direction as I crawled one way and the other to stay out of harm's way.

Cecil tossed his gun in my direction and it clattered to the floor but out of reach. The little man hauled a hand back and gave Carlos a mighty karate chop to the neck, a palm to the face and a kick to the chest that sent Carlos crashing into pantry shelves, which collapsed in a great roar and plume of flour. Cecil vanished into the white billowing cloud, and I heard a few other thuds before he emerged dusted in flour but holding Carlos' pistol. He stepped up and picked up his own weapon, so held one in each hand. Panting, he said: "I'm with the Royal Bahamian Poweeth. I heard what you told Carlos down by the dock, I was hiding just off the path."

Cecil was the inside man! I was bowled over – figuratively and literally. I arose from the floor, a little winded myself. "Bravo, Cecil. Talk about in the nick of time. Good grief, I've been through it today. Don't worry; I'll make my own cocktail." I began to slog toward the bar.

"Not tho fast, Linthenbigwer. We have to tie him up, and you have to head to Freeport."

Panting through open mouth, brow furrowed, I said: "Surely you must be joking, Cecil. I'm at the end. Freeport will have to come here, we'll call them."

He shook his flour-dusted head. "Carlos pulled the shunts on the cell tower and hid them. He also disabled the marine set. There's no way to get word out exthept by boat. I have to stay here. The other guests were sent out on a clambake, a picnic spot on another island. I have to protect them when they get back."

"How the dickens am I supposed to get to Freeport? It'll be dark before long, and it must be, what, four hours?"

"Maybe three. A full tank will get you there in a flats boat."

"What if I say no?"

"Fine, you can stay here and deal with the thmugglers when they come here angry. Those people at the submarine base will come here."

"I'll just get my phone and wallet, gas up and go."

CHAPTER 9

IT WAS SUNSET by the time I shot out toward the orange ball on the horizon in Elvis' boat. My phone's GPS mapping app would help guide me the forty-odd miles across the bay to Grand Bahama's East End, and of course, as it became dark Freeport would be the brightest thing ahead of me. It felt good to be escaping again and for the final time, felt good to leave all that danger in my wake. I had never spent any time in Freeport, and looked forward to treating myself to a nice hotel room and meal. By God, I had earned it, just lock the hotel room door and hang the "DO NOT DISTURB" placard on the nob.

To be sure, I was a little worried about what was going to go down back there at Banana Cay, a prickly situation.

Yet as worried as I was for Cecil, Tamara, the staff at Banana Cay and their guests, there was one bright and shining truth: this was up to the police. There was nothing I could contribute going forward beyond sounding the alarm. What was going on back at the lodge was Phillips and the RBP's bailiwick. As soon as I had a cell signal, I would call ahead. After that, it was out of my hands.

The sun turned into a cerise puddle on the horizon that dripped away, leaving a thin purple line of dusk that ended in the jagged black profile of East End ahead to my right. The only thing following me over my shoulder to the east was night and an emergence of stars.

I was so intent on what was ahead of me I didn't notice a boat approaching from the dark silhouette of East End until it was about a half mile away – a dark wedge with port and starboard lights. It looked much bigger than my flats boat, and it was angled directly at me. I tapped my throttle, adjusted my trim: I was going as fast as I could. To put distance between us, I would have to angle away, but that would make my trip to Freeport a lot longer, and I wasn't sure that eighteen gallons was enough for a longer trip. Well, the ship was coming not from behind but ahead. It couldn't have been smugglers, could it?

Then there was a sound like my skiff's motor was faltering, a pulsing sound. Playing with the throttled didn't seem to help make it stop, and the sound became louder. I looked over my shoulder to the left and a spotlight came on in the sky. The noise was a helicopter. Friend or foe?

One thing you quickly realize under such circumstances is that motoring a boat away from a helicopter on the open seas – or anywhere else for that matter – is a waste of time. If this was foe, I was done for. I throttled back, cognizant that I had three sub machine guns lying in the back of the boat. I could defend myself. Sure, and what were the chances I would be able to quickly figure out how to fire a sub machine gun? I didn't want to be that pathetic guy caught in the spotlight with a little machine gun when a big machine gun opens fire and makes him do a bullet dance as thousands of slugs tear up his body. No sir.

I throttled back and awaited whatever was in store. Damn it all, I had no cocktail, and there was even a cup holder right there below to the throttle.

The chopper slowed behind me to the left, and the ship to the right switched on its search light from a thousand feet out, dimly illuminating me. They had me wedged in.

I was suddenly drenched in the beam from the helicopter and it pivoted ahead of me, the water all around rippling in concentric waves from the chopper's blades. Instinctively, I held my hands up to the side of my head. If this were foe, I would likely be shot in the next second or two, and in some ways, I was resigned. There's only so much running and escaping one man can do. If they had caught up with me once more, well, they were better men than I, nothing for it, I had been caught up with a bunch of baddies. As an amateur, I found myself unable to wriggle free. So be it.

The chopper hovered five hundred feet ahead, light full on me, as the ship approached to the right at full speed, white caps surging at its bow. I could see now that it was about sixty feet long. It cut throttle and drew nearer. The copter drew slowly closer and I was engulfed in sea spray that absorbed the intensity of the searchlight. The raging blades of the chopper vibrated the air, my body tingling and wind whipped to the point where I was numb. I couldn't see anything except blinding white, salty mist whirling around my body, and in that instant I wondered if I were already dead, whether I had been shot and was about to move to the light, to the great beyond.

Then the helicopter pivoted to one side, and the storm of light and vibration subsided. The ship was broadside. It was grey, and amidships there were large white letters: P-60.

I bowed my head, leaning my raised hands on the windshield. *Well, God, maybe next time.*

It was a Royal Bahamas Defense patrol boat.

The helicopter turned out to be DEA. They were working a joint operation because the RBD doesn't have any helicopters for interdicting. They thought I was a smuggler's fast boat. The machine guns aft didn't do much to dissuade them from that notion, and they ferried me in handcuffs to the patrol boat on an orange zodiac. That was fine with me, by all means, just get me onto that boat and I am home free. *Old Boone is done with this caper.*

Once aboard, I was soon seated at a table in the wardroom of the patrol boat. The room smelled a little musty and was lit by low hanging fluorescent tubes that made the eyes of the five men sitting across from me glint. The retinue included three dark Bahamian officers of the RBD in tan uniforms and three Americans from DEA – two Hispanic, one white – in black stealth outfits. They had lowered from the helicopter on ropes.

I had told my story and they had verified who I was and that I was not a fast boat smuggler. They also verified the situation at Banana Cay via a satellite telephone intercept of Enrique. Apparently, something went south when Miguel and Tamara brought the money out to the plane – Enrique recognized Tamara as DEA from a previous encounter, and when he pulled a gun on her there was a struggle and a bullet went into the plane's engine. Enrique and Miguel decided to hold on to Tamara until they could get another plane in to get them out of there. The three of them and the pilot went back to the base and found me missing, picked up the submarine crew and some guns and headed to Banana Cay to wait for the plane. Our assumption was that the hostages were Tamara, the four anglers including 'Red', the chef, possibly Cecil and two guides. Likely Enrique, Miguel and the pilot would leave by plane, Carlos and the sub crew by flats boat.

The DEA agent in charge was named Diego, and he sat backward on his chair – a strapping man with wide shoulders, a thick mustache and powerful hands. His dark eyes were curious of me and likely bemused of my predicament. He said:

"You know the layout of the place, Mr. Linsenbigler. If we're going to go in there and save our fellow agent, the RBP officer and the rest of the captives, we're going to need your help finding our way to the various lodge buildings to see who is where, and then decide how to act. We know from the intercept that the smugglers have a plane or boat coming at dawn to remove them. When they leave Banana Cay, they will leave their captives alive? Maybe not. Or maybe only certain ones."

I cleared my throat and stood, steadying myself on the back of my chair.

"Gentlemen: prior to noon today nobody had ever tried to kill or kidnap me. Since noon, there have been two direct attempts on my life, and I have been shot at with a gun numerous times, and I have been kidnapped. I have had to make two escapes for my life. Prior to noon today, I have lived a life consumed with boozing and fishing and recently being a brand for Conglomerated Beverages. I enjoy a small amount of fame for being the front man for cocktail accessories. I am not, however, nor have I ever been, trained as a policeman or detective. I have no military training beyond Boy Scouts. On all accounts, I'm exceedingly lucky to have survived thus far. Yet you want me to go back to Banana Cay to resolve a hostage situation with a drug cartel?"

Diego grimaced at the floor, the weathered wrinkles of his face flexing. 'There are other options, but operations like this are full of variables and calculated risk. Unfortunately, we don't have the luxury of time, the luxury of reconnaissance or reinforcements. With your reconnaissance, our chances of success are greatly improved. A knowledge of the exact location of paths and sight lines are critical to stealth. So you coming with us greatly improves the chances that those people being held captive will not be killed. I would rather not have you along, frankly, as inexperienced members of a team jeopardize the safety of the experienced members. But given the stakes and the odds, I'm willing to risk my life to save those people. It's a lot to ask any man to risk his life for others, especially in your case, when that's not what you do for a living."

He looked up at me, poised to say one thing, and then I saw him decide to say something else, and he did so with a candid smile. "You know, I'm not always on duty. When I'm home with my wife and kids, I'm not thinking about gunplay and smugglers. I was a high school dropout, went into the army, and was busted for drugs when I got out, ultimately switched sides, starting as an informer, and then was recruited by DEA and worked undercover for years, until I became too recognizable. I'm all the people I used to be. And you know, every time before I go on something like this Banana Cay mission, or rope from a copter onto the deck of a fishing trawler, there's a part of me that's the scared kid on the first day of boot camp, wondering what the hell did I do to get myself into this mess. I want to go home."

I hung my head. Some situations seem to have a life of their own, and I knew that if I refused I would never forgive myself if anybody died. "Is there any coffee? If I'm going to do this, I need to get jacked up or I'll just pass out."

One of the RBD officers stood. "Anybody else want coffee?"

Everybody raised their hands.

CHAPTER 10

DRESSED IN BLACK commando gear head to toe, complete with mini radio headset, ski mask, gun belt and knife. I turned and handed my phone to Diego, who had just finished lacing his combat boots. "I need a picture of me in this outfit. My publicist is going to go wild." The other two DEA agents rolled their eyes.

I stood in front of a Bahamian flag on the wall of the patrol boat's locker room, striking a jaunty pose, arms akimbo. As long as I was going to be killed, I figured I might as well get to work on polishing the Linsenbigler legacy. I made sure that my nose and signature mustache were positioned over the edge of the ski mask.

He snapped the picture and handed the phone back. "Make sure you turn that off if you're bringing it with you. Seems obvious, but I can't tell you how many times you're out there trying to be quiet when someone's phone chirps. It's gotten more than a few people killed."

"Not to worry." I placed it in the locker with my fishing clothes, not taking any chances. "And this pistol? How many bullets?"

"Rounds. They are called *rounds*, not bullets. Fifteen." Diego put a hand on his holster. "You know how to use that weapon?"

"I'll have you know that in high school I was a member of the Pinwheelers Target Shooting club down at the Isaak Walton League. I have to work the action to chamber the first round, right?"

"Yes, but don't do that until you're ready to use it. In fact, if I were you I'd try not to even take it out of the holster. It's just there for an emergency. Once you lead us to the lodge and we case the place, you hang back, the three of us will go secure the hostages. If you hear shooting stay down. There should be no reason for you to do anything but collect and hold hostages as we free them, if that's the way it works out. A lot of times, they hold hostages in several places to complicate a rescue attempt, though they may not even think they have to worry about that. If they think you were going to Freeport and muster the RBP, the smugglers would figure that the time it would take the authorities to get out here would be too late."

"I favor the idea of me not being shot at or juggling a pistol in this whole plan, makes me feel like I might actually survive."

My three companions shouldered small backpacks, each hung with night vision goggles. I had none such as it was all they could do to equip me such as I was.

I followed the DEA agents down a narrow hall to a ships ladder that took us to the deck of the patrol boat. It was solidly dark and I'd wager about three in the morning. The patrol boat had anchored at the far side of Banana Cay out of sight lines with the lodge.

Red lights lit the way along the ship's deck to where some Bahamian sailors and an officer were standing at a ladder down to a bright orange zodiac. One by one we descended the ladder into the boat, then cast off and motored toward the hulking silhouette of Banana Cay, the patrol boat shrinking behind us in a sea of stars.

The bay was relatively calm and free of swells. The shore ahead was a barely discernable pale strip of beach backed by dark jungle, the black hands of coconut palms slightly undulating above. The men in commando gear around me in the zodiac sat in silence, folded in on themselves. I wondered if they were steeling themselves for the gunplay and quick maneuvering that lay ahead or reflecting on those they would leave behind if they died. This made me wonder what I should be thinking about, how I should be preparing. Well, the three cups of coffee were a good start. I didn't know how I should be preparing mentally since this was something I had never done. Boosting my sight and hearing and cognitive skills would be just the thing, if that was possible. How does one focus on innate perceptive abilities and make them sharper – through force of will? If that's what my companions were doing, I didn't want to be the one to interrupt for a quick lesson in tantric yoga. I needed them to be sharp.

A hundred feet from shore, Diego killed the motor and the man in the bow rolled over the zodiac pontoon into knee-deep water, pulling the boat the rest of the way in to shore. The rest of us jumped out ankle deep and hefted the zodiac all the way onto shore and under the palms. The inky jungle was quiet except for the gentle rustling of palms against each other. It sounded like waves of light rain on pavement, the way a summer shower sounds on a shopping mall parking lot in Paramus. There it was – I was thinking of home. Needless to say, it didn't smell like home. The breeze coming from the jungle was redolent with palm litter tinged with salt. It smelled vaguely like coffee grounds and peanut shells.

Our march from the landing spot took us up the beach, and we stayed as close to the tree line as we could. Even though it was louder walking on the crunchy flotsam and shells at the top of the thin beach, the white noise of the palms in the breeze had a cancelling effect at distance. It was more critical to stay out of sight. The three agents led the way toward a point where mangroves peeked around the corner and it took a good thirty minutes to get there. When we arrived, Diego crouched and so did the rest of us. He waved me forward from the rear, and we rose up slowly over a jumble of spikey palmettoes to take in the view around the point.

In the distance, I saw the main dock, the one where I shot Carlos in the neck with the flare gun. Zounds, that must have hurt! Hard to think of anything much worse than a flaming hot ball of gunpowder jumping around your shirt collar, swatting at it and burning your hands in the process.

To the sides of the dock were mangroves in a wide gentle crescent. To get there, we would have to either wade the shallows through mangroves or bushwhack through the jungle. Then again, Carlos had attempted to lead me up a path in the direction of where we were crouching.

I put my mouth to Diego's ear and whispered: "That's the main dock; the lodge is a short walk directly across the island to the ocean side. I think that there was a path leading this direction from the dock. We can see if we can find it – I did not walk up this way, I can't be sure."

He nodded and waved me to lead the team into the shadows of the jungle looking for a path. I had to trudge around the palmettos to find a way in, and meandered through the prickly underbrush looking for some dim path through the silhouettes of bushes, vines and tree trunks.

A burst of wings and a loud croak practically made my head explode – I wheeled and tripped over a vine. On my back, I saw the shape of a night heron fly up to the jungle canopy and vanish. Diego came to my side, holstering his weapon. I held up a hand and stood: *I'm OK.*

After about ten minutes of fumbling about, I heard a *pssst* behind me, and one of Diego's men was pointing down a faint, crooked alley meandering toward where I guessed the dock would be. I double-backed, following black forms of the three agents - shadows among the shadows. Ten minutes later, there was a dim patch of sky glow ahead framed by spikey plants. It was a clearing, the one at the lagoon dock. Diego held up a hand, telling us to wait. Down low and to the side, he crept down the path to where it met the track to the lodge. He knelt there, and didn't move for what seemed the longest time but was probably five minutes. I suppose he was listening, or just carefully looking, the way an angler does when he sets upon a trout stream and takes time out to just observe and see what's going on, where the fish are, and wait to see if any of the fish show themselves. Maybe there was a sentry at the lagoon dock and he would carelessly match a cigarette and reveal his location. It would make sense for them to have placed a sentry there, possibly just to the side in the dark. Diego's shadow flickered and vanished around the corner. I felt sweat trickle down my back, and the ski mask suddenly felt itchy, as if I was getting prickly heat. Damn it all, where had he gone without us? He appeared again at the clearing and waved us toward him. We trotted to where he crouched and he held up a finger and then made a fist, then pointed at the ground. I didn't know what the meant, but guessed that it meant he'd subdued a look out at the dock: *one down*. Good thing we took the inland path instead of wading the shallows to the dock. We would have been spotted.

I pointed up the main path to the lodge and put my lips to Diego's ear, whispering: "This comes to a spot that opens up behind one of the cabanas and to the side of the main lodge building and restaurant. When we get close, I think we should angle off to the right through the jungle so we come up not in the middle of it all but at the farthest cabana. That way we can check them one by one and clear our way to the main building where I would guess everybody would be gathered. Or at least some of them. I have to believe if they had a sentry at the lagoon dock that they would have one at the ocean dock as well. Something to keep an eye out for."

Diego nodded deeply and motioned to his ear, signaling for us to switch on our radios since I guess we might soon separate. I hoped so as I didn't want be in whispering distance when things went tits up. Through my ski mask, I turned on my earpiece and heard a gentle *bloop* signifying that the radio was operational.

We crept along the edge of the larger tunnel through the forest toward the lodge, and another sky glow appeared. The clearing ahead was dotted with the solar path lights of the main compound. Diego waved us off to the right, into the jungle. Fortunately, the trees were spread farther apart and there were fewer vines – possibly because it was ocean side and saltier, I don't know.

Yellow lights of the cabana windows winked at us though the shrubs, fronds and tree trunks until they stopped. Counting the lights, we knew we were behind the fourth and last cabin. Diego looked back at me and I pointed toward where the ocean waves dashed themselves on the sand.

Creeping to the edge of the clearing, we were directly behind Cabana 4, and only about fifteen feet away. Diego and his men scanned the area, and shortly Diego waved one of his men forward and pointed at the cabin. I heard in my ear: "Check the first one."

The agent slipped out from our cluster and scampered around to the side of the cabana, out of sight. I heard the agent in my earpiece. "Nobody."

Diego: "We'll check Cabana Three." He waved the other agent toward that cabana, and we received a similar reply.

Diego: "We'll check Cabana two." He motioned me to follow him, and I don't mind saying that I would have rather stayed right where I was. Cabana Two was mine, where my stuff was, and blasted close to where all the action was likely to take place.

Bent at the waist, we trotted toward the dimly lit window of Cabana Two, to the panes facing the jungle – the idea was to have the hut between us and the main lodge buildings.

When our backs were up against the stucco wall of the hut my heart was squeezing for all it was worth. This would have been sort of fun and exciting were it not for the fact that I might well get shot.

Then my heart stopped: I could hear voices inside the hut. Diego had what looked like an oversized telescoping pen in his hand, which he extended and put one end to his eye, the other to the window above our heads: it was a small periscope. I heard in my ear: "They have the girl in Cabana Two. Two bad guys with her."

Thwack!

Tamara yelped.

Thwack!

Tamara yelped.

Diego in my ear: "Bad guys torturing the girl. Consolidate here and we'll recon the main lodge. We can't move on the girl until we can lock down the other hostages. Boone: sorry, I wasn't going to get you involved, but I need you to stay here. Draw your weapon and chamber a round – *quietly*. Keep your finger on the side of the gun until you are ready to use it, if you even need to, then place your finger on the trigger to fire. When the shit hits the fan those guys in Cabana Two will come running out toward us, we'll have an eye out and take care of him. Only shoot if you have to or can't possibly miss."

I nodded, perhaps much harder than I needed to.

Really. This was just bonkers. This sort of thing just could not be happening to me. Just the previous morning, I was sitting right around the corner eating an egg sandwich in the happy Caribbean sunshine without a care in the world, so it seemed. And now all this.

The other two agents trotted past us headed to the back of the restaurant and bar, and Diego fell in behind them, leaving me alone and glued to the stucco wall. I was petrified.

Through watery eyes, I saw something move to my left. I could have sworn it was someone ducking behind Cabana Three.

Fumbling for my holster, I wrenched the gun out, and with trembling hands slid the action back slowly.

When I had it all the way back I could hear the bullet click into the action.

I slowly let the action go forwards and felt the bullet snug into the chamber.

My finger touched the trigger just to make sure I knew where it was.

Eyes still locked on Cabana Three, I saw a head duck out, looking my way.

"We have company," I whispered into the radio.

Diego: "Explain."

The person behind Cabana Three stepped out and trotted towards me.

I raised the gun with both hands, sweat stinging my eyes.

The person stopped about thirty feet from me, hands up.

I blinked and refocused.

I lowered the gun and Cecil trotted up next to me at the wall. For a plump little fellow he knew how to creep.

"It's Cecil, the RBP insider," I whispered into the radio. "He's armed."

Cecil put his mouth to my ear and quickly summed up the situation.

Me into the radio: "They grabbed the hostages before Cecil had a chance to secure them. He's been hiding in the jungle, watching, hoping someone would arrive to help. When he saw your team arrive, he took the liberty of subduing the sentry they had watching the compound on this side of the island. Now there are only Miguel and Carlos in Cabana Two with Tamara where we are and one submariner, the float plane pilot and Enrique watching the rest of the hostages in the dining room.

There was a pause before Diego said. "We'll get into position to storm the dining room from two sides, and you and Cecil get in position to storm Cabana Two. Copy?"

My trembling voice said: "Copy."

At that moment, I heard the screen door to the restaurant slam.

Cecil's sad eyes met mine, and we crawled to the edge of the hut to take a peek.

Someone with a machine gun slung over his chest was walking the path lit by solar torches toward Cabana Two. It did not look like a submariner – this man was taller, wore a sport coat. He was smoking a long, thin cigarette.

Me on the radio: "I think it is Enrique coming this way."

"Miguel!" The man shouted. "Carlos."

We heard the door to the Cabana Two open and close, and footsteps on the porch.

"Has she talked?" Enrique's voice was hearty, like an actor's. "What is the matter with you?"

Miguel groaned. "I don't feel well, and I'm having trouble seeing, I don't know what's happening, I believe I am ill. She has talked but I think she is lying."

The methanol martini taking effect!

Enrique snorted derisively. "*Fantástico*. Carlos cannot speak or hold a gun and you cannot see. Our friends had better arrive soon. Where is our sentry?"

Cecil put a gentle hand on my arm and squeezed. *Be ready.*

I didn't dare say anything into the radio, but hoped that the agents were close enough to hear this.

"Bah! I don't see him." Enrique continued, obviously disgusted with the quality of his crew. "You two go back to the dining room. You are worthless here. I will make the girl talk and then finish her."

The hut door opened and closed again, and I heard Enrique begin to talk, indiscernibly. But the baritone of his voice made the windows rattle ever so slightly.

We also heard footsteps heading back to the dining room on the path.

Cecil squeezed my bicep again. *Wait.*

Diego on the radio: "As soon as you hear the screen door slam shut on the restaurant, get ready for your man in Cabana two to come running out. Again, let us take care of him, just aim at his back in case he turns and runs. Copy?"

My mouth was so dry I had to repeat myself to be audible. "Copy."

Cecil whispered for me to go one way around and stand behind the door against the wall, and that he would go the other way and be the one to charge into the cabana.

My ears thrummed as I circled around the hut to the porch railing, relieved to see Cecil appear opposite me.

I lifted my gun, pointing it skyward, my trigger finger trembling, and my breathing uneven.

Then I saw Cecil climb quietly over the railing onto the porch, clearly intent on taking out Enrique as soon as he emerged. Which of course meant that there was going to be gunplay right in front of me instead of over by the dining room. At least I was below and not actually on the porch, but just the same, I was far too close to the fray for my liking.

We looked over and saw Miguel and Carlos through the palm fronds, climbing the stairs to the restaurant.

Cecil slid into position.

A gunshot went off at the restaurant, then another.

Cecil and I froze; timing was off.

Something had gone wrong.

Footsteps came quickly to Cabana Two's door and slid the screen door open.

The flashing end of a machine gun emerged first and it was already firing.

It was only by dumb luck that I'm alive – Enrique fired his first burst toward Cecil.

My pistol was at arm's length and aimed at Enrique's midsection as he swung toward me.

He was only ten feet away; I should have been able to kill him.

Finger off the side of the gun, onto the trigger. Eyes blurrily lined on the sites.

Enrique swung toward me.

I fired.

The explosion of my gun.

The jolt to my arm and shoulder.

The sight of Enrique's wild eyes as he dropped the machine gun.

It was an instant in time that for me will forever transcend a lifetime of minor inconveniences and problems. Laughable: all the flat tires, chipped teeth, stubbed toes, broken barware, bad backs, blisters, parking tickets, shingles, and cracked ribs.

I couldn't see Cecil. He must have jumped or fallen off the far railing.

My gun was still aimed at Enrique, a wisp of smoke rising from the end. Enrique was frozen in place holding his bloody hand. He had an oddly feminine face for someone his size, framed by long dark hair pulled into a ponytail. His complexion was very smooth with a thin drooping mustache and gentle eyes that tugged down on the sides. There was a mole on his chin, and the only trace of cruelty was in his wide lips, which were sneering at me, or was it just the pain in his hand?

Yet what struck me about him most was that viscerally he did not seem human. It was as if I were face to face with a centaur or some other type of primate – quite extraordinary. To this day I don't know how better to explain it. He was inhuman.

I rasped: "Don't move."

God damn it, he did.

After the fact, I cannot protest more adamantly about this. When the person holding the gun says not to move, the rules say you don't move, is that not correct? Well, apparently, that is not correct, that's the stuff of movies. In real life, you just kill the bastard. You don't say 'freeze' or any of that nonsense, but how was I to know? Clearly, it was enough for him to know I was a rookie.

He vaulted away from me over the railing, toward where Cecil had been, the machine gun still on the porch. I surged forward and fired again, missing. He rolled up onto his feet and veered out of sight, away toward Cabana Three.

'I scrambled around the porch, headed after him, but paused.

Cecil was propped up against the back of the hut. He had rolled there from where he'd been standing, but was slumped over. I rushed over and put a hand on his shoulder.

He fell to one side, eyes open, dead. There was a bullet hole in his neck, and probably more elsewhere.

Once again, I was favored with the eyes of the recent dead and the pit of eternity they contained.

Enrique's receding footsteps filled my brain with purpose.

By God, I was letting him get away.

With newfound energy – the kind of force of will that comes with indignation – I bolted after Enrique. In my ear, I heard: "Boone, you secure? Boone?"

I didn't want to spare the breath to answer, but barked: "Chasing east."

Diego said: "Halt, Boone. Let me go after him. I have the night vision."

I came to a shambling stop and watched through the shadows as Enrique crashed into the jungle in the distance, full tilt.

Leaning forward, hands on my knees, I tried to get my wind back. Frankly, I was glad Diego was going after Enrique and not me. I really wasn't up to this level of activity, especially having been up all night, not had any food to speak of except three cups of coffee on the patrol boat.

Footsteps trotted up from behind and Diego appeared next to me. I pointed toward where Enrique vanished. "That way."

"Does he have a weapon?" he asked.

"Not that I know of. He killed Cecil. Came out shooting."

"Boone, go help the girl, then head down to the lagoon dock and keep a look out in case Enrique circles back. If he's meeting a boat it will likely be there."

I gave him a thumbs up and he charged after Enrique.

Back at Cabana Two, I rolled Cecil onto his back into a more dignified position and folded his hands over his chest.

Afraid of what I might see in Cabana Two, I climbed the steps on the porch, picked up the machine gun and stepped through the open sliding doors. I was stung by the smell of rum.

It was my cabana, and my suitcase was still on the sofa on the left, though it looked like it had been ransacked. I could see my toiletry kit hanging in the dark bathroom straight ahead – my alarm clock, my rumpled bed directly in front of me – all exactly as I had left it. To the left in a little sitting area there was a single lamp on a side table lighting the room. A belt and a bottle of rum were tossed on another end table shoved against the wall.

Tamara was splayed backward on a large wicker chair, her legs through the holes under the armrests. Her arms were up over the back of the chair, and her naked back was toward me. Crisscrossing her back were about a dozen swollen bloody lashes a half inch wide. Blood and rum soaked the back of her white shorts – I guessed they'd used a belt to whip her and then douse the wounds with rum just for fun. Her tousled blonde head hung away from me over the back of the chair. She didn't move. *Please don't this be another set of dead eyes.*

Mouth like sandpaper, I stepped next to her and crouched. Her hands and feet were bound with belts from my suitcase, with my belts. She was effectively hog tied into the chair, and her wrists and ankles were bloody from struggling to free herself.

She jerked her head when she finally realized I was there – she may have been passed out when I entered. The eyes were not dead, but bleary, one eye blackened, her lips swollen, likely from a punch to the mouth.

I pulled the knife from my belt. "It's me, Boone. I'll cut you free. They're gone."

Sawing through her shackles, I tossed them aside. "Don't try to get up, let me get a towel."

In the bathroom, I grabbed a bath sheet and wet the center with cold water. When I emerged, she was sitting upright, working her shoulders, and I could hear them pop back into their sockets. Draping the towel over her back, the cool wet terry over her wounds, she hissed with pain. "We'll get some ice on that straight away." I came around to her side and draped the towel ends gently over her shoulders and around her bare chest.

"Boone?" Her voice was hoarse and thick. "I'm sorry I said you were an idiot."

Her bloodshot eyes met mine from under a shock of blonde hair. She put a halting hand on my cheek, and pulled me toward her, the trembling lips meeting mine. "Thank you."

It was all I could do not to fall to pieces right there. Methanol poisoning was too good for Miguel, and a flare in his neck was just the start of what I would have liked to do to Carlos.

I choked back the tears, jaw muscles flexing. "Let's get you out of that chair and start patching you up." I went around behind her. "Lift your arms. I'll just pull you straight back, pull your legs straight out and I'll set you down."

Lifting at her armpits, I heard her spine pop, and she whimpered from the pain in her shoulders until I pulled her legs free. I set her as gently as possible on the floor. Blood was soaking through the white bath sheet.

She needed a moment to collect herself, panting, twisting slightly with evident pain.

From the bathroom, I brought a hand towel with warm water. I knelt in front of her and dabbed at her face to clean up some of the blood, and blotted her wrists and ankles, which weren't as bad as I feared. She seemed a little like she was in a fog as I did this. "Do you think you're badly injured in some way that I can't see? Broken bones, dislocations?" She shook her head lazily, and I continued: "Do you think we can get your pants off?

They're a bloody mess; I can get you into a pair of my pajama pants."

Without word, she began undoing her pants in the front, and I went to her feet and said: "Put your arms back, and I'll just pull them straight off, OK?"

I'll spare her some dignity about the rest of the pants procedure, but we got her to her feet and cleaned up and into my pajama bottoms in a jiffy. They were too long, of course, so I did an alteration with my knife. The result was a thoroughly bedraggled specimen. To think this was the sex kitten of two days ago. My heart went out to her.

"Can you walk, Tamara? To the dining room? That's where the other DEA agents are, and of course the ice."

"My name is Tanya." I gave her my arm, and she reached out and steadied herself. "Get me out of this room." Tabatha, Tamara and now Tanya. Perhaps just 'Tee' would do?

Gingerly, we went down the steps and began a slow walk along the path lit with solar yard lamps.

We entered the lodge and shuffled past the bar and into the dining room – the place had the acrid smell of gunfire and panic. The two DEA agents were to my right, pacing, talking on satellite phones, likely calling in the patrol boat to evacuate us or possibly to chase down Enrique and halt his escape.

A chair had been pulled out in the center of the room. The four anglers, to include Red, were busy binding Carlos into the chair with clothesline. The prisoner certainly looked worse for wear. Bandages covered most of the left side of his face and neck. When he caught sight of me, his shaved head grimaced, eyes vengeful.

I motioned to Red, and he stood and approached me. "Could you fetch some ice for her back, lots of it? I'll get her situated in the lounge area on the other side of the bar." He nodded deeply and went to where the chef and two guides stood near the kitchen door. They all disappeared into the kitchen.

To my far left was Miguel slouched in a chair and he seemed to be having some sort of mild seizure, totally out of it and convulsing like he was being poked gently with a cattle prod set on low. Nobody moved to help him, and he was no longer a danger to anyone. I may not be able to shoot straight, but I know how to poison a man, that was for sure. I admit to some level of grim and amoral satisfaction for having laid low the man who shot Elvis. Better Elvis' quick death than Miguel's slow neurological collapse. They say two wrongs don't make a right, but 'they' didn't see Elvis die senselessly.

At Miguel's feet was the form of a man covered in a tablecloth stained with blood. My guess was that this was the third and last submariner killed when the agents stormed the place.

I shuffled Tanya back past the bar to a seating area comprised of yet more wicker furniture and floral cushions. "Here, lie on your front, face down, and they'll put ice on your back. I'll get you a drink."

"Not rum!" She croaked, gingerly lowering herself onto the sofa.

For someone who has been traumatized, many bartenders subscribe to the notion that a stiff drink is the ticket. I disagree. The last thing someone who is injured needs is some other extreme experience. Which is why I prefer to serve something soft and fruity at a funeral, for example. Behind the bar I found a bottle of Madeira, and in the fridge some fresh pineapple and an orange. I muddled some pineapple in the bottom of a tall zombie glass, topped that with ice, and topped that with five fingers of Madeira and a squeeze of orange. I proofed it up with some vodka and shook it against my palm – an impromptu cocktail shaker if ever there was. I finished it off with a long straw so she could drink it face down and delivered the concoction.

She sipped. "What is this? Good!"

"It's what Doctor Linsenbigler prescribes." I cleared my throat. "Look, I'm sorry if it was me that put you into this mess, Tanya. I really had no idea that the mere mention of submarines could cause so much trouble."

"It was the newspaper article," she croaked, and cleared her throat. "San Diego just popped into my head. Nobody ever told me there were submarines in San Diego."

"My blasted publicist placed that item in the paper, I had no idea. And believe me, I never had any notion about being a detective – that was all Terry's idea as well."

"Thought I might be able to steer you away with sex, send you on a goose chase. I just needed another day. That's why I drove so fast, and then I ran out of time. Miguel was calling."

"I would have been delighted to be part of your goose chase, my dear. Especially in retrospect."

She looked askance at me – as best she could. "You are a charming son of a gun in sort of a goofy way, you made it easy."

"Superintendent Phillips isn't really your brother is he?"

"No, I just didn't want him to see me. We've met. Never can tell what side people are on."

I patted her hand. "I know well that feeling!"

"The hotel desk told me they had been instructed to inform Phillips when you checked in. I knew he was he was coming to your room. That's why I was in such a hurry to seduce you. I mean, a little, anyway, show you the goods to steer you away." Her voice was distant and trance-like.

"Look, you don't have to explain anything just now."

Her voice thickened. "Working deep cover you can't be too careful. Enrique was someone I ran into before. I mean, that's just ridiculous. I busted up a gang he was working with eight years ago, but he escaped. He recognized me." She sniffled, and I could see the tears streaming down her cheeks, but she did not sob.

"Sip your drink and try to relax. I have to go check on something; here they come with the ice." I passed the chef and Red toting a bucket of ice as I went back to the dining room.

I walked up to the nearest DEA agent: "Diego said I should keep watch on the dock by the lagoon. I'll stay on radio and broadcast if I see anything. He thinks Enrique might circle around there to be picked up."

He put a hand over his phone: "I'll join you just as soon as I finish here."

I turned and strode past the barroom toward the door without even hesitating to think about having a drink myself – damned unusual. One always hears how desperate circumstances often change people, that under stress certain people fold up and other rise to the challenge. Me? I was just doing what needed to be done even though I would very much rather not do it. The alternative, under the circumstances, would likely have resulted in being killed. Or allowing more people to die around me, which was something I had never had happen to me before but found to be quite the grim motivator. Not blowing my own horn at all, I just wanted all this to stop, and if I had to do just one tiny thing more, so be it.

One tiny thing more like going down to the lagoon dock to see if Enrique's rescue plane was arriving.

Stepping out onto the porch, I saw the ocean horizon before me painted the cerise and yellow of dawn, stars directly above saying their adieus to the night. To the west toward the lagoon, the sky was still night. That's the direction I went, the foreboding tunnel of jungle leading to the lagoon ahead.

I had not heard from Diego on the radio in a while, and that worried me. Then again, he was likely consumed with a game of cat and mouse in the dark tropical thicket. I hadn't heard any gunshot, either, which I half hoped to hear – it would mean that he likely had killed Enrique and that this episode in my life was now really over. Over as in done. *Finito*. That's all, folks.

I crept into the shadows and mottled canopy of the jungle path toward the lagoon, my ears and eyes gone large with the potential for danger. Enrique could have doubled back and be hiding along the way and jump me. So I moved as quietly as I could, and along the left side of the path to try to stay out of silhouette to anyone looking down the path toward dawn's glow.

The path laid out before me like a jigsaw of greys and blacks, though my mind was drifting from my circumstance to my conscience. Elvis and Cecil's deaths bothered me. I felt I had somehow put them in mortal danger. It was Elvis' bad luck to get me as his sport even as much as it was mine to have mentioned submarines. He would not have died if he had not taken me for a customer, and I was the one who drew fire from smugglers. So it was my fault, at least through happenstance, that he died. There was some solace in the notion that I had avenged him by poisoning Miguel, possibly in the process saving other lives when the agents stormed the restaurant because he had been rendered virtually useless with a gun. And Cecil? Well, same thing, if I had gone around his side of the hut it would have been me that got a face full of lead. Well, I was glad it wasn't me, to be honest, but his bad luck wasn't my fault. However, it was my fault that the man who shot him escaped. If I had only aimed better and shot Enrique straight through the chest instead of hitting his hand, or had simply emptied my gun into him, he'd be a corpse and I would have to be skulking down a murky path paved with danger.

POW!

POW! POW!

Gunshots, off to my left. *Thank God. Diego shot Enrique.*

I broke into a full-on jog toward the dock.

Turning the corner into the clearing, I saw the finger dock on the left before me. About five hundred feet out in the calm lagoon was the silhouette of a boat.

Not just a boat.

A submarine.

And not a narco sub, but a real submarine, parked on the surface. How did I know it was a real military-grade submarine? Well, it looked like those I'd been seeing all my life on TV, on shows about war on cable. There was a conning tower in the center with antennae and diesel exhaust, and a long deck on either side of that. In the front was a machine gun turret, the kind in which the gunner sits behind a steel plate and looks through a slit window to aim his gun. I guessed if you had deep pockets like the cartels you could buy just about anything on the black market, so why not a submarine?

The turret abruptly moved — it swung to a point to the far left of me, and opened fire.

Tracer bullets sliced the twilight and jungle, and I could hear the slugs chopping up trees and foliage. The gun fired so rapidly that it sounded like a deafening buzz saw. It fired a sustained burst. When it stopped, there was a profound silence.

Cool! That was my first reaction, that of a ten-year-old, because I'd never seen a real machine gun in action, especially one with tracer bullets in the near dark. It was quite the spectacle.

Then I saw some movement in the water approaching the submarine. It was a man swimming toward it. It was Enrique trying to escape. Diego had fired upon the escapee only to draw fire from the submarine's machine gun. That means the machine gun fire was directed at Diego and he could be shot to pieces.

I whispered into my radio. "Diego, you OK? You there?" Nothing.

What was I going to do? I felt there must be something, but if I made so much as a peep that turret would turn towards me.

Yes, but Enrique is getting away, Boone!

If the turret did turn toward me, and Diego was still out there and not chopped to bits by bullets from the submarine, he could try a taking few more shots at Enrique. I could actually draw their fire. I could let them see my muzzle flash, and then run like crazy.

Unholstering my pistol, I worked the action and ejected a perfectly good bullet onto the ground. Oops. I had left a round chambered but out of nervousness cocked it again. Well, I didn't plan to fire that many shots anyway, and as far as I recalled I had only fired two rounds, so I had twelve left after tossing one to the ground.

I jogged as far right of the dock as possible and leveled the pistol at Enrique just at the same instant that a sailor on the sub's deck was reaching out to him. I fired three shots. I saw my bullets skip off the water to one side and well short of the target. Two of the rounds skipped into the side of the submarine with a *tink*.

Oddly, I saw the sailor reaching out to Enrique spasm. He stumbled backward and fell, squirming. The only thing I can think of is that one of my rounds skipped off the water and struck him by pure dumb luck. I couldn't hit Enrique's midsection ten feet from me but I could hit a submariner at five hundred feet! Remarkable.

The turret whirred, the barrels leveling on my position.

Time I should have spent running I had wasted staring in disbelief at my marksmanship.

No time left to run, just to drop.

I flattened to the ground for all I was worth, my face turned toward the jungle and pressed against the smell of coffee grounds and peanut shells. Between the submarine and me was the raised dock and a flats boat and some scrub at the shoreline. I hoped that would provide sufficient cover.

The sound of the machine gun didn't even reach me because there was a sudden storm of bullets thwacking into the jungle, chunks of wood and palm fronds exploding.

A pause as the turret whirred again, and lowered its aim.

The sound of the flats boat and dock being chopped in into shreds was a sustained and staccato splintering of *THWACKS, WHUMPS* and *PINGS*. It was as if some gigantic, clawed sea beast was smashing its way through the boat towards me, shredded fiberglass raining on me from above.

Had to get cute and play GI Joe, didn't you Boone? Any second the flats boat will be gone and so will you.

POW!

POW! POW!

Gunshots, off to my left. Diego was still alive and with any luck hitting his mark.

The rampaging beast stopped hacking its way through the flats boat and in the brief silence, small flakes of white fiberglass rained down on me like snowfall. I was flat to the ground as any flounder to a seabed. No more heroics from me, I had a newfound respect for turret-mounted machine guns on submarines. There was likely little left for me to hide behind, and even running away toward the lodge would not give me enough distance or cover from those bullets.

The turret whirred in the distance, and then opened fire – off to my left, at Diego again, flash from the tracers flickering on the fiberglass snowfall and torn jungle behind me.

Then it stopped.

A diesel engine coughed to life out on the water, and I heard the submarine kick into gear. I could feel the propeller through the ground churning, setting the boat to sail. I was tempted to take a look, but not enough to tempt the wrath of the turret.

When I had flattened to the ground, I smooshed myself so hard to the earth that my radio earpiece had popped out of my ear, but I could hear Diego command, faintly:

"Stand down. Sorry I lost communication. My radio shut off when I hit the ground. They got him in the sub. Call in the patrol boat for intercept, if they can before it submerges."

As I lay with twigs embedded in my face on the litter, my heart wheezing like that of a scared rabbit, I was sorry for Cecil, but I was also very relieved Enrique was finally

BRIAN M. WIPRUD

gone one way or the other. That horrible face, I'd never forget it. There was no way at this point that the DEA or the RBD or the RBP could possibly think I could be of any further assistance chasing down a submarine unless they had some wild scheme in which I was to become a human torpedo. Or perhaps drop me down in a bathescope with a pea shooter! I've got it: Old Linsenbigler can glide down from a transport plane in a wing suit, a knife in his teeth, and land on the submarine deck to single-handedly subdue the entire lot and sail the submarine back to cheering crowds on the dock in Nassau. Orbach would sign off on that in a second, wouldn't he just?

I stayed put for a long time, just enjoying the relative silence, watching the snowfall, listening through the ground to the retreating submarine until I couldn't hear it any more. Orange sunlight tickled the tops of the shattered palm trees, but there were none of the usual bird sounds, I think they all moved quite some distance away from all the gunplay.

I heard footsteps, but I still didn't move.

Enrique is gone. The turret is gone. Nothing left to do but lie here.

"Boone?"

I rolled over and sat up. The DEA agents in their black commando gear approached, a look of deep concern on their face. Diego said: "You alright?"

I sighed, calmly and methodically brushing the dirt, twigs, and leaves that had pressed into the side of my ski mask. Then I just pulled the ski mask off and held it out to Diego. "Please tell me I'm done here?"

The three of them laughed, chattering about how when they approached I looked dead.

"I could very well have been." I slowly got to my feet, a layer of white fiberglass cascading off my black outfit into a pile at my feet. To my right, the dock looked like it had been attacked by a rabid gang of lumberjacks, and the boat looked like it had been hit by a missile, cracked fairly in two.

Beyond I could see the patrol boat arriving too late to stop the sub from submerging.

Diego clapped me on the shoulder. "That was good work for an amateur, drawing fire so I could take a few more shots. I told these guys how you actually shot one of the deck hands out there. I couldn't believe it!"

I began shambling away from the dock toward the lodge, and the agents kept apace, again yammering excitedly about how successful we were, considering the last-minute planning and lack of manpower.

"But what the hell is wrong with that guy Miguel? Looks he's on death's door," Diego said. "And the other guy with the bandages on the neck and hands?"

I cleared my throat. "The second one you mentioned is Carlos – he was the lodge manager who tried to kill me and I shot him in the neck with the flare gun. The sick one, Miguel, I poisoned him yesterday afternoon with a methanol martini. It makes you go blind, and then your nervous system malfunctions and you possibly die, or wish you had."

Diego clapped me on the shoulder. "Well, taking both those guys out of action really helped, Boone. Good work."

Tired and annoyingly sober, I was in no mood to celebrate, as they seemed to be. "I have to admit, that revenge and self-preservation notwithstanding, I don't take a lot of joy in poisoning or seriously burning anyone. Much less being shot at more or less on a regular basis."

We walked in silence after that, the agents toning down their enthusiasm in the face of my petulant mood. Just before climbing the steps into the restaurant, Diego stopped me. His stubbled, lined face still showed the creases of where the night optics had been strapped to his forehead, the contours of his face made dramatic by the rising sun. "I hear what you are saying about all this violence, Boone. But we saved the lives of – what, the four anglers, the cook, the two guides, and the girl – eight? We saved the senseless slaughter of eight innocents, bagged two of the three bad guys. That counts for something. What you did to those two, believe me, they likely had it coming in spades."

"And we lost Cecil and my fishing guide Elvis." I was suddenly so exhausted I could barely stand. "I gather what you are intimating, Diego. It's going to take me a little time to digest all that has happened in the last twenty-four hours, the pluses and minuses, and what it all means."

We climbed the steps and into the lodge, sunlight drawing long shadows of the window partitions across the bar. I could smell breakfast, and heard the anglers and guides jump to their feet and begin asking the agents questions.

I turned away from all that to the bar.

And, pray tell, what cocktail is appropriate for a moment like this. *Ah!*

I poured a lager into a pint glass two inches from the top. In a shot glass, I poured vodka. The shot glass full of vodka I dropped into the pint of beer and it hit bottom with a gentle *klink*. Garnish: orange slice.

What could be a more appropriate cocktail after a harrowing encounter with a submarine than tippling a drink called a 'depth charge?' I managed a grim smirk in honor of my ingenuity.

Stepping from behind the bar, I saw that Tanya was still face down on the couch but that someone had placed a beach towel under her and had done some further cleaning up of her wounds, especially those on her face. A smaller new towel was on her back with plastic bags of partially melted ice atop them. What I could see of her back looked greasy like someone had applied some antibiotic ointment: good idea. She appeared to be asleep, and was snoring lightly and somewhat adorably the way some women do.

I pulled up a chair close to her, feeling at once protective of her and wanting to curl up into a ball and tune out.

Slouched down into the chair facing the sun, I realized it was almost twenty-four hours from when I had an egg sandwich and coffee on my cabana porch the day before – in the sun.

The day before, when I had some amazing permit fishing.

And then.

What a difference a day makes.

After a deep chug of the depth charge, I set the glass down half-empty next to my chair and let loose a gentle and protracted burp. My mind had gone blank, and in my black commando outfit bathed in orange sun, I deftly drifted asleep in the chair next to Tanya, my drink unfinished.

CHAPTER 11

LET IT SUFFICE TO SAY, we were all safely evacuated from Banana Cay. Miguel, Carlos and Tanya by medivac float plane, the rest of us by patrol boat, which put us back in Nassau that evening.

While under sail, I was able to compose a lengthy text to Terry Orbach informing him that his newspaper article had put me into the most dire of circumstances with drug smugglers. I had been shot at numerous times, kidnapped, escaped and had to both flee for my life and chase down and confront the most desperate and despicable characters imaginable. I had shot two people, poisoned another, and flayed yet another with a flare gun. Along those lines, I suggested that he secure me a competent law firm in case there were any legal ramifications of all this, as I didn't cotton to being sued by Carlos and Miguel. (Seemed unlikely given the circumstances, but in these frantically litigious times and Conglomerated Beverage's deep pocket, one never knows.) But most importantly, I informed him that this ordeal warranted me the nicest room and the nicest reservation in all of the Bahamas.

No doubt Terry was eager for the details of my heroics, so I further suggested that he dispatch some lucky soul to extract the entire gory tale from me as soon as possible so that I would not have to tell it more than once. Take it all down and let everybody read it, or edit it how you will for commercial purposes. Serialize it in magazines or plaster it on billboards or blimps. I didn't care, but I thought that Conglomerated was going to need to think long and hard about my next contract, that this sort of adventure was far outside the bounds of Article XXXVII, Subsection 3.2.3's verbiage 'and conduct various promotional and personal appearances as required."

With a flourish, my index finger poked 'send.'

Hours later, with Paradise Island and Nassau docks in view, I received a reply: "Driver waiting at docks to take you to Trident Club. Masseuse and bartender standing by, open tab, restaurant, too. Stand by on the rest. See you soon. T.O."

By Jiminy, Orbach fairly danced a jig for Ol' Linsenbigler! Rightly so! In life, you sometimes have to get pushy to ensure respect or they'll just trample all over you. I made demands and by God they met them – or else! I'm sure other beverage giants like Pernot Ricard or Diageo would pounce if they had any inkling my brand was available.

In due course, I collected my fishing tackle from Elvis' boat and along with my luggage was whisked in a limousine to the stately colonnades of the Trident Club, and further whisked to my room, where a comely young Japanese lady named Suzy awaited me with a daiquiri and a smile. She ran my bath as I stepped to the terrace and admired the north views and sea breeze of the ocean blue, sun setting portside. Somewhat to my surprise, Suzy led me to the bathroom and disrobed me. She gestured for me to climb into the spacious whirlpool tub that was bubbling away and so I did, whereupon she handed me a fresh daiquiri. Then she disrobed and put her slim trim pale body in with mine!

She set about massaging me, seemingly each individual muscle at a time, over my entire body. I hadn't realized how tense I still was, for she really had to work at my neck muscles to get them to let go. Yet they did, and before too long she had me completely unwound.

Eventually she left the tub, dried herself, vanished into the other room for a few minutes, and then came back in a robe and guided me out of the tub and dried me.

Emerging from the bath into the main room, I found that the sun had set, and the bedroom was alight with a dozen candle lanterns, the walls flickering with light and sea breeze. To the bed.

Decorum almost prevents me from describing what happened next, but it was so odd that I really must. Apparently, there's this Japanese 'thing' in which sex is simulated in a most extraordinary manner. The girl entwines herself with you so completely you can't tell exactly where the Old Man is, but apparently he is not inside her at all – though you'd hardly know it. She squirms and squirms and...well, all I can say, that for something that wasn't fornication it was rightly on par and with a very pleasing result, if I do say so.

And afterward...she massaged my feet, with another very startling result, I had no idea it was possible.

We showered and she dried me again, and put me in a robe and positioned me in a comfy chair on the veranda, the lawn below lit by torches, the sea beyond tossed up with a frisky westerly breeze.

There was a knock at the door, and Suzy went to answer it. Room service brought in dueling bottles of *Veuve Clicquot* and a shellfish tower and six giant flowering bouquets that they positioned about the bedroom.

It all begins to blur after that – I have snippets of downing oysters and gulping champagne, of Suzy rubbing my hands, and finally her sliding me between soft sheets into bed and rubbing my ears, of all things, as I fell asleep.

You know, I don't believe she said one word the entire time, or I to her, except upon meeting. What was there that needed saying with all that?

Moralizers might of course think ill of me for in all appearances submitting to a bit of harlotry. Call it what you like, but there's no denying that it was therapeutic, especially after the day I had endured. I suppose the puritans out there would find it preferable that I had locked myself up tight with a bottle of scotch and drunk myself over that episode, aye? As it was, I awoke alone but a new man the next bright and shining morning, the room redolent with blossoms. There was still much to sort out emotionally in retrospect to my adventures, but physically I was ship shape and fit for duty. Suzy was gone.

Breakfast arrived and was served on my veranda over the sea. The repast was comprised of strong coffee, fruit, mini-croissants and Prosecco. At the same time, my fishing clothes came back, all on hangers and pressed, and they hung them in the bathroom foyer.

Snug in my robe, completely unwound, slurping prosecco and amassing croissant crumbs on my chest, I thought to myself: *By thunder, Orbach, this all makes up for a lot!*

There was another rap at my door and I could only wonder what delight awaited me now. Eating a croissant as I went, I opened the door.

In the hallway was Terry Orbach in a seersucker suit and new Panama hat. Before I could say anything he lunged forward and embraced me around the chest – he's a good pint and a half shorter than I.

"Thank God you're safe!" He whimpered.

As I continued to chew on my croissant, I admit to some bewilderment over this show of emotion from a man who heretofore thought of me as a show pony.

"Terry, what in blazes are you doing here?"

He pried himself from my chest and held me at arm's length. "I had to come to make sure you were alright, Boone. What you went through is incredible. I feel responsible somehow." He dropped his hat on a plant by the door.

"Yes, well the newspaper article was perhaps a bit over the top."

"Press releases happen all the time without drug smugglers kidnapping anybody. Let's get you back sitting down, you need rest." He turned me and fairly shoved me back to my seat on the veranda, pulling up a chair at my elbow. Hands folded as if he were praying, Orbach said: "So you're alright? Not injured?"

"I admit to my share of bruises and scrapes, but nothing to write home about."

"Thank God." His lip trembled with relief, and from a pocket, he produced a folded document and a pen. "We're going to need you to sign this."

My glance at the document was suspicious. "What's this?"

"Nothing at all, Boone, just procedure, you know Conglomerated."

Brushing crumbs from my fingers, I took the document and perused the first page. Eyebrows raised, I said: "Indemnification?"

"Well, the lawyers need you to sign this to say that you were not injured while in the act of promoting the Linsenbigler product line. Has to do with workers compensation or something. I hate to bother you with this paperwork but thought we might as well get it out of the way. Did you enjoy last night?"

I took the pen, continuing to scan the document. "Outstanding homecoming, Terry."

"You deserved it, absolutely, only the best for Boone Linsenbigler."

The gist of the document seemed to be on the up and up, namely just certifying that I had not been injured and would not seek any kind of compensation from Conglomerated. Were I represented by a lawyer in the matter, he would have shredded the document and landed us all in court for the next ten years. But I don't cotton to litigation, and while they might have gotten me killed they hadn't, and I didn't see as to how anybody could prove that they put me in harm's way knowingly. Therefore, I jotted my autograph on the bottom line and handed it back.

"Thanks, and sorry, Boone, at a time like this doing business is crass, I know." He fumbled with his phone a minute and then pointed the back of it at me. "Just need to do a quick video for your Twitter feed."

I thumped the table in disgust. "Now? For heaven's sake…"

He lowered the phone, and poked that long proboscis at me. "I guess you've been isolated so don't know what's been going on, but that hostage video of you? It was second on every evening news program. All the talk show hosts mentioned you in their monologues. The tweets have just been pouring in. Boone, the nation thinks you are dead. They are planning candle light vigils."

I folded my arms. "Candle light vigils?"

"Well, we encouraged some bloggers to work that up a bit, but why not? Anyway, now they need to find out the indomitable Boone Linsenbigler is alive, just a teaser before we start to release details of all that you did to save the day."

Snorting, I said: "I saved my skin, not the day, Terry. There's a difference."

"But you said you shot people…and they told me you rescued a girl!"

"Yes, all of that but…"

"Where's this girl now? We need to interview her."

I leaned in: "N. O. You are not bothering her. You want some prosecco?"

"But first the twitter video – just say 'The reports of my demise are greatly exaggerated.' And give it some swagger."

Clearing my throat, I raised both my champagne glass and an eyebrow at his phone: "The reports of my demise are greatly exaggerated!" I added a smirk at the end, and sipped my drink.

"Great!" he squealed.

"OK, so, enough, Terry, I'm still recovering here. Want some prosecco? I think you need some. You need to relax."

"Maybe some coffee and a snack." He helped himself to some coffee and the rest of my mini-croissants.

Before I could protest the looting of my mini-croissants, there was a knock at the door, and Orbach leapt to his feet. "That'll be the doctor."

"Doctor?"

Terry scuttled through the room and beckoned me into the sitting room. From the hallway, he dragged an elderly black man in a tie and lab coat holding a satchel: "Good morning, sir, and how are we feeling? I'm Dr. Beckham."

"I'm fine. Terry, what is this? There's nothing wrong with me."

"I know you're fine, Boone." He pulled a chair over from a desk and pushed me into it. "But we can't be too careful, can we? What if you sustained some sort of damage that we can't see? Like I said, nothing is too good for you, so Conglomerated is getting you a physical."

"A physical? Here?"

Before I knew what hit me Doctor Beckham was in a chair in front of me with a penlight, one hand atop my head as he leaned in to inspect my retina. He said: "Have you had any dizzy spells? Seen any spots?"

There was another knock and off Orbach went to the hotel room door again, this time delivering a thirty-something hipster in yellow sunglasses poking at a smart phone. With him was a mod, sexy brunette wearing heavy black framed glasses, her hair in three pig tails.

Doctor Beckham wheeled to one side and probed my ears. "Any ringing in your ears?"

"Well, some, there was a lot of noise, machine gun fire..."

"Boone," Orbach wheeled the latest guests in front of me. "These are some creative people from The Coast, they're going to get the whole story from you like you asked."

The hipster and the mod girl made themselves at home cross-legged on the floor next to me, looking me over like some sort of specimen. She said to her pal: "Casting is going to be critical."

He looked sidelong at me and said: "Where were you born?"

"New Jersey."

Beckham: "Stick out your tongue." He jammed a depressor into my mouth flattened my tongue.

Hipster to Mod Girl: "We'll have to work around New Jersey."

Mod Girl to me: "You must have been in the military, right?

Hipster to me: "But you were forced out under mysterious circumstances, to be revealed later."

Mod Girl to Hipster: "There was a girl involved."

Hipster to Mod Girl: "Not just any girl, but a girl with tattoos."

They gave each other an exploding fist bump.

Beckham slapped a freezing cold disc of metal to my chest: "Deep breaths."

Behind the doctor I saw yet another man, one in a pin striped suit and a brief case, which he opened and began pulling out legal documents for Orbach to inspect.

Beckham: "I'm going to have to ask you to remove your robe."

I interjected: "Doctor, I have to go to the bathroom, why don't I fill your sample jars while I'm at it?"

He nodded gravely, and handed me two jars as I jumped from my seat. "Urine and stool, please."

Hipster to me: "Have you ever been to Alcoholics Anonymous?" To her: "We need to get him to one of their meetings, pronto. I can see a plot line here."

I held up a finger: "Be *right* back."

Specimen jars in hand, I darted around the corner of the sitting room and into the bathroom foyer containing

my clothes and suitcase. I quickly suited up in some
tropical casual wear and grabbed my wallet and phone. I
paused on my way out: Orbach's Panama hat fit perfectly.
It just needed a little brim molding to look dapper. In my
new hat, I slipped unmolested into the hallway and to the
elevators.

I asked the desk to send a car around, and walked the
palatial hallway past potted palms and colonnades to the
portico-covered driveway where a bell captain all in white
and white pith helmet saluted me. Incongruously, a
green, late model taxi pulled up, and the bell captain held
the door for me. As he closed the door, I happened to
glance back into the hotel – and saw Orbach running
toward me down the hallway, a look of abject horror on
his face.

I put a hand on the shoulder of the Rastafarian cab
driver: "Princess Margaret Hospital. Step on it."

The driver smiled: "Awright!" The little car lurched
forward.

As we zoomed off I saw Orbach waving his hands
excitedly at the bell captain, and another cab pulling
forward. I said to my driver: "Look in the rear view. I'm
being followed. What can you do about it?"

He flashed a gold tooth at me in the rear view. "That
the police?"

"No."

"Gangsters?"

"No."

"Loan sharks?"

"Worse. It's my publicist."

"Awright! I see what I can do. Hey, you look
familiar." The car swerved dangerously around a curve.
"I recognize the mustache. You that liquor guy?"

I smirked. "Yes, I'm Boone Linsenbigler. What's your name?"

"I'm Reginald. You all over the newspapers, Boone." We careened around another corner and zig zagged between traffic to a circle. "Cab behind us. Good driver. What's it like being famous?"

"It's like this, Reginald. Here I am running away from my own publicist."

"Why you run from him?"

"He's trying to make me somebody I'm not."

Reginald and I exchanged a look in the mirror and he said: "You Boone Linsenbigler. Just be Boone Linsenbigler, can't be anybody else."

I thought about that a moment as the tropical scenery and honking cars zipped by my window. Yes, I was Boone Linsenbigler. And just maybe it was time I started taking a little more ownership of that. I tapped at my phone until my Twitter page popped up. This was something I didn't do, my publicist had people tweet for me, but I had access to the account and had been encouraged to post missives. So I spun around took a selfie of me with Reginald behind me smiling in the mirror. I wrote: "Linsenbigler escapes yet again from the clutches of evil! My publicist in hot pursuit!" I attached another photo of the cab following us with Orbach in it.

Reginald said: "You OK if we have to get cute? I drop you off and then come back?"

"However you want to work it." I held up a hundred-dollar bill. "This is yours if you scrape them off one way or the other."

"Awright!" The gold tooth flashed at me in the mirror as he drove around the circle, the cab's tires squealing, and then we headed for the bridge to Paradise Island.

He shouted back to me: "We got some distance now but when we get to other side it's gonna be slow and he catch us up. So I have a plan. I let him catch me way down, but you not in my cab, he not know where you are."

In short order, we were in Nassau proper near the cruise ship terminals where two giant ocean liners had disgorged passengers that thronged the streets. Sure enough, traffic slowed as we pulled up next to an open plaza chock-a-block with hair braiding stalls. They were doing a brisk business as the tourists flocked to have their hair put into cornrows for some reason.

My driver yelled out his window at a beefy woman who was just being paid by a blonde tween with newly beaded hair. "Yolanda! Take this guy right away!"

She nodded and he pulled to a stop. "You run there into her chair and I take off and they follow me. I be back."

I threw the door open, dodged a few tourists and dove into Yolanda's chair, turning it away from the street.

She belly laughed. "You in a hurry!"

"I'm trying not to be seen, Yolanda. Being followed." I removed my hat and placed it on my lap.

She drifted her large frame behind me block me from view. "Got you covered, mister. Hey, you that liquor fella. I seen you on T.V. You're Ledbetter."

"Boone Linsenbigler."

Tugging at my hair she asked: "Boone, you want beads?"

"What?"

"You want beads?"

"No beads. Can't you just pretend to do it?"

"Pretend?" Another belly laugh. "I braid hair. How you want it done?"

"Frankly, I ...oh, fine, just do the one side or something."

"Oh, you want the Blackbeard. Fine, we fix you up, Boone."

It should surprise no one that I had never had my hair braided, and it was damned uncomfortable as she tugged, twisted and pulled at my hair. It didn't help that there were so many people packed into the plaza, that it was noisy and I was being jostled by tourists.

To think after all I'd been through that I had to flee not from murdering smugglers but from my own publicist. There's a line and Orbach was way over it. I was only going to be exploited so much. It struck me then that if what Orbach and others were saying about my popularity were true, that it was time to find an agent to look after my own interests separate from Conglomerated. It was clear I needed someone other than a Rastafarian cab driver to run interference for me. That would mean paying an agent fifteen percent, I guessed. Maybe just the threat of an agent would help. My resolve was building to take more control of my persona, of who I was. And perhaps who I was becoming.

A half hour passed of jostling and hair tugging before I heard a whistle and Yolanda patted me on the shoulder. "Reginald is back for you."

I stood and she held out a mirror. The left side of my head had been made into a cascade of braids the size of small asparagus. Yet, with the mustache, and the Panama hat, the effect was rather jaunty.

I paid Yolanda and pushed my way through the tourists to the taxi, safely lodging myself in the back.

The driver said: "Hey, dat braids bad like yaz, Boone."

"Feels odd. Did they catch up to you?"

"Sure they did. That little man with the nose, mon, he was very upset. I say I let you out and you jump in another cab."

"Good. Now the hospital." I handed over the hundred-dollar bill.

The gold tooth flashed in the mirror: "Awright!"

CHAPTER 12

SURPRISINGLY, I HAD LITTLE trouble reaching Tanya's third-floor room as everybody seemed to know who I was, even the Royal Bahamian Policeman guarding her door. I knocked lightly and pushed the door open as she said "In!"

She had a private room decked out in all the usual accoutrements found in every hospital in the developed world. There was the vague tingle in the nose of antiseptic smells covering up septic smells. Her bed had been turned to face the door and she lay on her front as if she were sun tanning, chin on a pillow, arms folded below. Her back from her hip to her neck was one big white bandage, and her lower half covered in light blue blankets. There was a stitch or two in her eyebrow and a couple on her lip. The poke to the eye was a deep purple with yellow around it, a peek of bloodshot eye within. Her shock of blonde hair was clumsily combed to one side.

The other bright violet eye was mostly clear and when it focused on me the mouth smiled. "Boone! I didn't expect to see you."

I stepped fully into the room, a brown paper bag under my arm.

"Sorry, I thought it was required for a knight to do a follow up visit on the damsel in distress."

The one eye rolled. "Distress? Yeah, just a little, I guess. Not used to that."

Wheeling a clanky chair in front of her, I sat with a squeak and pulled a chilled bottle of champagne and two glasses from the paper bag. "I also thought you might want a drink so I stopped at the store. Especially seeing as how last time I was unable to enjoy the champagne in your company."

"You still trying to get laid? When I look like this?"

I unwrapped the bottle foil and began untwisting the cork wire. "A gentleman is always trying to get laid. That's why he's a gentleman in the first place." *Pop.*

She snickered: "You really are quite the act, aren't you?"

"An act?" Reaching behind me, I plucked a drinking straw from an empty water glass and put it into one of the champagne flutes. "Well, we're all actors of one sort or the other. You should know that better than anybody, *Tabatha.*" I filled her glass and handed it to her, and then I filled mine. "Cheers?"

We clinked glasses, her eye inspecting me with suspicion.

"Well, it was no act what you did out there on Banana Cay."

"That, my dear, was improvisation, and so in effect acting at its finest. Diego and his team deserve all the credit. I am no hero, and the only time I played one was when I was a kid at Medieval Knights – a dinner theater in Ho-Ho-Kus."

"Ho-Ho-Kus?" She grinned. "Did you joust?"

"No, I was a broad swordsman. You know, swing the blade high and clang the other guy's sword, times three, then swing the blades low and clang the other guy's sword. Parry, thrust, dodge. I started out as the black knight – who always dies – but worked my way up to white knight – who always wins."

She was suppressing a laugh. "Ah, I see you do have training for this work, for freeing the damsel in distress, very impressive."

"Indubitably, clanging swords is prominent on my resume, but I am not and never will be some sort of super sleuth. In a jam, I did what I needed to do to save my skin and the skin of those around me. With notable exceptions."

The violet eye lost its mirth and was cast at the floor. "I'm sorry about Elvis. I tried to talk Miguel into simply kidnapping you both. He's an idiot. The narco sub guys already blew it when they shot Lundy, and making more people go missing just brought more heat on us. And just when Enrique was due to arrive." She sipped on her straw and suppressed a burp. "This is not the best position to drink champagne. The bubbles go the wrong way."

"Miguel is paying a price for killing Elvis, and you almost did, too."

Her eye was curious, so I continued. "Perhaps you hadn't heard, but I poisoned Miguel with that martini I made for him at the sub base. I almost made one for you, too, but thought better of it."

Her brow knit. "Poison?"

"I made his martini with rubbing alcohol from the bathroom."

"I thought Miguel was just sick or something. So you almost poisoned me just as I was planning for you to escape? Just as I was writing on the bar *I AM DEA*?"

I shrugged. "What can I say, I couldn't read what you wrote."

"That's just ridiculous. Now I'm getting pissed off at you again."

"At the very least give me credit for not poisoning you. And by the by, why is it you didn't let me play possum in Elvis' boat?"

"Because you would have motored right back to the lodge and right into Carlos, who would have killed you. I was hoping Miguel would agree to leave you on the island as part of the ransom agreement. When I realized that wasn't the plan, I had to make it so you could escape and take your chances with Carlos, there was no other choice."

"Damned good thing I had that little flare gun. So what has become of Carlos and Miguel?"

"They have them both in an upstairs room under guard. Carlos was really, really angry about you shooting him with the flare gun. His burns are terrible. You better hope he never gets out of jail. They tell me Miguel is in a coma. Good riddance." Her eye looked doubtful, but resigned. "Well, we both survived."

"An outcome worth toasting more than once." I clinked her glass.

"You know, we don't exactly train for torture, but I have read about how people have made it through by concentrating on something other than what is happening to you, something to pull your through it. What I concentrated on was needing to know whether your name is actually Boone, whether your father actually named you after Daniel Boone. I don't know why I chose that. It just popped into my head. I mean, your name sounds like it could have been made up. And I decided I had to know whether you were telling the truth."

I grinned. "You'll be edified to know that I am actually named after Daniel Boone, and that my sister is actually named Crocket, and that our last name is actually Linsenbigler. It's Bavarian."

"What the...what did you do to your hair? Did you get braids?"

"Indeed. I was forced to escape my publicists this morning and had to hide out in the plaza for a bit so Yolanda did some of her finest work with this Blackbeard."

Her face turned red as she began to laugh. "You're joking. Now you have to escape from your publicist? Why?"

"He seems to think my image needs retooling, and that my employer needs to indemnify the ever living daylights out of what happened so they don't get sued. Prior to this episode, I was a mildly famous front man for cocktail amenities. Now, apparently, my kidnapping and that video you took have made me a household name. I think my publicist is a little over-excited and needs a timeout."

"Pfft! That's a scream. More champagne, please."

I filled us both up, and asked: "So how does someone like you get into this line of work, anyway?"

She rolled her eye. "The short version? Was thrown out of the house at fifteen. I'm a wild child; I need excitement and danger to feel alive. So I was going to be either a criminal or a cop, neither was exciting enough on its own, but this way I'm both. Nobody who does deep cover is technically normal otherwise they would never do it. They would never trade a life of family and suburbs and barbeques and graduations for hanging out with depraved murderers and end up having most the skin removed from their back. Or in your case, vamping a complete stranger to get a desired result. I spent two years trying to find Enrique. In this line of work, you have to do whatever it takes. You do what needs to be done. That's the life."

"Sounds to me like a short life."

"You know, I was just thinking to myself, I've never had a Christmas tree. They don't exist in the underworld. Pfft. Enough about me. How long are you hanging around Nassau?"

"I'm not sure. As a bachelor, I'm generally footloose. It depends somewhat on Orbach – that's my publicist – and also on how I size up whether he and my employer will be more annoying here or back in The States."

"You're that footloose that you can just stay?"

"As long as I don't have some contractual obligation to fill. How about you? How much longer here at the hospital?"

"I'm here at least a week. And then…well, my undercover days are over. The bad guys have me made. I'll probably land at a desk job for a while before I'm a hundred percent and then be re-assigned to some other kind of lame field duty like as a liaison. Or maybe I'll train other agents at Quantico. But there's no more deep cover for me." Her brow was knit, eye on the floor, and I could hear her voice tightening with emotion. "If nothing else, after what they did to me, the nerves of steel just aren't there anymore. I can feel them gone. All it takes is a flinch and the bad guys know you're a cop. Funny, I can cheat at poker with bandits, throw knives, chew tobacco, crush a man's windpipe with one punch, shoot straight and vamp my way out of almost any dangerous situation. I've killed eight men. But I don't think I have what it takes to do Thanksgiving dinner."

"Having lost your nerve isn't such a bad thing, you know?" I reached out and stroked her cheek. "There's a lot of worthwhile things to do in life other than Thanksgiving dinner that are not dangerous but exciting."

She raised a suspicious eyebrow. "Such as?"

"Fishing."

"Fishing?" Her eye was moist when it met mine, and she tried on a smile. "Still trying to get laid, aren't you?"

I smiled back. "A gentleman to the last breath!"

"Well, I may let you buy me dinner one of these days when my back is healed, but if you're determined to bed me you'll have to wait a while."

"I'll drink to that!"

We tweeted a picture of us clinking glasses in front of Tanya's face so she could not be recognized: *Sharing some bubbly with the damsel I had the pleasure to rescue from certain death. Bottoms Up!*

CHAPTER 13

ON MY WAY OUT OF THE HOSPITAL I was admiring my handiwork on Twitter – the posts were getting favorited at a feverish pace – when I noticed I had about a dozen phone messages, all from Orbach, all within the last hour. I didn't need to listen to them.

Time to stop running and have it out with Orbach. I texted him to meet me at the British Colonial bar, a stately place with dark wood bar, wainscoted columns, high ceiling and giant crystal chandelier. An hour later I was halfway through a screwdriver (truly improved mixed with my bitters, by the way) under the chandelier when Orbach scuttled in – Diego striding right behind him.

Diego looked odd to me out of commando gear – he was in a tan suit, bright white shirt and blue tie, his thick dark hair carefully combed and parted.

Right out of the gate, Orbach blurted: "Did you get my messages?"

"My phone got them, I did not." I reached around Orbach and shook Diego's large hand. "I didn't expect to see you again, to be honest, but glad to have the opportunity to bend an elbow after our exploits. Bartender!"

Diego smiled, uneasily.

I placed the drink order: "A slow gin fizz for Terry here and...let me guess? An añejo with lime and a splash of orange juice for Diego. Another screwdriver for me."

Orbach tugged at the lapels of his seersucker suit, leaned in and said: "Look, Boone, you can't run off like that. We have things to do. I don't think I need to remind you that you are contractually obligated."

"And I don't think I need to remind you that I am the one and only Boone Linsenbigler, not Colonel Sanders. Boone Linsenbigler is my legal name and I still own it and my life. As such, I have some say as to what I will and will not submit. Perhaps I need to acquire an agent so that we're all straight on that."

"An agent?" Recoiling, Orbach looked at me as if I'd just spit on the floor. "Boone, how could you do that to me after all I've done for your career?"

"A talent agent, Orbach. I need one to prevent atrocities like that circus this morning in my room. Those two imbeciles from Hollywood! Diego, I'm sorry you have to witness this family squabbling. Did you two just happen to run into each other or something?"

He picked up his drink from the bar, came around the other side of me and sat on a stool. "I'd better state my business, Boone, so you two can conduct yours in private. I just came from a strategy meeting in which I was debriefed about Tanya's operation to locate Enrique."

"Who is he, anyway? You all seem very keen to grab him."

"Tanya worked two years to finally meet him. He's a liaison between the top man of a cartel and the distribution network. If we know where he goes we can get the top man, a kingpin named El Pescador. Tanya had placed a GPS transponder with the money Enrique was going to take back to Mexico with him. Once he recognized Tanya as DEA, there was no way he was going to take the money back without looking for and finding the transponder. She shot the airplane engine to prevent him from getting away so easily. Then we came and he escaped. But not before surveillance picked up his satellite phone signal from Banana Cay. The submarine must have taken him to an airstrip somewhere not far from Banana Cay because this morning we have located Enrique's satellite phone signal in Picazón, Mexico. Know where that is?"

"I do. Some good fishing around there, as I understand it." Picazón is in Quintana Roo, on the Yucatan near the Belizean border.

He took a deep sip of his drink and hummed. "Good cocktail, Boone. The orange juice is a nice addition. Anyway, if you know the area, it is on a giant bay called Chetumal. There's a canal connecting the bay to the sea, so there's a lot of ways to escape and move from Mexico to Belize undetected. So now we think this is where the cartel's top man El Pescador is located."

I cocked an eye: "El Pescador? 'The Fisherman' in Spanish?"

Diego nodded thoughtfully. "Translated, yes. Though we're not sure what that means figuratively. Most of these names are facetious. He may have once said he didn't like fish. Anyway, surveillance suggests that there are a number of small compounds or hotels in Picazón that are likely where we'll find Enrique and El Pescador and a bunch of soldiers. Finding which building is being used as the cartel headquarters is critical. The

Mexican Naval Infantry Force – the NIF are the Mexican Marines – storm the wrong place and they El Pescador will give us the slip. And of course there will be laptops we want to recover intact."

I sipped my drink, oblivious as to why he was telling me all this: "Well, I hope you figure out which hotel in a hurry. I'm betting that they don't always sit in the same spot for long."

"You're exactly right." He winced, finished his drink, and looked me in the eye. "That's why they've tapped me to step in – I'm here and they have no time to insert another field commander. But I don't know what Enrique looks like. Tanya does, but she's out of action. You see where I'm going with this?"

You could have heard a pin drop.

Or a feather.

Or a mote of dust settle gently onto a down comforter.

I was instantly transported back to that hellish moment at Cabana Two:

An oddly feminine face, ponytail, smooth complexion, drooping eyes, wide lips. It was as if I were face to face with a Centaur...he seemed inhuman.

Orbach clapped me on the back. "Isn't this great, Boone? Another adventure! Oh, boy! Super!"

I must have been quite the sight as I sat there examining my screwdriver, saying nothing for what seemed an eternity. Diego finally cleared his throat, adding: "We'd go to a local fishing lodge. Pose as anglers. The only thing we need to do is identify which of the hotels is the right one. The Marines will storm the place; we won't be anywhere near the estate when that happens. But we need to go right away. We've reserved spots at the lodge. Charter flight leaves this afternoon." He rolled his empty glass between his hands, watching me carefully.

I finally found some words: "I may have been wearing a mask, so he didn't get a good look at me, but he must by now know that Boone Linsenbigler was there. If he sees me…"

He said: "You'll have to lose the mustache, Boone. Cut your hair way back."

"Good, Lord!" I smoothed my whiskers. "Do you know the gravity of what you suggest?"

There was another pat on my back from Terry. "I've already looked into having a falsie made for you until it grows back."

"A falsie?!" I heaved a great sigh and settled my face into my hands.

Diego also sighed: "Look, we wouldn't ask, obviously, if this wasn't really important, or if we had any other person who knew exactly what Enrique looks like. You had a really good look at him, and we have to be absolutely positive. An opportunity like this may never come again to bring this cartel down, to capture El Pescador."

In my terror, the scene at Cabana Two played again in my head, ending with the sight of poor pudgy Cecil.

Dead.

I'd already settled the score on Elvis best I could.

I realized this one I could do for Cecil, and for Tanya. It hadn't escaped me that Tanya had spent two years tracking down Enrique only to have me come along and screw things up.

"Do you think we might actually get some fishing in?"

Diego smiled, wearily, and clapped me on the shoulder. "I'll try to make sure you don't even come close to getting killed this time."

I winced. "How reassuring."

Orbach raised his glass for a toast. "All for one, and one for all! This is going to be super!"

I furrowed my brow at him, and then at Diego. "Terry is coming?"

Terry leaned in. "Article XXXVII, Subsection 3.2.6 of your contract stipulates that on all promotional travel Conglomerated reserves the right to accompany you with marketing and promotional personnel."

I barked a laugh. "How is this promotional travel?"

He grinned, patting me on the shoulder. "Conglomerated paid for your trip to the Bahamas, as such this trip is an officially sanctioned promotional event. I'll get some super pix of you in action."

Head in my hands, I asked: "Won't this look suspicious with us suddenly showing up? Most anglers plan these trips far in advance. If they are watching who comes and goes..."

"We are filling in for a group of four anglers that the DEA contacted and asked to cancel so we could substitute for them. It was the only way to make it look natural. If we simply booked with one day's notice, it would have looked suspicious. As with Carlos, we can't know the lodge manager's loyalties. Terry is good cover, and nobody would expect him to be a cop."

"You're bonkers. Forget about believing he's a cop. Nobody will believe Terry is an angler."

"And why not?" Terry interjected, indignant hands on hips. "I've been fishing before. I caught a flounder. And besides, this way I can document the whole thing!"

Eyes shut, I inquired: "Who is the fourth angler, Diego?"

"Another DEA agent."

I shook my head in disbelief. "I know Terry has never picked up a fly rod in his life. Diego, do you or the other agent know how to fly fish? At all?"

He looked confused. "Is that important? I thought you just sort of flicked the thing out there, you know."

"How hard could it be?" Terry snorted. "You just wing it around and throw it out there." He and Diego seemed to agree that this should pose no problem.

Fly casting is only difficult because it is entirely counter intuitive. When you watch someone cast, you see their arm moving and the fly line moving through the air and so one assumes that the arm is making all this happen. In one sense, the exact opposite is true. The weight of the line activates the spring action of the fly rod to build the 'line speed' necessary to maintain the fly line and fly aloft. The arm initiates the motion that activates the spring action and functions mostly as a fulcrum thereafter. This is a fancy way of saying that fly casting is not like riding a bike. There is no eureka moment when you suddenly just 'get it' and are off like a shot. It takes a lot of practice to learn how to fly cast, a lot of muscle memory, especially to cast in variable conditions like wind that impedes the progress of the line through the air and requires different timing. Diego, Terry and the other agent had no chance at all of learning how to cast overnight. None. Zip. Nada.

My drink arrived, but did not survive more than a moment.

CHAPTER 14

I SPENT MUCH OF THE FLIGHT TO CANCUN from Nassau providing a crash course in fly fishing and lecturing my fellow anglers on the kinds of fishing we would be doing. There had been a mad dash in Nassau to outfit my companions so that they had the right equipment and clothes. There was also a fair amount to explain about the tackle, about the flies, and to set up their rods and load their reels with line. They would have to admit to the guides that they were complete novices, and there would be no fooling anybody otherwise. I must say it was rather novel to jet directly from Nassau via charter to Cancun, a dream flight if ever there were for anglers. There was of course lots of room to move around the plane as there were only four of us aboard. Though not enough room for any casting lessons.

In the van ride from Cancun to Picazón, we reviewed tactics. Diego was suggesting that we fish out in front of the estates where Enrique might be staying. My concern was that would look suspicious, that we would only have an excuse to pass by the ocean side of those places if on our way to or from Chetumal Bay to the main ocean-side dock. Likely all the sport fishing would be in the shallow bay. After all, could we really expect to see much without binoculars? And wouldn't that look suspicious? The conclusion was that he and the other agent – an imposing black guy named Tom – would have to do a little reconnaissance on foot first to get the lay of the land. They agreed to take a morning run along the beach and dusty road to see what they could see. My main dread in the endeavor was getting anywhere near where Enrique might put his hooks in me.

The van ride was brutal – a bumpy five-hour trek in the middle of the night. The good news was that Utopia Lodge was completely new and thus the plumbing all worked, which upon trudging to my cabana in the dark I indulged in immediately by way of a hot shower. The lodge also was rather forward thinking in that it was mostly single room occupancy. That's a rare accommodation at fishing lodges but one that is eminently desirable and usually costs extra. It is hard to imagine that anglers (other than couples) would really relish sharing quarters if they don't have to. Unlike the rather dowdy clapboard bungalows at Banana Cay, the thatched huts at Utopia were a little over the top with bold colors and huge paintings of flowers on stucco walls. It also had a mini bar. After washing off the road dust, I availed myself of a couple lagers on the porch. As I drank my beer and listened to the ocean off in the darkness, it dawned on me that this was my third fishing lodge in ten days' time. Had submarines not entered the conversation at the last lodge I might have had a full week of outstanding fishing with Elvis – RIP. I didn't hold out much hope that this little escapade on the Mayan Coast would be much different. I should have gone directly to bed but this 'mission' understandably had me a little nerve-wracked.

As did being clean-shaven for the first time in twelve years. I hardly recognized myself in the mirror, not only due to the lack of whiskers but they had cut my hair back to about an inch long all over, sort of like a crew cut. I had a new name, too: Chris Taylor. All put together, I had been made into a rather bland character, which was the idea I suppose. Mediocrity was taking root – for some reason I had opted for beer instead of an invigorating jolt of whiskey. What next? A rousing game of checkers? Rake the yard? Walk the dog?

This transformation was most alarming the next morning. In the mirror, I was confronted by a stranger, gave myself quite a start. Well, at least I didn't have to spend much time drying my hair or fussing with my mustache. Just towel off, dress and go.

Under slightly overcast but calm skies, I trekked from my round thatched stucco hut across the sandy compound to the round thatched stucco restaurant that served as the dining facility. Apparently, it was open to the public – unlike most lodges. This area of the Mayan coast was underdeveloped, and most of the eateries were extremely 'local.' That is, most Americans down there diving or fishing would be a little leery of eating at the local places for fear of contracting some whopping case of gut busting Monte's revenge. Personally, I defer to caution on these trips and never eat anything even mildly adventuresome. It just isn't worth the risk of becoming sick and ruining the trip.

The dining room had stucco walls draped with flamboyant Mexican tapestries, the tables and chairs all made of dark wood. I made immediate note of the smallish bar back and to the left, and the entrance to the kitchen to the back right. At a table to my left, I found Terry decked out in zip off fishing clothing, neckerchief and floppy sun hat – torn straight from the pages of an Orvis catalogue. He held his phone up and snapped a picture of me.

"Terry, don't post any pictures of me looking like this. We don't want anybody knowing what I look like."

He beamed. "Don't worry about a thing. Just saving all the photos for later, Chris. This whole thing is so super!" There was an empty Fiestaware breakfast plate and coffee cup in front of him.

I pulled out a chair and plunked down opposite him. "The only thing super about this is that it is super dangerous. I don't think you appreciate the gravity of the situation if Enrique figures out who I am. He would almost certainly kill me on the spot, and possibly you too."

"We've got Diego and Tom here. They'll protect us."

"Have you seen them this morning? They said they were going for a run."

A thick dusky Mexican waitress placed a cup of coffee at my elbow. "Break Fast?"

I nodded. "Whatever he had will be fine, thank you." I turned to Terry as she headed back to the kitchen. "Not sure I can even eat. Let's hope they get back soon and in one piece. These cartel people aren't idiots, you know. Two military-looking Americans just happen to go jogging past their hideout might set off alarms."

Terry kept poking at his phone, and said absently: "I'm sure they'll be fine, Boone. You worry too much."

"Worry too much? You bet your boots I worry after what I've been through. I'm damn lucky to be alive and I'm not keen to push my luck any further than I already have."

I heard footsteps and the restaurant door opening: it was four other anglers, not Diego and Tom. Terry and I introduced ourselves as Terry and Chris and I forgot their names immediately. My *huevos rancheros* arrived and as predicted, I managed only a few bites. My stomach was in knots.

I saw four Mexican fishing guides motor their flats skiffs up to the dock and tie up. Their second mates emerged from behind the restaurant carrying coolers with our lunches and beverages down the dock to the boats. We would be heading out before long.

The side door to the restaurant opened – it was Diego and Tom, head to foot in new fishing garb and carrying their hats. They saw us and sat on either side of me with mumbled 'good mornings', their eyes scanning the room. The waitress stepped up, filled their orders for breakfast, and waddled away.

After a second look around to see nobody was close enough to hear us, Diego said: "Good news. We spotted their hotel – it was completely obvious. Lots of expensive SUV's, men standing guard with concealed weapons. And get this – we spotted Enrique on a balcony smoking a long cigarette. He fit your description perfectly, has a bandaged left hand from where you shot him. Boone, you're off the hook. We called in the Mexican Marines. They'll raid the place tonight."

I was so relieved I almost threw up, which was not something I had ever experienced before and hope never to again.

He continued: "Sorry to have dragged you all the way down here for nothing, Boone."

I laughed. "A damn sight better than last time when I was promised to be kept out of the action and dropped in up to my neck!"

Terry groaned with disgust. "You mean I'm not going to get any shots of Boone in action? No danger? What am I supposed to do now?"

I made a suggestion: "Fish?"

All except Terry got a chuckle out of that.

And fish we did. As the agents gobbled down their breakfasts and Terry poked at his phone in a funk, I assembled their rods. In short order we were down the dock, in the boats and off into the briny blue. I was paired with Terry, who became even more disgusted when he started to lose signal and had to put his phone down and take in the scenery – the sun had come out, and the ocean to our left was a blazing topaz. To our right, a thin sandy beach, rustic shacks, half-finished cabanas, and palm trees. We veered this way and that through channels lined with scrub and palmettoes, emerging suddenly into the blazing white flats of Chetumal Bay, the shores pocketed with mangroves. There was a light chop on the water, which was just the ticket – if it's too calm, the bonefish and permit get spooky. The guide set us up on a course to drift a couple miles of shore no deeper than a foot, a stretch of open tan sand bottom that disappeared into and ever more complicated maze of mangrove.

We were looking for bonefish, a sleek fish so silvery and mercurial you can't really see them in a light chop just their shadows on the bottom. The bigger ones often travel in singles, and the smaller ones travel in packs that form chevrons you can see coming at you, either from straight ahead or angled toward or away from you. You cast ahead of the direction they are moving and strip the fly in short rhythmic movements. Sometimes you strip fast and sometimes slow, depending on how aggressive the fish are. I have boxes of flies for bonefish, but the go to lure is a pink and sparkly fly as long as your thumb is wide. Its called a *Gotcha*. I tie my own gotchas that have clear, barred rubber legs to make it look even more like a tiny shrimp. I've run into old anglers at lodges that have told me that's the only fly they've fished for many years. Yet like me, they bring boxes stuffed with every pattern you can imagine. An angler's worst nightmare is a scenario in which you arrive at a fishing lodge and don't have any of the right flies, any of the ones the fish are taking. Yet the bonefish I've seen always seem happy to chase my Linsenbigler Gotchas, the rest of my flies forlorn at ever having the chance to take the stage.

I stepped up onto the bow, rod in hand. "Terry, I'll go first, you observe, and think about how the line propels itself, that I really don't have to move the rod that far to make the line go."

"Whatever." He shrugged, slathering suntan lotion on his face like jam on bread. "At least I can get some shots of you in action, shots of you fishing."

"Don't you ever do anything just for fun, Terry? Don't you ever stop being a publicist?"

"Being a publicist *is* fun, and I'm having fun every waking minute as long as I am promoting something or someone super."

The stout brown guide grunted, pointing ahead of the boat. Technically, the guide is supposed to call out the location of a fish by the dial of the clock, with noon straight ahead, one o'clock slightly to the right, eleven o'clock slightly to the left, and so on. He's also supposed to say how many fish he sees and which direction they are going. Guides are supposed to do this because they spend every day spotting fish and the anglers they guide don't and so have a hard time seeing them. Yet most guides I ran into just pointed and said something like 'fish.'

Fortunately, I didn't have a hard time seeing the fish with my dark amber polarized sunglasses, my eyesight was good and I had an aptitude for picking the grey shadows of the fish moving against the direction of the grey shadow of the light chop.

There were five bonefish, long as my forearm at two o'clock and sixty feet out, poking around a small clump of mangrove. Bonefish have pointy faces that end in goofy lips angled down that they use to root around the bottom trying to scare up crabs or shrimp. They suck in sand and blow it out, which leaves pockmarks all over the shallow bottom. When you enter a flat you can tell if bonefish are around by fresh pock marks in the sand bottom.

I put the fly in the air, and cast longer than necessary to account for slack that would result in my line from the breeze. My gotcha landed politely about six feet from the one side of the mangrove and immediately drew the attention of the nearest fish. Being competitive, this drew the attention of the other fish. Stripping the fly toward me, line coiling at my feet, I watched as the five fish formed a chevron behind my fly. I slowed to let the lead fish catch up to my offering.

"Watch, Terry, this is the strip strike." When the lead fish takes the fly you feel a tap. Unlike many other fish, bonefish don't grab your fly, turn and race off with it. They just run up, take it, and usually begin munching on it on the spot. With their mouth pointed toward you, lifting the rod tip to set the hook usually results in the hook turning sideways and the fly sliding right out of their jaws. This is why you have to set the hook by pulling back on the line in one long strip and drive the hook into those goofy lips. Why precisely the fly turns sideways when you raise the rod tip is a little murky, but the fact of the matter is that you will miss hooking most bonefish if you raise the rod tip the way you do with a fish that turns away, so you have to consciously strip strike.

I glanced down at Terry, who was at my elbow with his phone. "And...action!"

The lead fish wriggled faster than the others up to my fly and I felt a tap. Left hand holding the line, I pulled it back in one long decisive strip, my left fist well behind me. The line went taught, throbbing, and I saw the fish shadow thrash, scales flashing sunlight in the water. That's the moment you raise the rod so that the fish is pulling against the bending rod, preventing him from snapping the line.

The fish raced around in circles for a moment – that's the time to make sure that the fly line collected at your feet isn't wrapped around anything, that you're not standing on the line, because the bonefish is about to go zero to sixty in two seconds.

True to form, the bonefish pointed himself at the horizon to my left and flicked on the afterburners. Loose line at my feet lashed through the rod guides and vanished. I swung the rod in a gentle arc toward where the fish was heading and let him run, my drag squealing. He shot out three hundred feet, paused and then shot out another hundred and fifty. Managing to slow his progress with some line pressure, I reeled him back half way before he shot off again. These lightning-fast runs are the appeal of bonefishing. As a meal, they make poor, boney table fare and ones that happen to die are sometimes made into fish balls, mostly as a novelty. Also, it is fun to watch them follow and take the fly, something called 'sight fishing.'

When I managed to tucker him out, kneel and get my hand under him, I lifted the fish up for Terry to see. It was a two-plus pounder. I've caught them up to five pounds, but they get much larger, though they are harder to catch. The stupid lips on the pointy face were pumping, the fish effectively panting. Little wonder what with the galloping they do. Probably because they are so exhausted by the time you boat them, they tend to sit in your hand rather politely until you release them.

Terry in his floppy sun hat and suntan lotion-streaked across his face was pointing his phone at the fish and me. "And...cut! Got some good video, anyway."

He never did pick up a rod that day. Which was fine by me, I don't really like teaching people to fly fish. Because fly casting is so counter-intuitive, students can't understand what you are trying to tell them, or at the very least they dismiss your instructions and do what seems natural. As soon as you put a fly rod in someone's hand they seem to go deaf – and blind. I cannot tell you how many times I have told someone "Don't bring the rod so far back, stop it at one o'clock, turn your head and watch how far back you are bringing the rod." They nod, and watch themselves bring the rod way far back to like four o'clock, rod tip practically touching the ground, and when they bring the rod forward the line ends up in a pile in front of them and draped around their heads. That's when they look at me with sad, bewildered eyes and whimper: "What did I do wrong?" I tip my hat to professional fly casting instructors as they are a marvel of forbearance. Me? I'd as soon stand next to the student with a cattle prod and say: "Every time you bring that rod past one o'clock you'll get the business end of this, numbskull."

I believe I mentioned that I am a nice person, one who likes animals and some people. Well, there you have it.

A dozen bonefish were to my credit that day, none over three pounds. We also stopped by a bit of reef and on a Clouser fly I caught a colorful parrot fish. His powerful reef-crushing teeth actually bent the steel hook.

I popped open a bottle of lager for the ride to the lodge and kicked back, Terry filming me in my reverie as I admired the glistening tropical sea and wondered how Diego and Tom did that day. Their poor guide would have his hands full trying to hook two complete novices into fish. I toasted Neptune's honor that this whole Enrique business was to be put to bed and that I was almost done with this misadventure once and for all. I admit that even thinking such thoughts, ones I'd had a number of times over that last few days, were thoughts that seemed to result in more mayhem despite indications, and my optimism wavered. I ran a hand over my clean-shaven face with trepidation: what could possibly go wrong this time? Based on experience, I was determined to proceed with the utmost caution. When the marines charged in the middle of the night, might some of the gangsters slip into the dark, and seeking a place to hide find my cabana? Might Enrique and some pals decide to dine at the lodge restaurant and recognize me? There was no room I would enter first, no corner I would not peek around furtively before venturing onward, until there were iron bars between Enrique and me.

Oh but for the mundane yet relatively danger-free (Camden excepted) confines of New Jersey.

As such, when we arrived back at the dock and we found the other guide's boats parked neatly at the slips, I took my time collecting my gear, watching the restaurant and cabanas for any sign of mischief. I saw none. Though I also saw no people. Usually you see someone, perhaps the caretaker raking the beach, or the laundress taking down dried sheets from the clothesline. *The anglers must all be in at the bar already having a fine time.*

Terry stood on the dock looking at his phone. "Finally, a connection. Hm. Whoopsie."

I was slowly stuffing my fly boxes into my boat bag. "*Whoopsie* what, Terry?"

"I had my phone set on automatic upload."

"What's so whoopsie about that?"

"The pictures I took this morning loaded up to the media sight automatically. And the ones I've been taking all day today are uploading to the media site automatically right now."

"Well, stop the damn thing!"

"Too late."

I paused. "Did it upload the picture of me from this morning?"

He poked at his phone, then wrinkled his nose at me. "Afraid so."

My sense of trepidation became intense. "You mean…Terry, do you mean that anybody keeping up with me on social media could see the picture?"

"Yes. And I'm location enabled so…"

I gasped: "So they know what I look like and where I am? People can see that on line? Anybody can see that?"

He shrugged. "Sure. That's the idea."

I fairly gnashed my teeth at him: "Don't you realize that means Enrique and his crew could have seen that?"

He rolled his head: "I think you're being paranoid, Boone."

I scanned the lodge. It was in the shadows of the palm trees, bathed in freckles of sunlight five hundred feet ahead of us.

Nobody.

Turning to the guide, I said in a low voice: "We need to get out of here. Now."

His English was remedial, and he knit his brow. "We go?"

I tilted my head at the lodge. "Banditos at the lodge."

He laughed, and heaved the cooler onto the dock. "Funny joke."

"I'm serious."

He looked askance at me, and then laughed again. "Funny joke." He hefted the cooler and began his trek toward the lodge, Terry following him, his eyes glued to his phone.

"Terry? If everything is ok when you get there, give me a wave with both hands, OK?

Over his shoulder he said: "Both hands, got you. Boy we got some good shots."

My trembling hands moved rods around, put the bag here and then there as the guide in his board shorts and thick brown feet went down the dock, Terry stumbling along in his wake.

Please let him wave two hands. Please let me go in and have a cocktail and share fishing stories.

CHAPTER 15

I WATCHED SIDELONG as the guide went around the back of the restaurant. He paused when he got there, looked back at me for a moment, and then stepped slowly behind the building. Terry marched straight up the steps of the restaurant, the screen door slamming behind him as he went.

I crawled up onto the dock, placing my tackle bag in front of where the bow was tied to a cleat. I untied the bow but left the painter draped over the cleat like it was still tied. Then I made it look like I had forgotten something, and climbed back into the boat as though I were searching for something. And I was: the key was in the ignition. Gas: third of a tank. There was a large bottle of spring water under the transom, half-empty.

I heard the screen door slam.

Terry stood on the porch.

He didn't have his phone with him.

He waved one hand slowly, turned mechanically and went back into the restaurant like some sort of glockenspiel.

No phone. One hand. The guide's look toward me from the back of the restaurant. Nobody else in sight. The whole thing stank.

The worst that could happen if I were wrong would be that I would take off with the boat and the guide and staff would rush out to see why. How bad was that versus the alternative? Versus if I were right?

I swept my tackle bag and rods back into the boat, pivoted and untied the stern. Turning forward, I wrenched the key, sparked the engine to life and threw the boat into reverse.

As the water surged at the stern and I drew away from the dock, a man with a rifle stepped out of the restaurant and leveled the gun at me.

Dear God, this can't be happening. Terry, you moron. Damn social media and automatic uploads and to hell with this endless promotion that was forever having people pointing guns at me. This is insane!

I crouched behind the transom and the plastic windshield splintered, a big chunk of Plexiglas falling on my shoulder. A split second I heard the gunshot cracking through the crisp salt air.

If I turned the boat, I would expose myself to the shooter from the side or the rear. Looking behind me at the ocean, my attention was drawn to a hatch in the aft deck. If I opened the heavy fiberglass lid, it would shield me at least somewhat from the rear. I did exactly that, my fingers trembling like an octogenarian's, the lid's hinges locking it in an upright position.

Reaching up, I spun the steering wheel, briefly exposing myself to the gunman.

More people with guns were pouring out of the restaurant.

I rammed the throttle forward, the compartment lid at my back swinging between my adversaries and me.

Bullets pinged against the steel poling platform, popped the motor housing and thwacked the compartment lid at my back as the boat lunged further away from the dock. In retrospect, I think I was helped by the fact that I was probably six hundred feet or more away from the gunmen, affecting their aim.

Go! Faster!

I put a thousand feet more between me and the gunmen in what seemed like seconds, the sound of bullets striking the boat stopping. A quick look back told me they were running down the dock to the other boats, to give chase.

Rising from my crouched position, I steered the boat in an arc to the south, toward the canal to Chetumal Bay, but also toward Belize, which if I guessed correctly was maybe forty miles to Cay Caulker. The only thing to the north was more Mexico coastline, and I didn't have any confidence in finding police or anybody else that would cross a drug cartel. You don't have to be an authority on Mexico, just a student of headlines, to know that the entire country seems to be in the pocket of drug kingpins.

What the devil was I supposed to do now? Make a run south for Belize? Duck into Chetumal Bay and try to hide?

I looked back at the motor and the hatch. There were holes in the motor housing but is seemed to be running fine. There were a handful of holes and dings in the hatch cover, and one corner of the hatch had been shot off.

That's when I noticed the blood.

It was on the floor at my feet and running down the back of my left leg.

Good Lord, I was bleeding and in my panic hadn't even noticed!

A tingle made itself known on my upper arm. Steering with my pelvis, I reached back with the other hand and found the wound – the broken-off corner of the hatch was sticking out of the back of my arm. Cursing, I eased it out and inspected the triangle of white fiberglass. Looked like it had stuck in only a half-inch or so. I slapped my hat to the transom and pulled my sun snood over my head. Doubling the snood over the wrist of the injured arm, I hiked it up over the puncture to stem the flow of blood.

Snugging my hat back on my head, I glanced aft. Two boats were indeed in pursuit.

I noted that although I was afraid for my life I felt less hapless than I had when I was kidnapped by Miguel. Just for starters, I had been sharp enough to elude easy capture. When Elvis was shot I was fairly cowering with fear in the bottom of the skiff. There was a meager and morbid satisfaction in knowing I was getting better at not being killed.

One could only imagine the scene back there at the restaurant. What would they do with Diego and Tom and the rest? And Terry? Can you imagine how well he would get along with a ruthless band of cutthroats? It would be comical were it not for the likelihood that they would all be executed, or worse, decapitated – unless the Mexican Marines showed up in time to save them. Then again, maybe with me dragging half the gang away, Diego and Tom might find some way to overpower their guards.

So was I supposed to try to help them or try to save my own skin? My phone was in my bag but I didn't exactly have the phone number of the Mexican Marines on speed dial. Who for the love of Pete would I call that could help me in – oh – say the next twenty minutes? And I knew from Terry's phone that signals out here were weak to non-existent.

This was a remote area; it wasn't like there were any kind of police for fifty miles. There might be some Belize Coast Guard boats straight south. Might be. Might not be.

There might be some of them in Chetumal Bay, too. It was not as if I had a solid grasp of the geography, I could not recall what Belizean towns were on the bay and where they were.

The irony of my situation did not escape me – this was the second time in a week that I was escaping a fishing lodge brimming with bloodthirsty hoodlums. I was a lucky dog to have survived the first incident, what were the chances I could duck out of this one?

In my gut, I did not like my chances on the open sea. With them in eyeshot, I had no idea if their boats were faster than mine or whether my fuel would hold out.

Since I did not know where to find the Belize Coast Guard, my best bet might be the Mexican Marines, and I knew where I would find them – at the smuggler's hotel in El Picazón at dawn.

A saying of my father's came to mind, and I had to guess it was attributable to some historic American figure: "The fox escapes the hounds by doubling back on a fence, not across open ground." For the life of me, I couldn't recall the circumstances under which he said that, but he was full of weird quotes, and they sometimes seemed to have absolutely nothing to do with anything except making him seem wise. He was as likely to have said something like that after getting a flat tire as he was finding the bread had gone moldy.

Adjusting the outboard's trim to get as much speed as possible, I was ears back and headed for the barn...or the canal as the case may be. My idea was to head into the bay, find a hiding spot in the innumerable nooks and crannies among the mangroves and then trek on foot back across the isthmus to somewhere near the hotel where the marines would invade that night. I wasn't sure what kind of ground I would be crossing, probably pretty swampy, but I had my wading boots and bug repellent.

In a slashing arc I lined up with the deep blue canal entrance – it was noticeably straight and deeper than surrounding waters. The boats in pursuit seemed a little more distant than before, so it seemed I may have had a slightly faster boat and an edge. If I were to hide, I needed to be out of sight when I beached the boat.

As I roared into the canal the thrum of my outboard reverberated against the sides of the canal. The tide may have been coming in as I felt like I was suddenly going faster down the barrel of the canal, the white and turquoise bay the size of my thumb in the distance. Zooming past a vacant navy marina on my right, I leaned forward as if that might add speed. *Faster.*

The exit from the canal didn't put me in the open bay but pointed the way to a buoy toward a mangrove island a mile or more distant. By the time I reached it, the pursuit boats seemed even farther back than before – my luck.

There was another channel sliced in an arc through the next mangrove island – this finally delivered me to a burst of horizon on the sapphire Chetumal Bay.

Immediately to my left a large catamaran motor yacht was steaming my way from behind the island. At the bow was a white-haired gent holding a cocktail and dressed in white slacks, navy sport shirt and Panama hat. Not a care in the world, the rich old so-and-so. He toasted the air with his cocktail and smiled at me.

I spun the wheel and pointed the flats boat at the yacht. Maybe they could get some sort of word out, hide me, something?

Spinning the wheel again, I came alongside the yacht and the old man, my boat's wake sloshing against the large hull just below her name: *Esmerelda.*

"Good day to you!" He barked, flashing his white teeth from behind a nice tan. Closer now, I saw that he was a fellow mustache fan, sporting a trim white handlebar beneath a noble nose. "Amigo, join me for a cocktail?" He had a thick Mexican accent.

"I would!" I shouted. "But regrettably I am being pursued by drug smugglers. Do you think you could alert some sort of authorities to help me?"

"Smugglers?" He looked amused. "Don't you mean the cartel?"

The yacht's engines stopped, and I put my boat in neutral, drifting closer.

"Of course. Could you do that for me? I have to get going."

He sipped his drink, scowled, and dumped it overboard. He shouted over his shoulder: "Manny?"

A waiter in a white smock hurried out of the cabin and up next to the old man.

The old man pulled a silver automatic from his back – must have been in his waist band – and pointed it at Manny's chest. The bartender's eyes went wide.

"Manny, you are a terrible bartender."

And with that, the gun cracked and blood splotched the white tunic at the small of Manny's back. He clung to the rail as he sank to the deck, groaning and gasping.

The gun was now pointed at me.

As were the old man's laughing black eyes.

"But you, Mr. Linsenbigler? You're a *good* bartender, aren't you?"

CHAPTER 16

MY HAND WAS STILL ON THE THROTTLE but I wasn't more than twenty feet from the muzzle of that gun. I had dodged many bullets in the last couple of days. This one looked too on target. And having just seen yet another man killed right in front of me I was too scared to move. Witnessing someone dying painfully – and piteously – is truly horrific.

The old gentleman laughed merrily, and while not taking his eyes off me, stepped over and put a foot on Manny's hip and shoved him under the railing and into the water with a splash. Manny bobbed to the surface gasping, and then vanished into a cauldron of red bubbles.

Like Elvis, it makes it worse to see a man shot and then drown, to witness the profound dismay on the condemned man's face, the faraway look in the eyes. It is as though he was watching something else other than his own predicament, perhaps his life passing before his eyes.

Perhaps glimpsing behind the mortal veil.

My stomach was in knots, and my mouth tasted like I was sucking on a penny.

"You see, Mr. Linsenbigler, it is me who is the top smuggler, the one the DEA is after. I could introduce myself by my actual name but you would not know it. I am known as El Pescador."

A younger man with yellow shooter glasses in white slacks, blue sport shirt and a rifle appeared at the door to the cabin, his eye looking down the barrel at me.

Game over. El Pescador, the cartel kingpin, had me dead to rights. And the boats chasing me? They were nowhere to be seen, they must have called ahead to have El Pescador intercept me.

I stammered: "I guess…I guess under the circumstances… I accept your offer of… a cocktail, El Pescador."

He returned the gun to his waistline behind his back and nodded approvingly, but glanced at Manny's bloodstain in the water and held up a finger. "But you will have to mix the cocktails. I seem to have lost my bartender."

Some crew all in white came around the other side of the dock and threw me a line. When I pulled my boat up to the yacht the little Mexican crew swarmed my boat and hoisted me up onto the deck of the catamaran. El Pescador strode toward me on bowed legs, chin high, but still smiling. I gestured toward the flats boat, my voice quavering slightly: "If you are going to kill me, you might as well take my tackle, I have some very nice rods and I'd hate to see them set adrift."

I know, odd thing to think about, but then anglers have some deep separation anxieties about losing their gear. And I wasn't lying, I would rather someone have my stuff than have it destroyed, even if he was my nemesis.

He waved a hand at the crew, barked something in Spanish, and they began to hand up my gear. Close to me now, the old man gave me a good once over from below – he was a head shorter than me, and not as old as I had at first assumed, probably mid-sixties.

When his eyes made their way up to mine he said: "I'm sorry to see you lost your mustache in your bargain with the DEA. No, Mr. Linsenbigler, I am not going to kill you. At least I don't think I am." He jerked a thumb back at the red stain in the blue water. "It all depends on your bartending skills. Hand me your phone."

I pointed at my tackle bag, he barked something in Spanish, and one of the crew fished around the bag until he came up with it and handed it to the old gent. He held it up, turned it on, saw wallpaper of me holding the permit from the other day. He squinted at the picture and then tossed the phone into the flats boat with evident disgust. He said: "Behind you is Hidalgo."

I looked over my shoulder at the rifleman – aside from the togs, shooter glasses and rifle, he had curly shoulder-length hair, broken nose and a bad complexion.

"Hidalgo is my top body guard. He does not fish, he does not drink or allow himself women. All Hidalgo does is watch my back. In Spanish, his name means *Gentleman*. The name is *chistoso*...what's the word? Ah yes: facetious. Don't do anything brave, Mr. Linsenbigler, I'd hate to lose another bartender so soon." He gestured to the cabin door behind me. "Shall we?"

I turned and Hidalgo receded into the brown shadow of the main cabin as I followed.

Removing my amber sunglasses, I blinked my eyes to adjust them to my shady surroundings. It was a wood-paneled barroom rigged out with brass hanging lamps and fixtures. On the wall were some elegant illuminated frames containing photos of El Pescador holding trophy fish interspaced with a painting, specifically vibrant Gauguin depictions of half-naked Tahitian women. At the aft end of the room was an elaborate mahogany bar proscenium, complete with furled wood and beveled mirror, an impressive array of bottles secured in brass slips and lit from above. Between the bar and me were three mahogany tables with chairs arranged in a triangle. Slouched at the closest table were three men like the one with the rifle except they were strapped with dueling shoulder holsters over their blue sport shirts. From behind sunglasses, they looked at me impassively, though I guessed in some way they were just hoping I'd try something so they could riddle me with lead.

El Pescador came abreast of me and gestured at the nearest picture of him with a sailfish. "I landed this one on Guatemala – have you been there?"

I gulped, wiping sweat from my brow, sure the next second would be my last. "No…I want to go there…or wanted…never did catch a sailfish."

He took me by the elbow and led me to the first Gauguin on the other side of his sailfish. "And are you familiar with art?"

"Gauguin," I muttered.

A toothy smile spread across his face. "You are a man of the world, yes?"

I gestured awkwardly at the bare-chested brown woman in a red sarong. "Originals?"

He spread his hands. "Mr. Linsenbigler, when you have as much money as me, why I would have anything but originals? For example, I have you! Why should I settle for just any bartender? Why shouldn't I have the most famous barman?"

Taking a deep breath, I let it out slowly, thinking to myself that I wasn't actually a bartender. I was no slouch when it came to making some favorite cocktails, but unlike a real bartender who remembers hundreds of recipes and makes his concoctions to exacting tolerances, I mainly made drinks by feel and by what was on hand. I hadn't used a jigger or measuring glass in years. I can eyeball a couple ounces in a Boston shaker, and I'm a big believer in splashes of this, a drip of that. In a traditional sense, though, I was no barman. Ask me what's in a Negroni and I know it has Campari and I guess gin in it but otherwise I have to consult a book – I never make Negronis, not a fan.

His words sunk in. I asked: "So you're not going to kill me because you want me to be your bartender?"

He thought about that for a moment, and then led me past the three dangerous men at the table to the bar, and gestured for me to go behind it. Woodenly, I did so, my eyes surveying the other men in the room before looking under the bar at the array of mixing glasses, strainers, stirrers and bar tools. El Pescador took a barstool front and center, the very picture of a white-haired, handle-barred gentleman. He removed his hat to reveal carefully crenelated waves of white, and placed the Panama on the bar next to him, his hands folded on the edge of the bar as if ready for grace.

Grace? How about a prayer for old Boone. I got the idea, all right. This was a test: make him the goddamn best cocktail he ever had or die. I'd come a long way from making methanol martinis, hadn't I?

Then I had to make the *worst* cocktail imaginable to save my life.

Now I had to make the *best* cocktail imaginable to save my life.

Clearing my throat, I asked: "Do you mind if I have a shot of something to calm my nerves before making you a drink? I...I admit to being frightened."

"Help yourself." He smirked, and glanced over his shoulder at his henchmen, then looked back at me and said: "It's funny, I'm so used to this life that it does not bother me that we are all cold-blooded killers. We really are. In this business, everybody is a murderer. Killing Manny was like nothing. Yet to you I imagine it was shocking, yes?"

The liquor before me was all from the upper top shelf, so I picked a rocks glass off one of the glass shelves flanking the bar mirror and poured myself a couple fingers of very rare 23-year Pappy Van Winkle bourbon and took a slurp. In a New York bar that slurp would likely have cost me a hundred dollars. In truth, I had only once had an 'Ol' Rip' version of Pappy Van Winkle bourbon, and it was the 10 year. Of course, the fine bourbon in my mouth, possibly the finest there is, was utterly wasted on me in that wretched state. Except for the fact that it did not burn going down, it tasted like bourbon mixed with the pennies in my mouth.

I answered my host. "I am not used to seeing people killed and it disturbs me, makes me think you are going to do the same to me." My trembling hand brought the glass back to my lips for another gulp. "After what has happened over the last few days, I can't imagine I'm very popular with you."

El Pescador chuckled to himself, searching the ceiling and walls for the right words.

"Mr. Linsenbigler, you give yourself too much credit. It is rather amazing that you have even made it this far given the fact that you are new to gunplay. The realities of this business model is that we expect and account for the DEA's little incursions into our inventories and infrastructure. They would have hit us one way or the other, and it makes no difference that you were involved."

I sipped the last, big gulp. "And Miguel? Carlos?"

He shrugged. "Little fish. They come and go."

"Enrique?"

"He's different, he's a big fish, but you didn't get him, he got off the hook with a sore lip."

What would happen, I wondered, when the Mexican Marines stormed the hotel or Utopia Lodge that evening and I did not warn El Pescador in advance? Likely the bad bartender treatment. I needed time to think.

"What drink did you have in mind, El Pescador?" I snatched the bar cloth from a hook, wiped the bar before him, and placed a coaster in front of his praying hands.

He squinted at me and said wistfully. "In New York many years ago I was with a woman at the King Cole Bar at the St. Regis. I had a drink there that would remind me of her and the time we spent together. When you get to be my age, Mr. Linsenbigler, sometimes memories of women, special women, are very important."

I ventured: "You have Gauguin on your walls, you've spent time at the St. Regis, you like cocktails and fish…I don't get it, how is it you're…" I waved a hand around, mostly at his thugs "…into all this?"

He chuckled. "Life sometimes has a life of its own, things happen you don't expect. I went to college. I was an engineer. It turns out much of what I do, much of smuggling, requires engineering and infrastructure. It is more of a fit than first appears. Mexico is also a country of stark realities. It is a country where success can be measured in the number of dead bodies you string from the lampposts. And there's having more money than you know what to do with. It becomes harder to be…to be amused."

I nodded like I understood but of course I did not – as such better not to go any further in that line of questioning and get down to cases. "So what were you and the lady drinking?"

"You cannot find them in the tropics, in Mexico, or if you do they are terrible, like Manny's. People here do not even know what a maraschino cherry is, much less a lemon."

In my limited tropical travels, I had noted that once you find palm trees you lose lemons. I once tried to explain it to a bartender in Belize and he said: *So you want a lime that is yellow?*

El Pescador leaned across the bar, one eyebrow raised, and whispered: "I have been wanting a Manhattan."

In a word: *Oy vey.* For the uninitiated, Manhattans, while seemingly simple, can be a minefield. Nominally, they are American whiskey stirred with ice and sweet vermouth, with a dot of bitters and a cherry. The devil – literally for me in that moment – was in the details. People make Manhattans with a wide variety of different kinds of rye-based whiskey, everything from rye to bourbon to sour mash to Canadian Club. The flavor profiles of each of those is vastly different, as is the proportion of sweet vermouth that people like. Having been to the King Cole Bar, I could imagine they may have made a rye 'perfect' Manhattan that also has dry vermouth. Some people like them with lots of vermouth, some with less.

Ever the iconoclast and contrarian, I prefer to make mine with wheat-based bourbon as opposed to rye-based. I think it has a cleaner finish and a brighter taste – like a martini – and is more forgiving in the proportions. I also deplore the use of sweet vermouth. Most brands you find are a sticky, fortified wine at the very bottom of my list and to me undrinkable on its own – except in some sort of post-apocalyptic or prison scenario. I prefer to use a tawny port instead for a nuttier, floral accent. If nothing else it makes a Manhattan glow like gleaming polished mahogany instead of resembling Welch's grape juice.

My father was the wordsmith in our family. My Uncle Jack was the family cocktail aficionado. He was a fussy man, an inveterate chess player and classical music fan who insisted on his Manhattans crafted with Makers Mark, a wheated bourbon. My bias was established early in life when I was afforded a taste of the adults' cocktails at holidays. My bias continues today, though I admit to enjoying the occasional Old Overholt (a venerable bargain-basement rye) Manhattan, made with ruby port and orange bitters. To me, rye cries out for a tweak of orange.

So, on the one hand, I could make him a Manhattan similar to the one he had all those years ago, one likely made from a rye whiskey. He had a bottle of Whistle Pig rye that would have made a dandy one. On the other hand, it sounded like the last Manhattan he had was so long ago that he really doesn't remember too precisely what it tasted like. I might do better to hit him with a cleaner wheated version, my strong suit.

Complicating matters, El Pescador was asking me to replicate perhaps the best drink he ever had many years ago and flavored with the memory of a gorgeous woman. How did I even have a chance of matching that?

I didn't.

As my father used to say: *When your shorts ride up don't try to fix the tractor.*

So I surveyed the bottles behind me again and then turned to El Pescador, the bottle of Pappy still in my hands.

"I'm at a disadvantage. Believe it or not, you don't have the right kind of whiskey for a really good Manhattan. Normally, I would make it with a wheated bourbon. It's better than rye for this drink."

He looked skeptical. "The Pappy is wheated."

I cleared my throat. "Of course, but its aged whiskey, and aged whiskeys don't usually mix well. To be honest, Makers Mark or another seven-year-old would make a far superior Manhattan than with Pappy. However, I have an idea." I poured myself another couple fingers of Pappy, sipped, and girded myself. *Come on, Boonie, you have to be brilliant at the bar, now or never.*

"And my idea is this. What you *do have* at your bar are the perfect ingredients for a Rob Roy, a Manhattan made with scotch. I will make you both a Manhattan with Pappy and a Rob Roy and see which you prefer." I didn't wait for an answer, I just took another gulp of Pappy and stooped down into the refrigerator under the bar, filling two mixing glasses with ice. I went about my business of pouring the ingredients, all the while the kernel of an idea brewing about my comrades in arms back at the lodge. Who knew what was to become of those captives in the interim between now and when the marines finally arrived, especially the DEA agents, not to mention Terry?

The Rob Roy idea hit me because I noticed a bottle of 25-year Macallan and a bottle of 40-year Taylor Port. A friend of mine once introduced me to a liquor brand ambassador – that's somebody who works for a company like Conglomerated and promotes their products by visiting liquor stores and bars to convince them to stock their brands. His name was George, a man with an elegant greying goatee, and in exchange for a batch of saltwater flies we tied for him, he invited us over to sample some really good bottles of whiskey. At a rather advanced stage of the evening, Ambassador George turned to me and said: "Do you like Rob Roys?" That's when he mixed 25-year Macallan and 40-year Taylors Port into a mind-blowing Rob Roy. I was quasi-sozzled at the time and even then it blew me away. In point of fact, it may be the best cocktail I ever tasted.

So why wouldn't I try to pop El Pescador's skull with the best cocktail I could possibly mix? At the very least, it would make a fitting last cocktail for yours truly were I to face the firing squad sitting at the table yonder.

Tossing out more coasters, I set four glasses between me and El Pescador and dropped a cherry in two for the Manhattans and a lemon twist in the other two for the Rob Roys. Stirring the cocktails consecutively and ambidextrously in the mixing glasses, I strained them into the appropriate glasses, one of each for us both. I had made them the way I like them, which is light on the wine. Some people like them swimming in the stuff, but there's a tipping point where the flavors don't meld, and the vermouth or port dominates the drink. Blech.

At least with two cocktails I had doubled my odds of wowing El Pescador.

Pleased as any kid in a candy store, he admired the amber potions arranged before him, smoothed his mustache, and picked up a Manhattan – as did I.

I had had two stiff drinks under my belt at this point, so was loosening up. I clinked glasses with him and said: "Here's to that woman many years ago."

His face melted into a gentle smile, and he sipped, closing his eyes. Was he imagining her? Would this Manhattan burst that memory bubble and get me keel hauled? At the very least, the Manhattan he was sipping was going to be smooth, with the Pappy it had to be.

Eyes still closed, he gently set the glass on the bar, and hummed.

He opened his eyes: "That Manhattan *es excellente*!"

In a half bow, I said: "Thank you, but I can do better with a younger whiskey." I sipped my Manhattan. Indeed, it was good, and thank heaven it sufficed as the King Cole Bar version eons ago. "Now the Rob Roy?"

We each picked our glass, clinked, and sipped. I saw him allow the sip to linger a second on his tongue before swallowing. Smacking his lips, his eyes bugged out at his glass.

Damn you, Linsenbigler, you should never have clambered out on a limb, just give the murdering cutthroat a Manhattan as he asked. But no! You had to get all fancy on him and he looks ready to gag! That Rob Roy just cost you your life!

His eyes lifted to mine, still wide, his brow furrowed, his mouth tight.

"Linsenbigler?"

I twisted the bar rag in my hands, still trying to smile. "Yes?"

"I cannot tell you how disappointed I am."

I just kept smiling and waited for the bullets to start flying. He continued:

"I cannot tell you how disappointed I am that I had to wait this long in my life to have a drink this fantastic!" He closed his eyes and sipped more deeply the second time. The sweat trickled down my back as I brought my Rob Roy to my lips and gulped half of it.

By thunder, that was a cocktail by half! It was in that moment that the alcohol in my bloodstream hit the level where I was suddenly relaxed, where all the stress just seemed to drain out of me. My eyes scanned the room, and the four thugs no longer bothered me. I was able to focus on the illuminated fishing pictures – and I could see that El Pescador was a fly fisherman – there was a picture of him with a fly rod holding a bone fish, and tarpon, and several other fish.

Conspicuously missing from his gallery of trophies was the flat's most annoying and most coveted fish: the permit. If El Pescador had caught a permit, he certainly would have that photo on the wall.

Yet he did not.

We sipped our cocktails in relative silence, the kind that accompanies the reverie of a taste sensation. It was akin to settling in with an entire tub of your favorite ice cream, slowly shaving down the ambrosia with a spoon.

When the ice began to rattle in his glass, I freshened the Rob Roys.

I cleared my throat. *Here goes.*

"El Pescador? I notice that you do not have a picture of a permit on the wall."

His gentle smile vanished. He opened his eyes and they were angry. "Are you trying to ruin the best cocktail of my life?"

I waded deeper, like the drunken maniac that I was.

"I take that to mean you have not managed to catch a permit. I know from personal experience, they are very difficult, aren't they?"

He practically shouted: "Difficult?"

I took another sip, waiting, and he continued, eyes wide, face red: "Those fish will not eat! I hate them! Do you have any idea how many times I put the fly right in front of a permit? How many times they have come up to my fly and just looked at it and will not eat? Do you have any idea..." he slammed his glass on the bar, drink sloshing, ice jumping out "... how many hours I have wasted on that fish? They are directly sent from God to torment me!"

His reaction may seem absurd, but this reaction is common in the angling world. One meets a number of haunted men that have spent weeks chasing this fish, even months, and not managed to catch one. Making it worse, some anglers catch one on their first try – pure, unadulterated luck. Haunted permit anglers can get rather agitated on this topic.

"As I said, El Pescador, I know exactly how you feel." I calmly strained more Rob Roy into his glass to replace that which had sloshed onto the bar. "El Pescador, is it possible I can make a deal with you?"

His brow furrowed. "You would make a deal with the devil?" He sipped the drink mechanically and rolled his eyes with pleasure.

"Yes, I would make a deal with you." *Now or never.* He had me by the short hairs anyway, and I would likely never escape his grasp if he liked my cocktails this much. It was better that someone, anyone, might escape this mess, even if it was not me. "And my deal is this: I will not only be your bartender, willingly, happily, for as long as you like, but I also guarantee that I can get you hooked up with a permit."

He snorted in disgust. "How can you guarantee that?"

"I caught three the other day, just before Miguel shot my guide. The pictures were on my cell phone but..."

His eyebrows practically arched into his hairline. "You have a special fly?"

I closed my eyes reverently, nodding deeply. "I do."

His eyes turned sidelong. "In exchange for what? I already have you. Hidalgo over there can make you tie that fly for me at the expense of your toes."

"Would it not be better to have Boone Linsenbigler as a willing partner? To have me as a companion to wade the flats with, to rejoice over a great day's fishing, sip Rob Roys and enjoy life?"

He leaned in. "In exchange for what?"

I sighed. "I don't know what's going on back at the Utopia Lodge, but I'd like the people there freed and unharmed. They are nothing to you, clearly. Yes, you could let Enrique torture the DEA agents, but what are they really going to tell Enrique that you don't already know? And my publicist is one of those captives, as are some other anglers. They are not your enemy, just citizens caught in the middle."

He rolled his eyes, clearly not moved, and took another sip.

"Enrique matters to you, am I correct?"

A sly, curious curl tugged at his lips as he waited for me to continue.

"Then I will tell you one other thing. There is a raid tonight. By the Marines. Enrique needs to get out of there." I pretty much had to tell him that to save my skin, and likely that of the captives. Think about it: I was a dead man once the marines stormed the place and captured Enrique. El Pescador would make me pay for not having told him and he would likely not believe my plea of ignorance. Also, there was too much time between then and whenever the marines arrived – time for Enrique to do way more to the captives than had been done to Tanya.

Slowly, El Pescador rose to his feet, his face blank.

From behind his back he drew the silver automatic, extended his arm, and pointed the gun at my face. Quietly, angrily, he said: "Would you lie to me?"

Friends, I would encourage you never to get drunker than the drug kingpin you're drinking with. Likewise, and at the same time, I would hope you never have to look down the barrel of a gun in the hands of a self-admitted homicidal maniac. But if you do, I recommend having a snoot full, because you're going to need it.

My voice quavering, standing tall as if ready for my execution, I replied: "I am a man of my word, El Pescador. I look forward to making you cocktails at every opportunity and tying you some amazing permit flies. With luck, maybe there is a Grand Slam in your future."

Among those who fish saltwater flats in the tropics, there is something called a Grand Slam. It is accomplished by catching a bonefish, a tarpon and a permit in the same day. There is also something called a Super Grand Slam that includes a forth fish called a snook. Either type of Grand Slam is very hard to do. An angler has to be very lucky to pull it off. Generally, one starts by catching the permit, usually the hardest fish of the bunch.

Any serious flats angler would give his left nut for a Grand Slam, much less a permit.

The gun slowly lowered, El Pescador's eyes softening. He whispered: "A Grand Slam? Me?"

"All you have to do is call Enrique, let the captives go, and have him vacate before the Marines get there. I trust that you, too, are a man of your word."

He barked a laugh. "Mr. Linsenbigler, you have some *cajones*, let me tell you. Of course, I am not a man of my word – I am a criminal businessman and by my nature I am dishonest. And yet – the one thing that businessmen like me respect is *lealtad*. Loyalty."

He tucked the gun away and settled slowly back onto his stool. "So I admire your loyalty to those who were close to you, even if some of them are my enemy. Also, as I said, I am a man who enjoys being amused. You have amused me by the very *excellente* drink, the permit idea, and your preposterous deal. For those reasons, I will make this deal with you. It pleases me that you are willing to sacrifice yourself nobly for others. It is…what's the word? Quaint? You really are Boone Linsenbigler, like on the commercials. Hidalgo? *El teléfono!*"

Well, he was half-right.

CHAPTER 17

THE REST OF THAT EVENING is somewhat of a blur, yet one can hardly hold me accountable if I did not contain my cocktailing – each drink I thought to be my last, and for me that is a dire prospect. At any juncture El Pescador could tire of me and put a bullet amidships and kick me under the rail. I remember some very delicious fried bird arrived at the bar for snacking, then some beef skewers, and later shaving nutmeg into an Italian aperitif called Ramazzotti, a dried anisette bud floating in the top. We smoked cigars on deck, the catamaran charging full-speed southeast, and talked flats fishing until I suppose I nodded off under an umbrella of stars.

I awoke the next morning to a rap at the door. My eyes opened to find myself in a small cabin in a single bunk with expensive sheets and lush pillows. A porthole told me it was daylight, likely mid-morning, as well as that we were still full-speed ahead as water sloshed over the glass and the room rose and fell with the waves.

There was the knuckle on the door again, and this time it opened. A little Mexican in a white tunic put his head in and said in faltering English: "You are to deck." He pointed up. "Must bite the dog's hair."

Brow furrowed, I quizzed over this odd interruption until it dawned on me that I was being called to duty to make some morning cocktail – to prepare the hair of the dog, as it were.

I swung my feet out of the bunk and waved the little man off. All in all, my head wasn't too bad given the circumstances. A bandage on my arm revealed that somebody had patched up my wound, the one from the hatch corner stabbing me. I didn't recall that.

Yet I made note that if I were to survive this indentured servitude it was imperative that I keep my wits about me and not be a drunkard. I did not kid myself that escape was a likely prospect as long as I was close to El Pescador and his Royal Guard, or that I might be in this situation for some time. In fact, I might not ever escape – alive. The mysterious disappearance of Boone Linsenbigler might go down in the annals of history akin to Amelia Earhart's South Pacific vanishing act.

As such, my mission was to be ingratiating and keep my head down and my spirits up. If I were to serve my master not in chains but at his table I could hardly expect more. For my insolence, I should really have been down there with poor Manny feeding the octopi. Yet I had miraculously survived. For that, I was thankful.

I found a closet with the blue sport shirts and white pants that seemed to be the crew uniform. I also found boxer shorts, and flip flops, both of which I despised but accepted as part of my new lot in life.

Once again I startled myself in the small mirror in the smaller ships head, and once again realized there was not much to do to get ready other than wash my face and brush my teeth, the latter accomplished from a well-stocked drawer of grooming necessities. I did shave, just not where my beard and mustache had to be regrown.

Dressed in an El Pescador uniform, I departed my cabin, and made a few wrong turns before finding the ships ladder to the dark barroom. I could see El Pescador on the foredeck where we smoked cigars. He was all in white, with dark sunglasses and talking animatedly into a satellite phone. Beyond him was a blue horizon rising and falling with the motion of the catamaran charging across the ocean.

I turned to the bar, and went behind it.

Hair of the dog is not my modus operandi the morning after. I understand why it is a potent weapon in the fight against a hangover, because the introduction of alcohol gooses the liver into finishing its job of cleaning the blood of toxins or some such. That said, I am keenly aware that my liver would likely have done better than to pick Boone Linsenbigler as its Lord and Master. So for the morning after a big night, I prefer not to tax my liver any further but to reward it with a whopping slug of the vitamins it needs to function. I tip my hat to Bloody Marys, which contain a spot-on paring of vegetables and especially horseradish. At the same time, I crave Vitamin C and citrus to quench my hangovers. I have devised a drink comprised of fruit and dark leafy vegetables – and what's called a headache powder. These 'powders' are hard to find in the United States but are common in England. They are powdered aspirin in small pouches that one pours into water and drinks. Alka-Seltzer is essentially the same thing but has fizz. I did not expect to find all my ingredients aboard *Esmerelda*. Yet I went to back down the ship's ladder to the kitchen to see if I could find them just the same.

I apologized to the two women cooks I startled in the cramped galley, and they more or less cowered at the far end as I searched their larder. No dark greens, but there was ripe mango, some cubed pineapple and a big fat carrot that I brought back to the bar along with some aspirin from my cabin.

I blendered the ingredients thoroughly, poured the mixture over ice, added a splash of soda water (it needed thinning) into two tall glasses and garnished the cocktails with lime. Well, I hit El Pescador's with a shot of vodka and Cointreau. He did ask for hair of the dog and I dared not disappoint.

Before going out on deck, I found a small silver tray behind the bar for El Pescador's glass and a white bar towel for my arm as is customary with private bartenders. My drink remained on the bar. The intent of the formalities was to make sure I did not presume any social station other than crew, all part of my vow to keep my head down.

I weaved through the door along the side of the catamaran to the fore deck. El Pescador was pacing away from me shouting into the phone in Spanish and waving his free hand in the air. I stopped and waited for him to turn and pace back toward me. When he did, he seemed surprised, strode forward and plucked his drink from the tray. He eyed it – clearly not knowing what it was – and then eyed me. Between shouts into the phone, he took a sip and smacked his lips. I got a simple nod of approval before he continued his pacing and shouting. I retreated to the barroom and drank my smoothie at the bar.

Yes, *smoothie*. I dislike the word, it ruins a delicious drink by tainting it with the notion that it is designed only to be healthy. To be sure, we all want to be healthy, but I ascribe to the notion that treating your body like a chemistry set is anti-epicurean. There's a reason things taste good – that's the body's way of telling a person what to eat, and what you need to eat. Granted, the proliferation of junk and frozen food has been engineered to fool the taste buds into thinking you need a bucket of 'cheese product' in every bite. There is, however, nothing false in a craving for beef. Or if you distain cow and crave only plants. So I put my faith in the taste buds with which God – in his infinite wisdom – saw fit to carpet my tongue. Amen.

Watching El Pescador pace and shout, waving his peach-colored drink around with his free hand, I could see that he was a hard man to please, that he was demanding, and I wondered about the poor soul on the other end and what his ultimate fate might be in the organization. Searching the distance, I also wondered where we were going. Esmerelda had been full steam since the previous afternoon and we'd lost sight of land, but now I thought I could make out land off the starboard rail, at the horizon. That would suggest that we were still off the coast of Central America. I sipped my drink and did a little internal calculation. If the boat were traveling thirty miles an hour since five the previous day that was – let's see – sixteen hours or so – times three and add a zero – four hundred and eighty miles. It's not like I had an atlas in my head, but heading southeast would take us across the front of Belize and Guatemala and to the coast of Honduras, then I thought Costa Rica might be next and then Panama. (Sorry, Nicaragua, I forgot all about you at the time.) Beyond that was Columbia, Kingdom of Cocaine. The map in my head was not to scale so I really had no sense of how long it would take to get to any of these places on a boat at my assumed speed. There were some islands off the coast of Honduras that we should see eventually and possibly give me my bearings. The name of the islands escaped me then (Bay Islands) but I recalled that there were some flats fishing there. Might be a good location to stop and get my new boss a permit. Not sure what opportunities there were farther south as I had not heard of flats fishing down that way, certainly not off of Columbia. Though you never knew what little hideaways might have flats fishing that had just not been popularized yet.

I admit to feeling a little lonely and afraid, not knowing how far we were going or if I would ever be a free man again, if I'd ever find myself in New York again sipping some Michters by the fire at Fraunces Tavern, the snow swirling through the urban gloom outside the windows.

El Pescador stomped into the room, interrupting my reverie. When he caught sight of me he scowled: "At least there's one person around here who can do something right." He came over and handed me his empty glass and stormed out of the room.

I wasn't entirely sure what I should be doing when I wasn't in the act of serving drinks so I went behind the bar and started to inspect what exactly was in inventory. By jiminy, whoever stocked his bar did so with the best of the best, it was all top shelf, and when I went in the cupboards, I found backups for the Pappy and Macallan. The bar tools were mostly to my liking, though the citrus threader – it carves lemon peel into strings – was a piece of junk. Not surprising. Most lemon threaders come with dull blades and just mangle the peel. There were Boston shakers, the kind with a pint glass that fits into the silver shaker and are my favorite. I collected the canister-type shakers and tucked them out of my way – I don't like them, the lids get stuck when they get cold. There was a condiment tray with folding lid that looked like it had never been used – I had no need of that either unless I was going to tend for a party and needed to pre-prep my fruits, so I tucked that in the back of a cupboard as well. When I was done, I had freed up a considerable amount of room under the bar, so I could store six shakers down there and not have to rinse in the small sink to one side.

I turned my attention to the waist-high fridge. There was a jar of Spanish olives in there that had sprouted life so into the trash that went, though that left me without any olives. In a drawer I found playing cards, corkscrews, cigarette lighters, condoms (!) and a note pad and pen. I started a shopping list, with olives at the top. Delving further into the fridge I pulled out the maraschino cherries and drained the bright red liquid from them into the sink and refilled the bottle with port to improve them. I jotted down on my pad cherries and Luxardo – I would make my own cocktail cherries at my first opportunity and do away with the store-bought treacle. There were some half-used bottles of seltzer that I junked, and jotted down Italian mineral water – I wasn't sure I would find Pellegrino wherever we were going. I also wrote down club soda. To many, seltzer and club soda are the same, but not to me. I actively dislike the coarse bubbles in seltzer and always use club or Pellegrino in my highballs.

Once I had cleared out the dreck from the fridge there was room now to put martini glasses in there – it is absolutely essential to have the glasses properly chilled. When I was done, other than the cherries, the entire fridge was filled with martini and pilsner glasses, as it should be. The fridge door I stocked with citrus from the kitchen, much to the dismay of the two ladies cowering once more in the corner. I don't know why, but they always did that when I came into the kitchen.

In the freezer, I found the ice tub I had used the previous evening to make drinks. It needed refilling, but I noted that the ice was blown ice. That is, made by a machine very quickly. No wonder Manny had been shot – this type of ice melts very quickly and waters down a cocktail in a hurry. Fortunately, my drinks the previous evening were made from bold ingredients and stirred rather than shaken. If you shake up a martini with blown ice, especially in the tropics, you end up with a watery abomination. I did not see any ice trays around so made note to shop for those along with spring water with which to make proper ice. Obviously, tap water, unless it comes from a low-mineral well, and especially if it comes from a municipal plant, is – as my Uncle Jack would have said – *an anathema*. I may sound fussy, but ice that has chlorine, orthophosphates and fluoride add those tastes to your cocktail, subtle as that may be. Those components also have the capacity to chemically bond with the alcohol and bitters to form Lord-knows-what compounds. Also, the ice tub was made of plastic, which when frozen gives off a chemical taste, too. I made notes to purchase a Pyrex container for my ice, noting approximate dimensions.

When all at the bar was customized to my liking, I wiped down the bar top and felt somehow better about my situation, like I was at least a little in control.

Deck hands and some of the soldiers trotted up both sides of the boat toward the fore deck, and for the first time in about an hour, I looked up and adjusted my focus to the sea around us.

A grey and white patrol boat approached, soldiers on deck holding machine guns.

I noted that our soldiers did not have weapons drawn, so I checked my impulse to grab the bottle of Pappy and sink behind the bar to say a final prayer.

The crew threw a line when the patrol boat drew near, and when the boat was alongside, an officer appeared on the patrol boat's deck. He was lighter skinned than his compatriots, and wore a crisp short sleeve-uniform, peaked cap, reflective aviator sunglasses, baton and black rapier mustache. His men parted, and when the officer stepped forward, El Pescador's soldiers hefted him aboard the Esmerelda.

The officer was lead directly into the barroom, where he sat himself at a table and removed his sunglasses. He did a double take when he saw me, squinting suspiciously.

I nodded contritely, and mustered my best Spanish. Mind you, I don't speak the language, but there are some phrases for drinking that are essential. Like *cerveza*. I said: *"Cóctel, Senor?"*

He slid his baton back and forth though his hands as though wondering what it would be like to beat me to death with it. Perhaps I was being insolent?

As such, I was a tad uneasy when he slid back his chair and strode toward the bar, his shiny boots making a sharp tap with each step. When he came to a stop in front of me, he raised an eyebrow at the bottles behind me. He reached out and tapped the edge of the bar and said: *"El Daiquiri congelado."*

I noted that among the various badges and such on his uniform was a patch that read *Guardocostas de Guatemala.*

I gave him a crisp nod as opposed to a snicker. This guy looked like a hard case, like a Hondo who would want tequila, straight up. Instead, he orders a frozen daiquiri! Perhaps there are places where lumberjacks and oil rig crews like nothing better than to belly up to the bar for a round of frozen daiquiris.

El Pescador strode into the room and greeted the officer with a hearty handshake. He offered him a seat at the table where he had been sitting. I filled the blender with ice, squeezed a handful of limes and tossed in some powdered sugar. I hit the blender with a splash of Cointreau for fun and then with a healthy dose of Añejo and a splash of Pusser's Rum for oomph. I know you're supposed to use white rum but that's really rather boring. To be honest I like my daiquiris to taste more like margaritas.

I didn't have the proper glass for the daiquiri which is supposed to be stemmed like an aperitif glass only slightly larger. So instead, I put it into one of the chilled martini glasses, and garnished with dueling small orange and lime slices.

Towel over the one arm, I delivered the drink on the silver tray, and the officer eyed the glass curiously as he took it, that eyebrow high again.

I turned to El Pescador: "Señor?"

He waved me off, and so I returned to my safe place behind the bar. I poured myself a smidgen of the daiquiri. Indeed, it tasted a lot like a margarita, and the Pusser's gave it a bold molasses accent.

My boss and the officer spoke genially in Spanish, and though I didn't know what they were saying, it looked to me like chitchat. At one juncture, the officer waved this baton at me and they both gave me a glance. When the officer finished his daiquiri, he began to thump the edge of the table, and then slid his chair out and stood. They shook hands and that's when El Pescador's left hand presented the officer with a thick envelope.

The payoff.

El Pescador was taking care of business and making sure he had the Hondurans' protection while in their waters. I wondered if this scene would replay itself in each country on our way to, say, Columbia. It also occurred to me that my passport was in with my fishing gear – I always took it and my wallet out on the water with me just in case there was some calamitous mishap, and likewise I didn't always trust the maid service. Though I'm sure when it came to customs, El Pescador and his retinue breezed past the entire process.

Once the Guatemalan patrol boat had shoved off, our yacht resumed full speed ahead as did El Pescador. He paced the foredeck in his Panama hat, a large square silver cellphone clamped to his ear. My guess was the phone was like none I had seen before because it was some special kind with encryption. As I was to learn, he never spoke twice in a row on the same phone and he must have had two-dozen of them, no two alike. Some plugged into something on his belt, while others seemed to be normal cell phones housed in some other electronic device. He was not shouting this time as he paced, but his free hand seemed to be checking off items on an invisible list in the air.

From my perch behind the bar in the shadowy barroom, I fell into a sort of trance watching him pace, with the deep blue sea behind him rising and falling as the yacht surged forward. Eventually, I realized that the straight line of the horizon had acquired a ragged green jot that eventually grew into what seemed a mountainous island dead ahead. Likely some part of the Honduran Bay Islands, which I had never seen. The trance made my eyelids heavy with the bright sun and motion. I folded my arms on the bar and rested my head upon them, my mind blank of the horrors of the previous few days, save for sitting at the hotel bar in Nassau drinking a Boone Linsenbigler screwdriver. My mental exhaustion, I think, had caught up with me.

I awoke to the yacht's horn bellowing softly.

When I raised my head, I saw that El Pescador was flanked by his security detail on the foredeck, a wall of green jungle and a pier beyond them. On the pier was a complement of brown people in white uniforms waiting for us. Behind them was a staircase that led up the side of the green wall at an angle. The deck hands trotted up the sides of the yacht toting sacks of laundry and suitcases, including my gear.

Standing, I came around the bar, white bar towel still over the one forearm. I could see that the green wall of jungle went up some distance – this was the mountainous island I had seen before dozing off. I slid out through the side door and around the crew, positioning myself well behind El Pescador and his squad, hands clasped before me.

Lines were thrown and the yacht tied off. The boss and his men stepped onto the gangplank first and strode to and up the steps. I didn't know what if any protocol there was for the bartender when disembarking, so I lent a hand with the crew transferring baggage and such onto the dock whence others whisked it away and up the stairs, of which I guessed there must be a considerable number to get to the top of that cliff. The bearers didn't look like Sherpas but perhaps they should have been. When at last we had it all piled on the dock, the crew took to helping move it up those stairs. I retreated to the yacht's bar.

By my estimation thus far, this island was likely El Pescador's lair. The assumption was based on the protection of the Guatemalan Coast Guard and likely their Navy, too, but also by what seemed like an ideal natural fortress from which to run his business. Would the DEA dare infiltrate Honduran territory to abduct this drug kingpin? And even if they tried to cut a deal with the government to do so, how likely was it that the old fox wouldn't hear about it in advance and be absent by the time they arrived?

As this was a homecoming for my employer, it was time for his manservant Linsenbigler to be proactive with an appropriate libation. Nominally, my choice would be prosecco, though there was only 1996 Bollinger and 2000 Krug champagne in the larder, so I made do with the Bollinger. I'm not any kind of expert in wines by any means, but anybody who hangs out with drinky people on New Year's Eve knows that these two vineyards knock out some spectacular bubbly. I guessed the Bollinger was a five-hundred-dollar bottle of champagne. Yet as the man said, money really was of no object so why not have the best all the time? Therefore, it was without trepidation that I popped and bucketed the bottle with ice and a few flutes, and some tangerine slices for fun. It all slid nicely onto my silver tray, and I marched it across the gangplank and up the staircase behind the crew.

Of note was that there was a white flats boat tied up opposite the yacht, as well as one of those super-fast cigarette boats, all black.

My calves were pretty tight halfway to the top by the time the stairs took an abrupt turn into the cliff face through a rocky archway. On the other side of the arch was a lush, cool jungle draped with vines and alive with the creak of frogs and twitter of birds. The occasional curly yellow orchid, droopy fuchsia, or magenta bromeliad rosettes dotted the way along a steep rocky path. Mixed in with the flowers was the occasional surveillance camera making sure the jungle and anyone in it behaved. Unlike the low reef islands, this sultry green environ smelled moist, woody and mossy. I glanced back at the archway and could see that there was a massive iron gate that could be closed across it, secured in place by gigantic steel pins through iron U-bolts into the rock.

Holding the tray with both hands as we trudged on, our caravan turned a corner into daylight. The jungle parted, relenting to a path through an open, manicured lawn. A glance back revealed that the edge of the jungle was pegged discreetly with some sort of sensors. They resembled camouflaged tuna cans and were strapped on trees.

Ahead? Behold the grand manse: at the crest of the lawn was a low, white-columned mansion with a red Spanish tile roof. It was framed by blue sky and puffy white clouds. And to think that the DEA thought El Pescador would stoop to staying in a beat-down hotel in Picazón!

The procession wound up the path, and as we neared the mansion, I could see that there was a stylish patio and ornately shaped pool tucked into the right side of the house, the kind meant expressly for lounging and drinking, not for laps. I noted an adjoining outdoor bar from which I would no doubt be spending many hours delivering drinks.

The crew wound around to the left, away from the expansive main French doors into the house itself, and likely toward some sort of service entrance. So I broke rank and marched in the front doors. I wasn't sure my station in the hierarchy of help, but I was pretty sure it was above that of the rank and file. Best to cement that right off the bat if I could. El Pescador and I were chummy the night before but less so today. As such, it was essential to ingratiate myself so that I didn't get a pink slip from the barrel of a gun like poor Manny.

The entryway was stacked with suitcases at the base of a stairway that wound up on my left. To my right the marble floors stretched off into a sizeable oval living room. As you can imagine, this living room was plush by half. In the corner, there was a rock formation with watery cascade into a tub-sized pool. From the pool, an open stream flowed circuitously between the furniture and out a wall under a substantial fireplace that danced and crackled with flames. The stream was only about a foot wide, and as I drew nearer I could see that it was lit from below and topped with tempered glass so nobody tripped over it. The clear green water wriggled with ornamental fish.

Above the fireplace was a steel shield, like a family crest, that was laced with four swords – like something you might see in a castle.

The wall facing the patio was all glass, as was the ceiling. The other walls were stucco and hung with more Gaugins and draped here or there with burgundy and royal blue silk.

I skirted around the living room to a stately dining room, table and chairs in the Spanish style, and yet more colorful Gaugins. The far wall had a glass partition into a combination wine cellar and humidor – all obviously climate controlled. Steering down a hallway to the right, I found a game room complete with a card table, duck pin bowling alley and vintage pinball machines.

Further down I found offices, my trip culminating at twin doors laid open into the boss' wood paneled office. He was sitting on the edge of the desk, hat on a leather sofa, and he was glancing quickly through some papers like any other boss who might have just returned from a business trip. He looked up at me, his brow knit.

Then the brow unknit. "Linsenbigler. You *are* a man of your word!"

"A homecoming deserves a little champagne."

He waved the papers in his hand at me. "You would think that a man like me could be freed from the chains of paperwork, and yet here it is."

I set the tray on a glass coffee table in front of the couch, poured him a glass with a tangerine wedge in the bottom. Handing him the glass by the stem, I said. "Welcome home, El Pescador."

He smirked and took the glass, but tipping it at me. "Join me. I insist."

And so I poured myself a flute as he rounded the desk and dropped into a high-back brown leather swivel chair. He gestured to the guest chair opposite him and I sat. We toasted the air and he said: "*Salud*. So what do you think of my, how is it called? My hideaway?"

I snorted. "Damn fine set up you have here, sir. And I have to say, I realize now that all those other things called champagne are a sham. This Bollinger is a completely different animal from my price range. I could get used to drinking this if were a billionaire."

He chuckled. "Fortunately for you, Linsenbigler, you know just such a billionaire, and are his bartender."

"It is OK I opened this bottle, isn't it? Or was that impertinent?"

He chuckled again. "I don't know what impertinent is, but as I said, whether this bottle is five or five hundred dollars a bottle makes no difference to me. The wine cellar, though, is different. I will select which bottles to open from there."

I nodded. "Good, because I know nothing of wine, and to be perfectly honest the whole subject I find forbidding."

He squinted at me. "You know, Mr. Linsenbigler, I think you may learn more than you think as my...as my bartender... and fishing guide. I haven't forgotten about the permit."

"If I might be so bold, sir, I think that there is likely much we can learn from each other, and by the looks of things I am not going to be restrained here. I am honor bound to fulfill my obligation to you for sparing those people back at Utopia. I have no ideas of trying to escape."

He looked at his flute, sipped, and then cocked his head at me. "That's good to know. It would be stupid in any case – there is nowhere to go. The Guatemalan navy would only return you to me. Then there's what happened to poor dumb Manny. And as you see, life here and aboard the yacht will be a standard of living that you will find unparalleled in your previous life."

I sipped, and raised an eyebrow at him. "Just so I know, what level of participation am I supposed to have here in what goes on? I mean, I know first and foremost I am your bartender and fishing guide, and will – as with the champagne – anticipate your wants and needs. But at the same time, I think we are kindred spirits of a kind, we like to fish and we like cocktails. Yet I don't want to be presumptuous. That is..."

He smiled knowingly. "I will invite you when to participate, how is that? I will usually invite you to dine with us and recreate, so long as you bartend. However, when I have business associates here, you will be on your own when not serving, and out of sight unless called upon. I like you too, Linsenbigler. But you are still part of the staff, and so should wear the blue sport shirt and white pants during the day like the rest. When joining me for dinner, you wear what you like, but never casual. No T-shirts, and remain groomed, appearances are important. You may of course regrow that mustache. You look odd without it."

"Understood."

"Cocktails are at six." He looked at his gold Rolex. "In two hours. Dinner is at seven, on the patio unless it is raining. Cork the remainder of this bottle for this evening. Drop in the kitchen for your room assignment and get settled."

I finished my Bollinger and stood. "I have begun a list of items I'd like for the bar here and on the yacht."

"Items?"

"Things you don't have that would help make better cocktails. Beyond all the terrific bottle stock you have."

He grinned. "You can give that to the staff in the kitchen, they will take care of it."

"Great." I took his empty glass and mine and placed them on the tray, but before leaving asked: "Manhattans tonight?"

He flashed a thumbs up and I turned and went back down the hallway. I found the kitchen off the main dining room.

CHAPTER 18

MY ROOM WAS NOT in the main house but at the end of a row of square white huts discreetly placed behind it. This area was where the housekeepers hung the laundry, where the groundskeeper had his tools, and where the back entrance to the kitchen was located. It was where all support staff lived and could be found doing the behind the scenes work that kept a kingpin's lair operational.

My hut was a tidy single at the end, with a small patio and peeling deck chair on one side that had a glimpse of ocean far below through some palms. I noted that behind my hut there was a path leading off into a patch of forest strewn with boulders, though it had a chain across the entrance with a hanging sign that read: *PROHIBIDO*. I supposed it was off limits either because there was some sort of dangerous cliff that way or that it lead to some sort of secret storehouse. In any case, I had to assume it was fully rigged with cameras, and my curiosity was not going to get this cat killed.

I shouldered the hut's door open and was pleased that though it was quite rudimentary it did not smell musty. The windows were all pebbled glass slat windows that opened with a crank. There was a single bunk, a closet filled with uniforms and tropical wear (tags still on), and a small bathroom with a smaller shower, the kind you almost can't turn around in, with an electric showerhead for hot water. There was a small dresser and mirrors on one side, and a writing desk on the other under a window.

Notably, the desk was arranged with fly tying gear: a vice, bobbin and tool array, stacks of plastic boxes filled with feathers, spool, racks covering the rainbow of tinsel and chenille. It was plain that this had all been hastily put in place and no doubt was installed in anticipation of my arrival. My boss was clearly intent on my tying that secret permit fly, the one that did not yet exist but properly doped would have the fishies fighting over his offering the way they had when I fished with Elvis.

There was always a pang of guilt I felt when I thought of that guide. It happened just days ago and yet it seemed an eternity. I dumped my fly gear next to the tying desk and sat on the edge of the creaky bed, ceiling fan wafting overhead and the sound of muted voices of the maids taking in the laundry directly behind the house.

So this is it, aye, Old Boone? Never thought you'd end up like this. Had the near perfect set up as Conglomerated brand, didn't we? That's all gone now, better get used to it and make the best of things. This is still better than what we had before the bitters, back when we made vodka martinis with Popov drained through a Britta filter in that basement apartment in New Jersey.

I bounced on the bed, the springs creaking. Not an ideal bed for entertaining as it was a bit too musical. I snorted to myself – better forget about all that, too. Lord knew when I might have a shot at any companionship. By the looks of the maids, there wasn't any pickings that were of remote interest, and I wasn't sure what penalties there might be for fraternizing, as it were.

There was no TV, no computer. In fact, I was to find there were none to be found anywhere on the entire campus. And no cell phones, either, except for El Pescador's menagerie of satellite phones.

Fighting off the depressing circumstances of my new abode, I determined that the room was strictly for sleeping and tying flies, that I had better find a way of ingratiating myself so that I could spend all day at the bar, at the pool or fishing.

So I shaved, tracing out my nascent mustache, took a brief shower, and dressed in a black guayabera shirt, white pants and sandals. My short hair I just left sort of spikey as there was nothing else I could do with it. Key in my pocket, I left the rooms and curved along a line of pavers around the far side of the main house, the side I had not seen.

I stopped and surveyed the ocean view where the trees opened up to another expanse of lawn leading to the edge of a steep forested slope. In the middle of this lawn, lower than the house, was a leveled asphalt patch painted with a white circle – a helipad. Just beyond that was a tennis court, also set below the house. The island was effectively a rocky lump. The island on the dock side and two others was a sheer cliff straight up, but this far side was a steep and forbidding jungled slope with intermittent escarpments that you would bounce off as you tumbled down to certain death on rocks or beach below.

My guess was the main house sat several hundred or more feet above whatever beach there might be below – I couldn't see it. From what I could tell, the only safe way out of the compound was back through the cliff face and archway down to the boat dock. Or through the air from the helipad. Not that I had any plans. No sir, I was a believer: the only way out of El Pescador's service was if he let me go or if he put a bullet in my chest and fed me to the sharks. I continued to circle around the house, past a large raised deck with commanding view, to the patio, the bar coming into view.

I noted that on this side of the house the lawn stretched some distance behind the bar to the edge of the forest, and that there was another row of cabanas halfway across – these built on stilts and more stylish than the row I lived in. They actually matched the main house. My guess was that some of the soldiers lived there. At least some of these guys must live in the mansion itself and close to the boss as he slept.

The lay of the land established a security perimeter around the house where nobody could really sneak up from the jungle – they had an expanse of lawn to cross. The soldier cabanas were raised so you could see under them, shoot under them. The closest forest was at the backside of the mansion where my bungalow was established. From what I could tell, the terrain behind my hut was pretty rough and rocky. I had to assume there was some impasse from that direction. Through the slats of my bathroom window, I could only see boulders and vines.

By the pool and seated around a glass table were the boss's thugs. They looked the same as before: like Dobermans on the chain, eyeing me suspiciously and wondering what it would be like to take a bite out of me. Standing beyond them with binoculars was Hidalgo, who paused his inspection of the forest and ocean to bestow me with an almost imperceptible sneer. Almost. I could understand why they did not like me: I was a variable that they now had to consider, to watch, to scrutinize, to make sure I didn't go after their boss with a steak knife or poison him. As I passed the fun bunch, I gave a friendly nod, for all that was worth. To have told them plainly that I was not going to be any trouble seemed like a good idea until one considered that they might only speak Spanish. Or until one thought about it in terms of approaching a gang of Rottweilers with your hand out saying "Good boy!" Keeping my distance seemed the best policy until such time as I might be able to remove a thorn from one of their paws.

The bar was a sleek white-tiled affair, freestanding, with a red-tiled roof to match the house. The bar top was brasserie-style, armored in zinc. It was nicely appointed, including a built-in barbecue. If I felt bold I might try my hand at making some bar snacks on that puppy, make myself indispensable. The bottle selection was if anything even better than on the yacht, yet with more vodka for some reason, heavy on the Grey Goose and Belvidere. I'm a traditionalist when it comes to vodka. I like Stolichnaya, and haven't much use for the French varieties. They have a strange mouth feel to me and taste flavored. Not that they need me for a customer – an associate of mine call these 'frosted bottle' vodkas 'chick vodka' based on the perceived notion that women flock to them, and that when ordering bottle service at a club, it is the honey that draws near the bees.

Checking the ice machine, I found a sizeable bin of blown ice, so made a mental note to gently stir the boss' Manhattan. I didn't know if the soldiers other than Hidalgo were permitted to drink but I doubted it. I had not seen any guests. So far as I knew, I would only be serving El Pescador and myself. I didn't know what I really had to prepare other than a couple of Manhattans, which I decided to concoct with Willet instead of Pappy. I went across the patio to the open doors to the living room, across the in-floor creek, through the dining room to the kitchen. Once again, the lady chefs eyed me with trepidation as I raided their larder for fruit.

Juggling some lemons and oranges, I made my way back across the patio to the bar.

I did a double take: At a stool at the bar was a raven-haired beauty in a blood-red cocktail dress with matching lipstick and fingernails. Likely about forty, she wore black heels, a necklace of dark gems and a curious look in my direction. As I approached, chin up, she tossed her hair to the side and said in a thick, sultry accent: "You must be Boone."

She was the last thing I expected to see that evening.

I smiled graciously and circled around to my safe place behind the bar, where I drew opposite her and nodded courteously. "I am one and the same, madam. What can I get you?"

Her nose was long and slightly upturned, her face acorn-shaped with large brown eyes and fulsome lips. She showed me some teeth and reached a hand across. "My name is Paola."

Shaking her warm hand gently, I replied: "A lovely name for a lovely lady. Is there a cocktail I can make you?" Leaning in, I could smell her perfume, something on the order of lilacs tickling my nose.

"You are the same man from the commercials, yes? Lindenvogler?"

"Linsenbigler, yes."

"I like the one where you take a cocktail and *boom* the burglar falls to the ground!" She was one of those women with a slightly hoarse voice. "How is it you are here?"

Eyebrows raised, smiling, I said: "Um, just on vacation, sort of."

She scrunched up her lovely lips in a dismissive way, waving the red fingernails toward the house. "Alberto knows some very interesting people. It does not surprise me to see you here very much. I like vodka, though I am allowed only one or two. What vodka cocktail can the famous Linsenvogler make Paola?"

"You look like you might like a Cosmopolitan."

She winced large and made a hissing sound. It's funny how some Latinas can be very attractive and yet they are so dynamic facially and verbally that they have a tendency to don an alarming array of less-than stellar expressions. Paola looked like she was doing an impression of a tire going flat: "Manny makes them so sweet, the poor man. Is he coming back?"

I took a breath, and tried not to betray any alarm: "He's moved on to a better place."

"That is good. He to make Alberto angry."

I hoisted the nearest Grey Goose. "This your brand?""

"Yes, Boone."

"Shall I try making you a cosmo, see if you like it, and if not we can move on to something else?"

Hands thrust toward me she said: "*Perfecto!*"

Few drinksologists are worth their salt if they have not hit upon the essentials of a first rate Cosmopolitan simply for the reason that they are popular with the ladies, though it helps that I like them myself. As ever, I have a few substitutions. First, I never ever use triple sec for the very reason the lady stated: too sweet. Instead, Cointreau or preferably Grand Marnier. Second: Cranberry juice strikes the right bitter balance yet there's a sour undertone to pomegranate that I prefer, and I use one of the liqueurs of that variety. Many people seem to enjoy dismissing vodka as having no discernable taste, a contention easily dismissed by the popularity of certain vodkas over others. It is a delicate flavor, and so is easy to drown out with sugar and juices for those who don't really like hard spirits. In a cosmo, it is important not to kill the vodka's essence but to enhance it and blend it into a unique flavor that becomes the Cosmopolitan. Moderation in the mixers is essential, as is a hearty squirt of lime at the end to make it pop. I stirred her drink vigorously to bring the proof down – she was slim where it counted and I could see why 'Alberto' limited her to one or two: it was likely her senses would be quickly overwhelmed by platoon of cosmos.

I found a chilled martini glass and poured her drink with a flourish. A cosmo – even made with cranberry – should start out cloudy and then slowly clear into a limpid, sexy pool of pale pink. If it is bright red it is too sweet, send it back. Unless you don't like vodka.

Paola clapped like a little girl as I set it in front of her. "Bueno!" She swept her dark locks to one side and held it there so she could lean over and sip the drink without lifting it, affording me a rather advantageous glimpse of her fine cleavage and another waft of her perfume. I held my breath: *steady, Old Man. Alberto would blow your brains out all over the patio for what you're thinking.*

She sat back and thumped the bar with one hand, gesturing forcefully at the cosmo with the other. "*Perfecto!* This is what Manny could not do."

I detected motion in my peripheral vision and swiveled my gaze toward the white guest houses. Coming up the path was yet another female swaying slowly toward the patio. When she saw me look in her direction, she looked away, self-consciously poking at her honey-brown hair that splayed lazily across her shoulders. She was in a patterned indigo sun dress and espadrilles, bangles on her wrists and hoop earrings on small ears.

Paola noticed me noticing and smiled. "Boone, I think this one is for you."

I raised an eyebrow at her, sidelong: "For me?"

"But of course. Alberto is good host. You do like women?"

I felt hot and realized I was blushing, which made Paola laugh softly at me. "You know, I sometimes think Americano's are too, how is it? Too uptight about sex. The man likes the woman and is manly, the woman is sexy for the man, making him desire her, and there is energy, you know? Like, um, electricity."

Should I have guessed there would be women? What billionaire would seclude himself on a ritzy tropical island bastion with all the best booze and surroundings and yet not include comely companionship? My 'therapeutic' interlude with the Japanese girl in the hotel notwithstanding, this 'arrangement' left me feeling awkward. Moralizing had nothing to do with it, mind you. The pretense is what bothered me – the pretense that the ball is still in fair play and the refs haven't been paid off.

Refusal was not in the cards in any case. Imagine the potential outfall with 'Albert' Pescador if I were to spurn his offering? I would be demonstrably excluding myself from being fully-vested member of the team, with this lifestyle. By accepting the girl, I would be accepting a place in his criminal enterprise – which I'm sure was much to the point. Aside from making me a happy bartender, he would not have to worry as much about Boone taking flight or undermining him in some way.

For me, there was really only one way to play this out, and I girded myself inwardly. After all, I had embraced Conglomerated's absurd pretense of Boone Linsenbigler being the world's best barman. Indeed, not just the world's best barman, but a grand gentleman and adventurer. Why would I not approach this situation with my namesake savoir-faire and accept she was not already mine.

Just the same, it occurred to me that even if she was bound to bed down with me that really didn't mean she was mine at all and I did not want an unwilling partner. For me to take the stage, and for her to accept the pretense, I would have to charm her so in the same way I approached other women of interest. All romance has conceits, after all. As such, it was a matter not of capturing the village and burning it to the ground but liberating the village and entering Main Street lined with cheering crowds. I tried smoothing my mustache and realized once again that it was not there.

As the girl swayed closer, she held her chin up, as if in defiance, and did not turn her gaze away as she had before. This one was not like Paola, who was clearly one of the converted, one who had made a career as a courtesan. For starters, she was in her late twenties, and less pumped up. The hair had not been expensively cut, curled and coiffed. The dress was not tight, and the shoes were appropriate for poolside. The makeup was nominal save for mascara and some light eye shadow. Her skin was *café au lait*.

I pried my eyes away from the girl long enough to produce the pre-opened bottle of Bollinger and poured a flute to coincide with her arrival at the bar. This was not the cosmo type girl; she had white wine written all over her. She slid onto a barstool next to Paola, who embraced her lightly and said: "*Ciao*, Karina. This is Boone."

Sliding the champagne in front of her on a napkin, I deftly raised my hand and held hers briefly, my eyes meeting her large oval ones — the pupils matched her light brown hair and were golden. A graceful neck supported a round face with high cheekbones. The eyes were set wide apart and smiled – cautiously – even if she did not. The nose betrayed some native blood and was small and slightly wide. The lips curvy were naturally very pink all on their own. She cocked her head at me and said quietly: "*Ciao*." She picked up the flute and sipped, looking away toward the pool.

I believe it was the infamous cad, Hugh Heffner, who redefined "the girl next door" as a female attribute rather than a state of being. Karina had it in spades, and rather than being the gushy and forward party girl, it seemed to me like she was playing it a bit coy, which for me was ideal: the pretense would be mutual.

Anybody who has spent as much time as I around bars, and in the company of ladies with whom I would like to establish some rapport, is likely to be familiar with bar tricks as a way to break the ice. As my father was fond of quoting Mark Twain: *Actions speak louder than words though not nearly as often.*

Simple sleight of hand magic using objects commonly found in a bar were conceived mostly as a wager to obtain a free drink from a dupe. However, they can (and often are) merely used to impress the ladies. I did not know whether these idiocies existed in whatever Latin countries these girls came from, but something told me Hispanic men would not stoop to such chicanery as bar tricks to gain the respect of women.

So I opened a jar of maraschino cherries and placed a stemless one on the bar with a flourish. The ladies looked at me suspiciously.

I held up a brandy sifter, the type of stemmed glass that is like a squat wine glass, wide in the center but with a narrower rim.

"I can put that cherry into this glass without touching it."

They looked at each other, then back at me, uncertain whether they correctly understood my English.

I placed the glass over the cherry, paused for effect, and then began to move the glass in rapid circles on top of the bar. The cherry began to spin around the inside of the glass, and as I went faster, the cherry went higher and higher into the glass. Abruptly, mid spin, I raised the glass and turned it upright, the cherry rolling slowly to a stop in the bottom.

They gasped, and I saw Karina smile for the first time, though it was a guarded smile.

Paola screamed with laughter. "That is *fantástico*, Boone! Can I try? I want to know how to do this."

I smiled at Karina, then at Paola: "Of course." I placed the cherry on the bar and handed her the glass. Kids at home: you can do this trick with an olive but it is much harder because the stickiness of the cherry helps prevent it from flying out at the end when you turn the glass up right. Which is exactly what happened when Paola tried it, the cherry landing in Karina's hair. We laughed at that, and the next couple of tries were also a dud until she finally managed to throw the cherry directly up in the air but catch it back in the glass.

While this had been going on I had surreptitiously taken a matchbook from under the bar, folded back and lit one of the matches and then shook it out. The match was still attached to the matchbook, but I had it folded back so that it could not be seen.

Paola was beside herself with triumph and laughter: "I am going to practice every night until I get it in the glass to stay in the glass!"

I think it was safe to say they had never seen this trick, or likely any of the dozen or so other ones I had lined up.

"I have one more for tonight." I held up the open match pack. "A full pack of matches. You see?" I tore out an unlit match, and struck it on the back of the pack, back where I had the burnt match folded and where it could not be seen. I held the lit match up to Karina: "If you would, please blow out the match."

Hesitantly, with cautious eyes, she did so. This of course is the moment of diversion where all eyes are on the match being blown out. Meanwhile, my other hand folded the burnt match back into the matchbook and closed it.

I held up the smoldering match and threw it over my shoulder. Gone.

"Now, Karina, hold out your hand. No, all the way out."

She looked at Paola then at me, suspiciously: "You are not going to injure my hand?"

I laughed. "Of course not, it's a lovely hand, why would I do that? With your help I'm going to make that match reappear."

Paola slurped her drink and nudged her: "Put your hand out, I want to see what happens!"

Karina put her hand out, palm up, and I placed the closed match book on her palm. "Now close your hand and turn it over, holding it straight out."

She did so, those big golden eyes blinking at me.

It was at this juncture the proceedings that El Pescador appeared next to Paola, both eyebrows raised.

I gave him a courteous smile and nod, and then looked back at Karina, held her outstretched hand in both of my hands. I looked her in the eyes: "Now repeat after me: Oh Wah."

"Oh wah."

"Ta gooz"

"Ta gooz…"

I know I know – corny as all hell, but they had never seen any of this stuff. When she said the magic words faster it was Paola who first realized I was having her say "Oh what a goose am I" and she erupted in laughter and blurted out in Spanish: "*Usted es un ganso!*"

Karina laughed also, but dropped the matchbook on the bar with mock indignation.

My eyes still on hers, I pointed to the matchbook: "Open it!"

She looked at me askance, picked it up, and when she opened it her eyes went even wider than normal when she saw the burnt match stick in the book – presumably the one she'd seen pulled from the match book and that she herself had blown out: "*Como hiciste eso!*"

"Bravo!" Paola cheered. I glanced at the boss – he was clapping and smiling as well. He gave me a curious look, like this was unexpected but a welcome diversion.

"I will show you and Paola how these are done and then you can amaze your friends. But later. I believe I need to make *el caballero* a Manhattan."

Paola proceeded to show her paramour the cherry trick, once again catching it in the glass to much laughter as I served El Pescador his Manhattan.

Fancy that! By pure miracle, I had stumbled upon people mightily entertained by bar tricks, clearly completely new to them. And I could not have done a better job of breaking the ice. You'll note that the last trick had the advantage of allowing me to have increased physical contact with Karina, holding her hand in mine, which helped me become more physically familiar.

The dulcet tone of the dinner bell was soon in the air and thus we were summoned to the veranda overlooking the sea, where a circular dinner table had been set out and dressed with a yellow tablecloth and ornately-folded napkins. In fact, I believe they were supposed to be folded into the shape of swans, so as I pulled out a chair for Karina to sit, I nodded at the napkin and said: "Here is that goose we were talking about." Paola snickered, and Karina smiled and swatted me playfully. Red wine had already been decanted and placed on the table, and El Pescador went around filling our glasses, which he seemed to enjoy thereby taking complete ownership of his wine selection.

It was just the four of us at the table – the soldiers were out on the lawn patrolling the edges of the jungle as the day slipped into twilight.

No sooner were we seated than Paola wanted to know about my name, and when I told them about my father and my sister, etcetera, they all found this mighty strange, and they wanted to know if Crocket was pretty because her name was not. I said she was indeed pretty and was a professional athlete and they could look up a picture of her sometime. Gazpacho was ladled into our bowls, and as we slurped I realized that I would have to assume much of the brunt of conversation that evening. There was no talking about what El Pescador did that day: *So, how many narco subs made it to their rendezvous today, E.P.? Any notable beheadings worth mentioning?* I was only able to ask him about the Pinot Noir he had served. I asked Paola about where she grew up, which as it happened was Mexico City and Los Angeles, an urban girl from the get go. Karina was from Guatemala City but had grown up on a cattle ranch, so had gone from punching cattle to modeling. El Pescador said he had been thinking about getting horses for his island retreat but wasn't sure there was room for a barn, and then there's the matter of importing all the hay and feed. The main course was whole snapper with a thick spicy tomato *racado* sauce. It was accompanied by black beans and dirty rice. The girls began to discuss shopping in Guatemala City – apparently El Pescador had arranged for them to go there in a few days to shop, and so they were fairly excited about this, and lapsed into Spanish from which I only picked out words like *galerias, plazas, parque commercial*.

El Pescador waved his wine glass at me. "How do you like the wine?"

"Like the champagne, it tastes above my grade, but likely its quality is wasted on me as I'm not much of a wine enthusiast. I thank you for sharing it with me, as with everything else." I gestured with my glass at the table of food and vaguely to my right where Karina sat.

He gazed at me, self-satisfied. "To hold you in my employ without companionship would be inhumane. My inner circle needs to be happy. The guards work nine months, get three months off to be with their families."

"They don't have…companionship?"

He shook his head. "As I said, they are family men, fathers who are devout to The Church. Every time they leave home to come here they leave their wives pregnant."

I had read of such people, the kind that live two lives that are radically different and perhaps diametrically opposed. Doubtless, a little time in the confession booth and making their families strong makes up for a life of crime – assuming there is anybody really keeping score.

El Pescador leaned in. "So tomorrow we go find that permit, yes?"

"Absolutely."

He squinted. "Your promise is a bold one; I am not sure how you can be so confident. I have been an angler a long time, seen many fish, but nothing like these fish from hell. What is this secret fly that you have?"

I blinked slowly, reminding myself that I really needed to sit down at the pile of fly tying gear and make something up, pronto. Any of the flies that I already had in my kit was a standard pattern that he would recognize. I had to come up with something unique that a permit would ingest. God willing, they would eat no matter what I threw out so long as it was doped. The way they attacked the flies Elvis and I were throwing I had to believe you could throw out a used tissue that was doped and they would throw themselves at it. It came to me then and there what I should tie, something perfectly simple that to a permit would not look like a purple Martian with three horns, a duck beak and one eye.

"It is really so simple. As it turns out, permit do not really like crabs that much." His eyebrows shot up and I continued. "True, they will come over and look at them, and sometimes they will eat newly molted crabs, but everybody is wasting their time throwing crab patterns at them. What they really like is a small eel."

His jaw dropped and I continued, sipping my wine and lying for all I was worth.

"So my fly is just a small strip of tan bunny fur, slightly weighted at the front on a number four hook." I held up my thumb and forefinger to show him the size of about two inches.

He cleared his throat, and uttered: "Amazing. And just how did you discover this?"

"I was throwing crabs at permit, like yourself, and seeing that they would not take them, only look at them. I started to experiment, and finally tied on a striped bass fly, the kind we use in New Jersey, that imitates a small sand eel. That's how I discovered this. And instead of letting it sit on the bottom like the crab where they can study it and not make up their minds whether to eat it, I stripped this fly through the water like it is swimming, and they chase it down and take it."

He shook his head: "Mother of Christ. Who would have believed such a thing? And here everybody is casting crab flies! Food they don't want!"

I shrugged: "Though when you think about it, this is pretty obvious, is it not? I mean, they won't eat crab flies, you've seen so yourself, which means they don't like crabs, they only like to look at them, and we mistake this for genuine feeding behavior."

He held out his glass and we toasted: *To tomorrow.*

Dessert was something like Puerto Rican mofongo – mashed fried plantain – but rolled into balls with sweet black bean filling and sprinkled with powdered sugar, and it was served with ruby port. Afterward, we retired to a round table poolside with cushioned wicker chairs, where the women continued to chatter and my boss doled out the cigars. It was a rather large stogie, much larger than the cheroots I prefer. Yet sharing a smoke with the old man was a male bonding ritual that I did not dare pass up with my erstwhile benefactor. He waved his cigar at the women: "I send them to the city to shop when I have business to conduct. There will be men coming here to discuss commerce, and it is customary to supply them with women. Also, it is best that these men not be seen in my company by outsiders. You will be on duty to provide drinks, of course, and there will be much tequila to pour. Your skills will not be tested, and I will be drinking margaritas. But you may be very busy. As I said this afternoon in my office, there will be many nights like this and then there will be nights like the one in a few weeks' time were you will be an employee only."

I blew some smoke. "Understood."

The girls rejoined us, remainder of their red wine in hand, Paola saying to El Pescador. "Alberto, when I first saw Boone, he was coming out of the house juggling fruit!"

"Is that so?" he said, eyeing me.

I nodded, glancing at Karina, who seemed relaxed and looked at me inquisitively, in the way some women do when you can see they are sizing you up, wondering what kind of man you really are.

I nodded. "Yes, when I was a kid I worked at a place called Medieval Knights, which was like theater where I was an actor playing a swordsman." They didn't seem to understand, so I mimicked waving a sword. "I was supposed to be a knight, and I wore armor, and I would fight a bad knight and win."

The girls suddenly understood: *Ah si si si si.*

"Well, I sometimes had to stand in for the jester, the fool who entertains the king. So I had to learn how to juggle to play that part."

The irony of this description under present circumstances was suddenly quite palpable, though I guessed only to me. Who was I but El Pescador's jester, his personal entertainer?

The girls thought this was funny, and Paola said: "So, you wore the tight pants, the stocking pants?"

I spread my hands humbly. "When you're young you need to work, and this was work."

El Pescador blew smoke and then thumbed his cigar, looking askance at me. "So you are a swordsman, too?"

I barked a laugh. "Not at all. It was play-acting. They taught us mostly how not to hurt each other or ourselves. We mostly just made a lot of noise: *clang, clang, clang!*"

"I am sorry, this is very funny," Paola said, a hand on my arm. "To imagine you as a boy doing this! In the funny clothes!" She and Karina shared another laugh at my expense, and I accepted being the brunt of their hilarity with nonchalance.

I took the opportunity to excuse myself, so I stood.

"And with that, I am going to take my leave and say good night. I admit that I find my eyes suddenly wanting to close. It has been a long day and we are fishing tomorrow early, so I really should say goodnight."

The girls chorused an *aww* of disappointment, and I detected a little consternation from Karina, so I circled around to her and kissed her on the cheek: "I will see you tomorrow when we return and show you some new bar tricks."

Karina brightened, smiling, and I think a little flattered that I was being gallant when perhaps I didn't necessarily have to be. I wasn't sure to what she was accustomed, but as a model, if that's what she was most of the time, one could only imagine the liberties some men would take with her. Or try to.

Back at my cabana, I set my cigar outside on the small table by the patio chair to let it extinguish itself and possibly smoke it the next day. There was little doubt that it was Cuban and I could not see just chucking it in the bushes.

Inside, I sorted my stuff a little, and there was no doubt that I was quite tired. If nothing else I was mentally exhausted from being 'on stage' all day. It was nice to be alone, and also nice to sit down to the tying vise and whip off a couple of eel flies for the next day. Fly tying is a ruminative activity, and I wondered how things would go with Karina, about what it would be like to embrace and kiss her. She was certainly a sweet kid. How she ended up in this assignment anyone could guess, but one had to imagine that it was quite lucrative and might bankroll her way out of the life of a model.

After tying four flies, I clicked off the desk lamp, brushed my teeth, washed my face and rolled into bed. I drifted to sleep quickly, my mind's eye captivated by Karina's golden eyes looking at me inquisitively.

CHAPTER 19

IT WAS THE NEXT DAY that El Pescador finally caught his permit – two of them on eel flies. It wasn't easy, his casting was a little clumsy, and he spooked the first fish we saw cruising a small mangrove cay, but the fly dope made up for a lot. Mildly spooked fish, those that did not have the fly dropped on their head, would turn back. Hidalgo at the helm, the black cigarette boat full of soldiers flanking us, we roared back home in the late afternoon sun, my boss positively over the moon.

Imagine, friends, if I had been an honest man and not brought crab scent for my flies? Imagine that I was truly an honorable sportsman and demurred catching permit except by sheer, idiotic forbearance? At the very least, I'd be in less optimal circumstances, and at the most the captives at Utopia Lodge would have been killed. So anybody who tells me that honesty is always the best policy is an unmitigated nincompoop.

We found the ladies poolside and decked out in white bikinis that I can only describe as Brazilian. They cheered the permit triumph, and when El Pescador whispered something into Paola's ear, she giggled and excused herself – they retreated to the main house and presumably his chamber for a post-permit romp.

I stepped to the bar and hollered to Karina if she would like me to make her something.

She pushed aside her magazine and sauntered over to the bar, swaying her dandy curves toward me. Yet I hardly noticed as I was in a fine fettle for having worked some permit magic for El Pescador as I had promised. *Thank God the eel flies worked! Next, a Grand Slam!*

Karina rested gently at the edge of the bar and lifted her sunglasses, the golden pupils once again inquisitive.

I sloshed some Willet into a mixing glass with a half a lemon and half an orange and packed it with ice. I gave the cocktail a quick shake to chill it down and dumped it into a rocks glass. I sipped: a simple yet spot on old fashioned.

"Boone?" She pushed back her honeyed hair on one side.

"Yes, Karina, what can I get you?"

"So this is a celebration, yes?"

"I cannot see how it would not be."

"Alberto, he is celebrating, yes?"

There was an awkward pause as I thought how to respond. "If not now, I can see him having more than his share of cocktails this evening."

She studied my rugged hand, then reached out her smooth brown one and placed it atop mine. Her eyes lifted coyly to mine. "I think we should celebrate."

I took another sip before her meaning became clear and the bourbon went down my gullet with an audible gulp as she played with the tip of my finger.

Before I could formulate a clever rejoinder, her hand slid off mine and she drifted back to her pool chair, slipping into her shoes and shouldering her beach towel. She bit her lip and said "*Mi cabaña?*"

As I followed her back to her cabana, permit were the farthest thing from my mind. I need not elucidate as to the proceedings that followed except to say that by the time I emerged from her abode an hour and a half later I can honestly attest to having had the best celebration I had ever had without a hangover. While it had been my intention to string out the courtship, I don't believe it ever pays to disappoint a lady.

I will add that while Latinas have a reputation for being moody, many have an innate sense of sultry in the extreme and manage to continue seducing a man all through the clinches. In deference to decorum, I'll leave the rest up to the imagination.

As you might imagine, when the troops reconvened at the bar, high spirits prevailed, and the '96 Bollinger flowed steadily. Karina was now close to my side and at turns rubbing my thigh under the table at dinner. There was an after dinner skinny dip in the pool from which we all seemed anxious to retreat for more celebration of the amorous variety behind closed doors.

When my eyes popped open the next morning in Karina's cabana, her soft warm brown body curled around mine, her hair's floral scent gracing my nostrils, I watched the ceiling fan spin and thought to myself: *You know, Boone, this situation is really not half bad at all. What kind of lunatic would struggle free of this straightjacket and escape?*

As such, I made my way mid-morning across the path from the row of cabanas under sunny blue skies to the patio and bar. El Pescador was seated at bar in a terry robe reading the newspaper, Paola floating on a raft in the pool behind him. She seemed to be fast asleep as she was snoring rather loudly – I supposed the old man had put

Paola through her paces. He looked at me over his reading glasses, smirked and said: "You're late."

"My apologies. What can I get you?"

"Something like you made me the first morning, only more fruit. Paola will have a mimosa. When she awakes."

I nodded, pulled a bin of fruit from the fridge, and began slicing and hacking pineapple, mangoes and oranges.

After a moment, my boss took his eyes from his paper again to look at me over his glasses. "I trust the girl and you are entertaining each other?"

I smiled: "Indeed."

Packing the blender with fruit and ice and a bold shot of madeira, I blended the living daylights out of the ingredients and poured the old man a tall glass, garnishing it with a sizeable wedge of pineapple and a straw. He continued reading the paper as he sipped, and I searched for champagne for the mimosa and found a half-done bottle from the night before. I set about squeezing an entire bag of oranges – fresh squeezed is the only way to go. Is there anybody, other than those in TV commercials, who think juice from a carton is even remotely comparable?

Half way through the bag, El Pescador once again raised his eyes from his paper. "When was the last time you picked up a sword?"

"Many years ago – probably when I was nineteen?"

"I need a sparring partner. Hidalgo is a good man but he is too big to be a good swordsman."

"Sparring?" My pile of spent orange halves was growing larger.

"Yes. For exercise, I practice *destreza*. Do you know what that is?"

I shook my head and he continued. "It is an ancient way to fight with swords and I need you to be my sparring partner."

I cocked my head at him. "You want me to...well, of course, but I have no idea what I'm doing. It was all play acting, swashbuckling."

He blinked: "Better you than Paola, yes?"

Through all that had happened in the last couple days, I had not forgotten that the man reading the paper, the man with the carefully crenelated white hair looking at me over his glasses was a self-professed homicidal maniac. This was the man who had pointed a pistol at my face and likely almost blew my brains out all over the yacht for lying about permit while drinking the best cocktail of his life. So it was with some trepidation that I amiably agreed to let him go at me with a sword.

Like most people, I'm accustomed to seeing swashbucklers in old movies wielding rapiers and jumping on furniture, swinging from chandeliers and fending off whole squadrons of Hollywood extras in chainmail armor. Or more occasionally the prissy-looking French fencers dressed all in white waving wobbly foils at each other. Or like what I had done as a kid – two knights in full armor laboriously swinging heavy broadswords at each other.

So it was that in the afternoon I found myself sweating in the bright sun on the helipad wearing what for intents and purposes was a baseball catcher's padded apron and a rusting fencer's mask. I was facing El Pescador, who was similarly attired and standing in the center of the painted circle of the helipad. We both held what I can only describe as medium weight swords with two-post hilts and plastic handles. Three feet long, the last half of the things was sort of whittled down and flexible, likely as they were practice swords and not for actual combat. Though I'm sure if you jabbed someone in the chest who was not wearing a catcher's apron that it would warrant a 911 call. A fat lot of good that would do you in the middle of the Bay Islands.

Oddly, El Pescador began his explanation in English and then, unable to find the proper vocabulary in English, lapsed into Spanish, though he positioned me and demonstrated physically what he could not adequately explain. The gist of destreza swordplay seemed to be centered on circular motions around your opponent so that you could force his sword down and step in close for the kill with a dagger or a debilitating jab to the kidneys. When I saw it demonstrated it made a lot more sense tactically than all the flailing one sees on TV. This was not about art and form so much as about actually trying to kill the other person. The trick was in the defense against these offensive outflanking maneuvers, so that you could in return outflank your opponent. As El Pescador demonstrated, the best defense was a fluid one. When the opponent circled to one side you had to turn to prevent him from forcing your sword down and stepping in. When you were squared to each other, you used thrusts and slashes to try to gain an advantage whereby you could outflank the foe, force his blade to the ground, step close and finish him off. I'm sure the self-respecting destreza aficionados out there are gnashing their teeth at my over simplification of this noble endeavor, though as a novice being instructed in a language I did not understand, I would hope that I might be afforded a little slack.

Likewise, for all I know, El Pescador had his own style of swordplay. I did start to get the hang of it. Admittedly, I was more ready to defend than attack, finding that I had some aptitude from my previous experience. Defensively, I was relatively adept at parrying – that is to wield my blade to the side to thwart slashes and thrusts. I found out quickly that such maneuvers opened myself up to having my boss suddenly close to my side poking a mock dagger into my ribs, him chuckling softly at his victory. In essence, I stood in the bullseye of the helipad's painted circle while he moved around me. I tried to make sure I turned to whatever side he tried to outflank me on and the rest was parrying, intercepting and pushing his blade away with mine. The sweat poured off us and I could see how this had the old man in fighting trim. He killed me at least ten times that first afternoon, and it really seemed to make him happy doing so. Well, what else would you expect from a homicidal maniac?

For the next week, we continued to spar most afternoons, and he began to add practice drills to make sure I clasped the hilt correctly and usually made downward strokes. He also showed me the advantage of not trying to reverse the direction the blade was going, but to move it in a circle, or even to spin your body to bring the blade back to bear on the opponent. The week after, that El Pescador would even sometimes laugh with surprise that I managed to thwart one of his kill moves. He was older with less stamina and overall strength, but if he really wanted to, I had no doubt that he could outwit and kill me in thirty seconds.

As the weeks passed, swordplay and fishing set the tempo for the day for the men, while the girls played tennis, sunned by the pool and met us for cocktails, more bar magic, dinner and increasingly, indulging Karina's appetite for salsa dancing. The weather was the same every day, warm, with an increasing afternoon breeze from the south east, with clear starry nights.

El Pescador spent much of the time between leisure activities with one of his many phones clamped tightly to his head, pacing, and often shouting. You could see by the end of the day how welcome one of my Manhattans was as a stress reliever. Yet, I began to detect something more with his cocktail ritual. He would sip, and close his eyes for several beats. When he opened his eyes his gaze was far away, and the dark eyes sometimes moist. I had come to believe that in his mind, he was visiting with that lady at the hotel in New York, and I could tell there was more to that woman and his relationship – far more – than I knew.

I had not yet managed a grand slam for El Pescador, but on a number of occasions we had bagged a permit and a bonefish. And once we caught those two and a small snook, sort of a Not-So Grand Slam. The yard-long silver tarpon that we were finding in the mangroves were the variety that roll and porpoise, yet act as if they do not see the fly even when you put it on their nose. The sticky brown crab scent I had been using for the permit was useless on the tarpon. In my fishing career, mangrove tarpon had been every bit as uncooperative as permit, and now even more so. We just had to get lucky, and after one of those days in which we were cheated out of a grand slam by yet another tarpon, he just stopped casting, put down his rod, fished a beer out of the cooler, and sat and watched the tarpon roll. He wasn't angry, just pensive, but inwardly calm. It seemed like the right time to see if I could probe a little deeper into this complicated man.

"Captain?" I had begun to call him that and he didn't seem to mind – it sounded a lot better than 'boss.' "I have been noting how much you enjoy my Manhattans. That lady in New York…she must have been special."

He scowled at me. "She was my wife. Esmerelda."

I nodded at the boat floor. "I'm sorry." I was guessing she had died, and was going to leave it at that. But his scowl dissolved as he turned his attention back to the silver backs of tarpon slicing the surface of the lagoon.

"Boone, have you had a great love of your life?"

I picked up a big black tarpon fly and began to stroke the feathers. "No, Captain, I have not."

"Good. It is a curse."

He was silent for a minute or two before he continued.

"Esmerelda was mine. We were at a family picnic when rivals of my cousins showed up with guns and shot up the place. Esmerelda died in my arms. It was then that I was no longer an engineer. When something like that happens, you take sides, so I joined my cousins in the trade to kill the men that did this. Your heart becomes hard when your love is taken from you and killing makes your heart harder, protects you from the pain of being alone." He studied his beer, then turned his tired eyes to mine. "But as I get older, my heart is softening, and I miss her. I begin…" He sighed, shaking his head slowly. "…I become less afraid of death because I want to be with her, and that is the only way. My soul and hers need to be together. I can feel that she is out there waiting for me."

What does one say to that? *Bummer?* I had no idea, yet I had to say something.

"That must be a great burden, Captain. I am sorry."

He smiled sadly at me: "Do not be sorry. I have eternity with her that awaits me. I have just become a little impatient. Hidalgo? *Vamonos!*"

CHAPTER 20

KARINA AND I BEGAN to fall into a couple's pattern whereby we would turn in by ten and sleep in her bed at her cabana. I would retreat to my shack in the morning to shower and dress, arriving by nine at the bar to whip up fruit smoothies. It was fortunate that she and I took to each other the way dogs sometimes do – strangers who soon after they meet like the smell of the other and wag our tails. Even though our relationship had been engineered by El Pescador, we did not ask how the other came to be there as I think we both realized that such matters were irrelevant and our coupling was a *fait accompli*. I had to guess she was being handsomely compensated, and likely as not that money was earmarked for some career move, such as out of the modeling business, which in Guatemala was likely not entirely modeling. So God speed.

Her English was rudimentary, though our talks became more intimate as the weeks passed. As I suggested, she loved to dance, and she was so excited to be teaching me how to salsa and pleased that I was a willing and able partner. In bed, she would drape herself on my chest and ask me about my family – I made her laugh with my father's nonsensical sayings, particularly: *When your shorts ride up there's no fixing the tractor.* She also liked *some men are burgers with no buns* and *weasels and beavers – same thing.* Of course, she didn't know what a beaver or a weasel was, she just liked the sound of it. She would tell me what it was like on a cattle ranch with three brothers and a blind father running the whole show, and about her uncle who showed up one holiday dinner cross-dressed. Apparently, many of the ranchers had had problems with *el narcos* but her family had been spared being terrorized because there was a shrine or some such nearby. She would ask me about other women I had been with, but I demurred – it has been my sound policy never to discuss such matters, as I am convinced nothing good can come of it. Karina would only have fretted about whether she was better than they – so I simply answered that they are in the past and no longer exist – only <u>she</u> exists for me now. She had a way of cooing, then purring when I said something sweet like that. For all intents and purposes I meant it, too.

Good Lord – what a sweet girl. I found myself sometimes wondering if I was falling in love with her, then wondering: how could I even think of partnering with anyone if I were not freed by El Pescador? Presumably, Karina was only contracted for a while and then would be replaced by another courtesan. I tried not to think about all that, but was finding it harder and harder not to.

As the weeks trailed on, Paola and Karina were getting increasingly petulant about their postponed shopping adventure to Guatemala City. My sense from little snippets I picked up here and there in El Pescador's conversations was that his organization was having security issues that kept prompting a delay.

Finally, one evening over cocktails El Pescador announced that the next day the girls would fly out and spend two nights and two days in Guatemala City, and that there would be two body guards and a driver to meet them upon landing.

They gasped and cheered.

Then he handed them each a credit card, with the admonition: "There's a ten-thousand-dollar limit on each, but the company penthouse is paid for."

They gasped and cheered again.

Karina drank more than she usually did – I had been right, she was only into white wine and bubbly, but she drank a bottle and a half, and after some protracted dancing and dinner she all but collapsed into my arms and I toted her fireman-style to her bed.

When I returned to the pool Paola was gone and only El Pescador was sitting at the bar nursing the last of another in a long line of fantastic reds from his cellar.

I went behind the bar to tidy up.

"Boone, my associates arrive tomorrow evening. You have enough tequila? Any supplies you need? Let me know. There is a shipment of food arriving tomorrow morning by float plane."

"Now that I have my ice trays and as long as I have plenty of fruit, we're good. I'll chill a lot of glasses. Do they drink it on the rocks, or do they want margaritas?"

"On the rocks with lime, mostly. Better chill down many cans of beer as well."

I nodded. "Will do. How many are coming?"

"Ten. And as I said before, you should keep to yourself while they are here, and you will just be the bartender. They will not like that you are a gringo. They will think you are DEA. I will drink margaritas."

"I understand, Captain. Do you think we have time to fish the outgoing tide tomorrow? I wanted to try that creek mouth for tarpon when the tide is going out. Perhaps they will be more inclined to take a fly in that deep trough when they aren't rolling."

He tilted his head, uncertain, but then with a wave of his hand decided we would do it. "Just make sure your girl is up and ready to fly out by eight in the morning."

Which I did, by awaking her at six thirty, and I had to resort to dragging her by her feet out of the bed to get her into the shower to recover from the previous night's dance party. Meanwhile I dressed in baggy fishing clothes, long brimmed fishing hat and a sun snood around my neck. Packing her gear of course was a nightmare. She could not decide what to wear while away – until I sagely advised: "You have ten thousand dollars to buy clothes – buy it there!" She liked that idea, and this of course greatly advanced the process of delivering her to the helipad where a military helicopter sat waiting in the cool morning shadows. I had to hand it to El Pescador, the Guatemalans were like his own army to do with as he pleased. Here they were as a taxi service for his girlfriend!

Paola was already in the helicopter, clearly eager to get the trip going. El Pescador was nowhere to be seen. I handed the co-pilot Karina's bags (even without substantial supply of clothes there were three bags!) and the blade began to spin overhead as the pilot began flipping switches on his console. I led her to the open helicopter door.

She turned before climbing aboard, cupping my face in her hands, and kissing me gently. Color came to her cheeks, and she bit her lip, her golden eyes searching mine. Then she hugged me and whispered in my ear: "*Te amo, Boone.*"

My heart literally stopped just for a few beats. As she pushed back, Karina smiled awkwardly and climbed into the helicopter.

I believe it was the thump of the helicopter door closing that started my heart beating again.

I drifted back away from the aircraft as the blade turned faster, wanting to prevent my head from being chopped off.

When the giant raging machine rose from the ground, I saw Karina look back down at me from the window and I blew her a kiss.

She blew one back as the helicopter pivoted away, tilted, and roared out over the ocean, the forest canopy in-between lashed by propeller wind.

I turned toward the bar – it was time to make smoothies for the morning fishing trip. Placing one foot in front of the other, I thought I might faint, my heart thumping in my chest.

This was bad.

I was falling in love, and under very dangerous circumstances.

Yet my childlike brain just played over and over her dulcet words: "*Te amo, Boone.*"

A tarpon was right where I predicted it would be that morning, and it took a Black Death fly when El Pescador swung it into the current right in front of its nose. The silver king jumped and jumped and I was deathly afraid it was going to throw the hook.

But Hidalgo heaved it into the boat, and it was a big one: fifty-two inches, seventy some-odd pounds. After the pictures, after the fish was back in the water and finning slowly away, El Pescador turned and gave me a bear hug. "*Fantastico!*"

By Jove, I did also believe I was coming to love this murderous old man, too.

I clapped him on the shoulder: "To the flats!"

To make a long fish story short, he did it.

El Pescador got the grand slam.

And when he did, tears of joy cascaded from his eyes, and as he blubbered, he shook my hand, and he even shook Hidalgo's.

Overall, it was a big day.

Te amo, Boone.

CHAPTER 21

THAT EVENING, THE DANGEROUS MEN began to arrive. Most were ugly, short, thick brown men with mustaches and darting black eyes. All to a man had nasty facial scars and prison tattoos. It didn't take a criminologist to figure out that these were El Pescador's captains. These were the ones who oversaw the brutal, dirty work of terrorizing the opposing cartels and bending the government and everyone else to their will.

They arrived trailing two henchmen who were even uglier and more dangerous looking than they. All of them were dressed in what they likely thought was fashion forward, but to me they looked like relics from the disco era with loud print polyester shirts, beltless slacks and patent leather slip-ons. Gaudy gems bedecked their fingers, and heavy gold chains were around their necks. As they passed on the way to the cabanas, I made myself busy wiping glasses and cutting fruit so as not to meet their murderous stares aimed at the gringo.

It was genuinely disturbing to see how drastically the mood of the island was changed by their arrival. All the staff – the maids, the gardeners, the wash women, the cooks – were scuttling from view as they arrived. I was the only one that needed to stay visible.

Unfortunately.

A huge spread of food had been laid out by the pool on folding tables, and I had filled some buckets with blown ice and Gallo beer to flank the buffet, which was loaded with *tamales, chuchitos, tamalitos* and *paches*. I also put a couple of bottles of Don Julio añejo in a sizeable tub of ice surrounded by chilled shot glasses and lime slices so they could down the stuff themselves if they chose to without having to ask the gringo. Of course, what I was hoping was that the self-serve station would greatly limit my contact with them.

The first group arrived to approach the pool didn't even see the self-serve station and so came directly to me. The headman had an eye patch and acne, his lower lip disfigured – from what I did not want to know. His two henchmen were uneasy with the surroundings, and gave me the stink eye. Eye Patch didn't ask for what he wanted, he just snarled and thumped a hand on the bar. Now it could have been he was ordering a Pimm's Cup, but I went out on a limb by lining up frozen shot glasses with lime wedges and filled them with ice cold tequila.

If they had a Pimm's Cup in mind they did not say so as they reached in unison to take their shot.

"*Cerveza?*" I asked.

Eye Patch grimaced at me. His thick brown fingers slid his empty shot glass back toward me, and I refilled it.

One of his sidekicks asked: "*Que tipo de cerveza tiene usted?*"

I waved a hand at the beer selection, the three brands that I had put behind the bar for just such a question –we had Dorada, Gallo and Monte Carlo (a dark beer.)

He ordered the Monte Carlo, and when I went to pour it into a glass he grunted and shook his shaggy head, so I handed him the bottle. After the second shot, the group of them wandered off to the pool and affixed themselves in chairs there. They were almost immediately replaced at the bar by a second group more hideous than the first. And those were replaced by another surly trio. And so on. All drank two shots and then left, some asking for a beer, but none would take it in a glass. Perhaps they were accustomed to compatriots trying to poison them, or perhaps drinking beer from a glass was too fey.

In the end, the ten men that El Pescador said were coming really equaled thirty because of the henchmen, and when they were all assembled by the pool, I began running trays of frozen tequila shots out to them, and then finally put more bottles of chilled añejo within easy reach. The cloud of aftershave they created was likely visible from the space station.

It was dark before El Pescador made his appearance, and the assembled hoodlums were, at this juncture, more relaxed and even telling jokes and laughing.

The crowd cheered him and raised glasses, one or two making some sort of toast. I shuttled a margarita to Captain from the bar, and he took it without even looking at me. That was fine. I wanted to disappear into the furniture. I could only imagine what would happen when this gathering of cutthroats were thoroughly plastered and started playing games with knives, or worse still using me as target practice.

Needless to say, it was a damn fine thing Paola and Karina were not there, and I don't think I need to clarify as to why.

It seemed the first evening was just a meet and greet party, and I guessed that the next day would entail meetings or some such to review what El Pescador's salesmen were up to these days.

Party lights in the trees were turned on and as the group became louder, Mexican ballads began to play through the fake rock speakers, and the men would sometimes begin to sing along. By this point, I was mostly out of the picture except to keep chilled glasses moving in and out along with fresh bottles of añejo, limes and beer. At one point, a particularly nasty scarecrow-like man intentionally tripped me, much to the amusement of his pals. I didn't fall flat on my face, but almost. That was the point where I realized I'd do better to stay behind the bar. They were beyond needing their glasses chilled.

It was about ten I think when I looked up to see a tall man with a ponytail approaching the bar. I stood ready to serve him, and when he came into the light I saw he had a cast on his left hand and murder in his drooping eyes.

It was Enrique.

As cold as frozen tequila, my blood chilled at the sight of him.

He noted my trepidation, and smirked.

"Champagne," he rumbled.

From the refrigerator I popped a bottle of '96 Heidsieck – the worst we had but still better than anything I had ever had prior to becoming a billionaire's bartender. I poured it into a flute, the one I kept cold for Karina, and it bothered me to see him take the glass with his good hand and put his malevolent lips where hers had been. He whispered: "*Fantástico.*"

It was in that instant, watching his wide lips curl on that glass – and in his mind pulling me apart like a daddy long legs – that I realized I had to escape this place and find Karina and take her back to New Jersey and never fall into the grasp of gangsters ever again. This violent, vicious circle of psychopaths would eventually kill me.

He motioned for me to hand him the bottle, and when I did so, he glanced at his cast, at the hand I had shot.

Then he cocked his head at me, smiled with his teeth and toasted the air with his flute.

The message couldn't have been clearer: *I owe you one.*

He turned, his ponytail drifting back into the shadows toward the rest of the depraved hoodlums by the pool.

I had been drinking lightly while at the island. I had promised myself I would when I arrived – that is, mostly wine and beer so that I had my wits about me at all times and did not get drunk and make outrageous or reckless proposals to my boss, like about grand slams, or perhaps super-duper grands slams with a shark and a wahoo thrown in.

I reached for the Pappy 23 and poured myself a stiff one. Once again, I was drinking perhaps the best and most expensive bourbon in the solar system when I was in no shape to enjoy it. But who knew, it could be my last?

At that juncture of the proceedings, some of El Pescador's soldiers led a procession of prostitutes along the path from the boats, and the congregation of criminals cheered their arrival. The girls slithered into the group, dropping their robes and sliding into the swimming pool. The hooligans whistled, and some immediately began to disrobe and slide into the pool with the girls.

The scene developing before me was going to devolve into nothing short of an orgy, of which I had little enthusiasm to become a spectator. It was going to be revolting.

I was startled by the sudden appearance of El Pescador at the bar holding his empty glass. I had another margarita already made in the freezer, and fetched it for him. My manor and expression must have betrayed my trepidation over the bacchanal, and he grinned, eyeing me coldly as if to say: *And what did you expect?*

Then he said: "You can go... if you like." He turned and walked back to his sordid gang and their exploits.

Yes sir, Captain!

I practically ran back to my hut, bottle of Pappy tucked under my arm. As I headed for my cabin door, I spotted in the gloom the white sign at the head of the path, the hanging sign behind my hut that read: *PROHIBIDO.*

I had hardly paid the sign or the mysterious path any attention up until then. Now I felt I had to know what was beyond that sign – it could somehow help me escape this place. Maybe it led to a submarine or a boat for an escape in an emergency, something like that. I just had to pick my time carefully and get as far as fast as possible and outside the reach of the Guatemalan Navy.

While my pillow was not enough to completely insulate me from the roar of the drunken orgy on the other side of the mansion, the bourbon rushed me into sleep anyway.

CHAPTER 22

I AWOKE EARLY, the room filled with the grey light of dawn, and reached for Karina's warm curves that were not beside me.

The previous evening's dread returned with the suddenness of boney hands grabbing me by the neck.

With apprehension, I crept from my cot and peeked through the window slats, afraid of what I might see. But I saw only the cleaning woman and the groundskeeper whispering and drinking coffee beside the kitchen door.

A cursory birdbath, tooth brushing, sport shirt, white pants and ball cap on my head had me presentable enough to venture forth. I checked my new mustache in the mirror before stepping out – it was coming in a little sparse on one side, but the old dashing Linsenbigler was coming back strong enough. I snagged a cup of coffee from the kitchen and then walked around the side of the main house toward the pool and bar. Nobody was there except for one of the housekeepers, who was sweeping up the last of the debris from the orgy. By all appearances, it seemed the staff had arisen early to get things ship shape.

They had even swept up behind the bar, though the bottles were in disarray and the bar top itself a sticky mess. Sticky with what, exactly, I dared not imagine as I liberally sprayed it with ammonia and used a huge wad of paper towels to wipe it down.

The trash can was full of beer bottles and a few pairs of underwear, so I gathered that up, put in a fresh bag and hefted two full bags back around the side of the house to the dumpster next to the kitchen door.

Heading back around the house again toward the bar, I stopped and gazed down the steep slope and jungle canopy out over the blue ocean, which had the orange light of sunrise twinkling on it even though the campus was still in a cool shadow. I hoped Karina was having a good time out there. I would have given anything to be with her just then.

I turned to continue back to the bar when I saw something move in the forest.

No, I didn't see anything in particular. I didn't see any of the iguanas move, the ones that sometimes set off the alarms. I stared at the forest the way I stared at the flats, looking for something that worked against the patchwork pattern of colors, in this case the greens and browns of the jungle.

Nothing.

Just as I was turning away, something moved again.

Some part of the forest definitely moved, and a chill gripped my spine.

I stared.

My eyes bugged out at the shape of three men crouching and motionless, head to toe in camouflage and combat gear. They were looking back at me, and now that I saw them, their eyes looked impossibly white.

They were holding military weapons, machine guns I guessed, and were still looking right at me when the one in the center lifted his hand slowly and put a camouflaged finger to his lips.

Shhhh!

Ice crackling through my veins, I scanned more of the forest, and began to make out the shapes of dozens more soldiers crouching at the jungle's edge, weapons at the ready. I tore my eyes away, searching the compound not for the shape of soldiers but for an avenue of escape. I wanted to sink right down into the earth and vanish with a low moan.

I started for the bar again, heart bouncing around in my chest. Then I turned back and then back again – I didn't know what to do. Anybody watching me would think I was pacing.

Were these soldiers my rescue or my doom? Were they some rival cartel here to massacre everybody? Perhaps the Honduran military changed sides with another cartel and had come to wipe out El Pescador? Whoever they were, all hell was about to break lose and I had to make myself scarce. If I went to the bar, I would be between the men in the jungle and the cabanas with all the hoodlums snoring off their binge. So I curved around the main house and aimed to cut through the living room and kitchen, out of the line of fire, and straight into my hut.

As I marched through the house, the shield over the fireplace caught my attention – there were four swords laced into it, weapons that I could use if anybody came barging into my hut. I shoved a chair over, stood on it, and unsheathed one of the swords. These were not practice blades but the real thing: sharp and sturdy. Holding the sword at my side, I marched through the kitchen past the cringing lady cooks. Out the back door, I headed toward my hut, my eyes blurred with panic.

I smelled cigarette smoke when I arrived at my hut, and looked over my shoulder.

The far back edge of the mansion's deck was visible, and sitting on the railing was Enrique, smoke streaming out of his nostrils and his head cocked at me and my sword.

His eyes could see in mine that I had been caught doing something I shouldn't.

He jumped to his feet, and flicked his long, thin cigarette off the railing, eyeing me like a hound waiting for a rabbit to run.

But he didn't wait.

He disappeared into the house, likely saying to himself: *Fantástico.*

And I was pretty sure he wasn't headed for a cup of coffee.

My hut suddenly seemed more trap than refuge and I backed away from the door, my mind feverishly calculating places to hide. In the dumpster? On the roof? Behind my hut? Under my hut?

That's when I saw the *PROHIBITO* sign and path.

Now the rabbit ran.

I vaulted over the chain barrier, sword high, and scrambled across the boulders into the thicket along a lightly-used path that became more hung with vines the further I went.

Behind me, I heard shouting, and a helicopter roared overhead.

Gunfire sounded.

It went off like popcorn, the pops at first slow – just one or two – and then happening all at once. A few bullets zipped and thwacked off the boulders around me as I crested a mound of rocks down onto a path that cut diagonally and across a downward slope to my left.

I could smell – but not see – the ocean and hear waves crashing against rocks down the very steep jungled slope to my right. At least I was out of the line of fire. Where the path led, I had no idea, but I didn't rightly care as long as it took me as far away as possible from that battleground.

In the distance behind me, I could hear volleys of gunfire, automatic bursts and explosions.

I'm not a religious man, but if ever there was a moment when the Almighty might have stepped in on my behalf, it was when he gave me the gift of seeing things. The ability to see bonefish, see things that are camouflaged, sure as Queen of Sheba, it saved my bacon. I would have been cut to ribbons at the bar had I not noticed the movement in the forest.

I trotted along the path, hoping that Enrique had been shot and was not in pursuit. The trees to my right thinned, giving me a glimpse of the ocean. I could hear military helicopters circling the island.

The path turned steeper as I rounded the east side of the island and was bathed in orange morning sun. With any luck, the path would lead me to that boat I imagined parked and ready to go. Yet the path took an unexpected turn upward, and became so steep that I had to help myself along with my hands and the sword pommel. As I crested the steep part, a face full of ocean breeze and sunlight hit me. Shielding my eyes to discern my path, I saw that the trail led down again to the edge of a cliff.

Where the path stopped.

At a rope bridge.

The bridge was about sixty feet long and connected the edge of the cliff to a thick free-standing pinnacle of rock about a hundred feet above where the ocean crashed onto rocks around it. The top of the pinnacle was probably twenty feet square and planted with ornamentals.

What the devil was this? Where was my boat? Why on earth would someone build a path that led to a dead end? And a rope bridge dead end! This was insane! I trotted down to the small open area at the cliff edge and looked down – there was no way to climb down to the ocean, and the briny blue water was not deep enough to sustain a jump. As a denizen of New Jersey, I was keenly aware that even jumps from the George Washington Bridge into deep water were almost universally fatal.

Perhaps, I thought, if I backtracked I could find a way down the steep jungled slope to a secluded bit of shoreline and hide.

I turned just as Enrique crested the path behind me.

A sword was in his bandaged left hand, a silver pistol in his right hand. He was puffing from having chased me down the path, yet he seemed pleased with himself: he'd cornered me. His overly smooth face and wide lips grinned hungrily.

He quickly raised the pistol at me and before I could react he pulled the trigger.

Click.

His laugh, like his voice, was baritone: "Linsenbigler, I seem to be all out of bullets, I used them all back there in order to escape, so I regret that I will have to kill you with this sword. I cannot let you be rescued, you understand. Nobody shoots me like you did and lives." He tossed the gun aside and switched the sword to his good hand.

There was nowhere for me to go.

I had to stand and fight or throw myself over the edge of the cliff.

At that juncture, there certainly didn't seem to be any percentage in crossing the bridge to the pinnacle – that would be just bad to worse. At least where I stood I might be able to bypass him and rabbit back toward the compound. Perhaps the battle at the compound would have ceased and I could be rescued from Enrique's vendetta.

He held his sword out lazily and began to come toward me, closing the fifty feet between us. His eyes seemed to glow like a snake's with the anticipation of killing, and I swear to Perseus that Enrique actually began to hiss as he stalked toward me. As I said, he seemed to me not entirely human – perhaps it was an act, but the man approaching me was for all the world like some sort of half-snake half-man creature from Greek mythology.

Granted, I had been sparring with El Pescador for weeks, but there is a world of difference in practicing and actually fighting for your life. I did note that Enrique was not holding the hilt correctly, or at least the way El Pescador had taught me. And as he drew closer I noted that he was not taking an angled stance. It looked to me like he had no sword training at all, which I surmised might give me at least some advantage.

The problem was I was terrified and he was not.

A situation as dire as this sets the mind on all sorts of paths looking for options, as well as searching vainly for past experience with which to resolve the crisis. Having not had any experience in fighting to save my life, I was short on reference material. Unfortunately, the only thing that came into my head was one of my father's useless sayings, the one about the shorts riding up and not being able to fix the tractor. In that moment, you might be surprised to learn that it suddenly made sense. He was talking about was fear. If you want to fix that tractor you can't be afraid to do it, whether or not your shorts are riding up. I mean, how do the shorts actually prevent you from fixing the tractor? Sure, it's not comfortable, those shorts are wedged way up between your butt cheeks like an owl roosting in the fork of a tree. But damn the shorts, that tractor needs fixing!

Enrique was my broken tractor; my fear was the shorts.

I'm aware that doesn't make perfect sense, but neither did the situation or my father. He possessed a certain insanity that allowed him to be supremely confident no matter what. That's what I needed in that moment, and it was his mantle of insanity that I dredged up from the depths of my psyche for courage.

As I had been taught, I extended my sword straight out at Enrique, looking down the sword at him, hilt and thumb up.

His drooping eyes betrayed some curiosity at my stance and resolve, but I could see by his swagger that he was confident his killer instinct could easily overcome any skill I might have with a blade. *"Hissss."*

Yes, he began to hiss!

He sprinted at me, blade swinging, taking me by surprise, the sun at my back flashing off his blade and blinding me.

Instinctively, I responded with the standard circular parry of my sword, spun and brought my blade full circle toward his side as he rushed past me.

My blade caught his flank and he staggered, stopped, and put a hand to his hip. Blood smeared his hand.

In spite of myself, I grimaced and said: "Good Lord, sorry."

He was incredulous of my apology, and even more so that I had been able to damage him. Of course, he clearly had no idea what he was doing and I at least had some unremarkable defensive moves. Rushing me like that, he could have startled me from reacting but in truth left me with nothing but to do exactly as I was trained.

Pointing my blade at him as before, I circled to his left, away from his blade hand, forcing him to turn with me, my back to the hillside.

Hissss.

He lunged and swung low at my legs and again I parried, this time pinning his blade to the ground. He stumbled as he tried to pull his blade free and I took that opportunity to knee him in the side.

He fell and rolled, dragging his sword with him.

I stepped forward, swung but hit the ground behind him, and then jumped back, my blade ready.

He staggered to his feet, sword in hand, his eyes red with murderous lust.

Hissss!

I circled further left, my back to the cliff, the ocean breeze chilling the sweat on my neck. The way the combat was going, all I had to do was wait for him to attack. He was his own worst enemy in this fight.

He charged again, swinging his blade up at my face.

Mistakenly I swung my blade in the same direction as his slash so did not force his blade down or halt it. I was only able to deflect his blade away from my face.

I swung in a figure eight, coming at him in the opposite direction as he slashed again, caught his blade and stepped toward his left side, my hilt sliding up into his and forcing his blade to the ground in classic form. I was right next to him and could smell his body odor – it was like battery acid.

The maneuver that brings you close to the opponent's side was the one designed to deliver the deathblow with a dagger in my other hand. As I was without a dagger, I rammed my forearm into his face but he shoved back and away at the same time, so my jab had little purchase.

Stumbling backward, his foot caught on the edge of the cliff, and he waved his arms trying to re-center his balance and not fall.

He seemed to teeter there for a long time, like he was doing an imitation of a bird flapping his wings, but it could not have been more than a second before he fell forward onto his knees, his sword on the ground.

This was my moment, victory was at hand, and yet I hesitated.

I'm not a killer, I'm a drinker and an angler and a lover. Killing doesn't suit me, and yet this was something I had to do. The tractor would not be fixed until this hissing freak was dead and I was the one who had to make him that way.

As any professional fighter will tell you, combat is one thing, and winning is another.

My blunder, my pause, allowed him to pick up his sword and launch himself at me – literally, he sprang through the air like a cobra, blade aimed at me, and my defensive parry was no match for the entire weight of his body. I spun away from him, again to his weak left side, his blade grazing my pant leg.

Blood shone brightly on my white pants, and the sight of it brought me the resolve I had lacked in the moment of hesitation.

This was no sparring match; this was the real thing.

He fell to the ground to my right and rolled away from me.

I gave chase.

When he spun to his feet I deftly flanked him, his blade on the far side of his body.

And I lunged.

My blade went in under his left arm, the one with the cast on the hand, and I felt the steel crunch as it slid between his ribs. I could feel the tissue snap as the weapon sliced muscle and then I could feel it punch through into the hollow of his lung.

Many hideous trials had happened on this adventure, and that was one of the worst. Feeling the blade enter his body and to see the look of horror on that weirdly smooth, droopy-eyed face almost eclipsed seeing Elvis die. I am absolutely earnest when I say I felt no sense of victory in that moment, just one of utter revulsion.

He shrieked like banshee, and when I yanked out the blade and sprang back, he coughed a spray of blood into the breeze that sparkled like red glitter in the morning sun.

Half standing, arms tight to his torso, he staggered toward the edge of the cliff.

At the brink, he froze as if he'd been turned to stone.

Without a sound, without even a hiss, he tipped sideways and out of sight.

Gone.

I stood panting, my bloody sword tip resting on the ground. Wild eyed, my ears full of the sound of the waves crashing on the rocks below, the morning sea breeze in my sweaty hair, I took a moment to revel in a moment of calm, the sun warming my face.

I yearned for calm.

The sound of the ocean was replaced by clapping.

To my right and behind me I heard a slow, deliberate hand clapping.

When I turned and squinted toward the sound, I saw El Pescador standing at the crest of the path. Dressed only in a smudged sleeveless undershirt and torn sweat pants, his hair was mussed and he was breathing hard. His old brown hands clapped mechanically: "Olé! Swordsman Linsenbigler, olé!" His voice was hoarse.

He stopped clapping and plucked his sword out of the ground beside him. Shambling down the path toward me, he was limping on his left side. As he came, he took a few practice slashes through the air in front of him: *Swoosh! Swoosh!*

I just watched him come toward me, trying to gauge his mood and intent. My guess was he had narrowly escaped the mansion, possibly by jumping from a window and thus the hurt ankle. The question in my mind was whether he blamed me for the assault, and likely for his downfall.

It was as if he read my mind: "No, I don't blame you for this catastrophe, Mr. Linsenbigler. You were not the cause. They were coming for me eventually anyway. I am diseased, an aging gangster and you are merely a symptom. I have grown old and sentimental, characteristics that are fatal in this business. I should have made my own Manhattans. I should have continued to kill bartenders. Bringing all my captains here? The right thing to do would have been to gather them elsewhere and stage an attack attributable to the opposition and then replaced them all with their lieutenants. You need to clean house occasionally. Perhaps not if you are old and sentimental."

By the way he was waving his sword, I could tell that he had some sparring in mind. Sparing? Likely an actual duel. "We're not going to duel, are we? I know you don't mind killing, Captain, but I do."

He cocked his head and raised his sword, pointing it at me. "Then die."

I stepped back and to the side, toward the rope bridge.

Crossing the bridge seemed like a really bad idea just moments ago. If you have ever been on a rope bridge, you know that they are idiotically unstable. If more than one person crosses, you have to step in cross-synchronized strides to prevent the bridge from swaying. If you want to make it sway for some insane reason, you could easily do so by throwing your weight side to side. So if I crossed the rope bridge and he followed, I could make it difficult for him to cross behind me, or perhaps even cause him to fall off and join Enrique. Not that I looked forward to swinging a bridge like that over a chasm, suspended high above wave-crashed boulders.

"Don't do this, Captain. You have an injured foot, and I'm not accustomed to taking advantage of another man's injury. For whatever reason, if there is one, this is all over. Time to lay down the sword – not pick it up."

Swoosh! He lunged in a feint and slashed the air at me.

"You foolish imposter! You think that after a few weeks you can outmaneuver me in *destreza*? You are nothing but a front man, an actor, my lowly bartender. You are mine to kill."

My father used to say that overconfidence is like an ink pen in your shirt pocket – just waiting to explode and ruin a nice shirt. Wordsmithing aside, he had a point. This old man, like Enrique before him, considered battle with me done deal, and yet I was far younger and in better shape than he. If I circled to El Pescador's left, away from his sword hand, he would never be able to turn fast enough on that ankle to thwart me. And he was gaunt and tired. Yet stabbing an old man? This one, a man I'd come to like?

Yes, but what kind of man had I grown fond of? A self-admitted psychopath willing to kill over a plug nickel or just a bad cocktail. And he just made it clear what he really thought of me. Either that or he was trying to make me angry – and we saw how far anger takes you in a fight, RIP Enrique.

Inwardly, as I backed onto the bridge and glanced down at the roar of the ocean sloshing far below, I wasn't sure I believed what he said about me.

Had you asked me a scant fourscore days prior I would have barked a laugh and bellowed: *But of course I'm an imposter!*

Yet consider what I had been through thus far and managed not to get killed. Many a lesser man, many a lesser angler and cocktailer would be pushing up daisies by this fine juncture, I dare say. How much of a fraud was I now? I guess I was about to find out as my curtain call seemed at hand.

A military helicopter roared overhead and out to sea, and behind me I heard it bank and start to come back around.

Mid-bridge, El Pescador sprang forward and slashed.

I would have followed my training and circled to the right but there was no room on that narrow bridge to do so. The rope handrails impeded wide circular motions of the blade. I realized El Pescador had it figured out that way, too. Yet I managed to parry overhand as the tip of his blade stung my cheek under the left eye.

I leapt backwards away from him and felt the blood begin to tear down my cheek.

The bridge went wild when he lunged, bouncing down about five feet and then up five and angling to the side. I threw my weight back and down to keep from flying off. It was all both of us could do to hang on and not be tossed into the turquoise washing machine below.

In fact, El Pescador lost grip of his sword briefly. When he sprawled across the planks to snatch it, he almost bought himself a one-way ticket to Boulderville.

Yet he clung on and collected himself.

I staggered to my feet before him and scrambled more or less on all fours toward the rocky pinnacle, my guts sloshing around inside me with the motion of the bridge. Another episode like that had the distinct possibility of putting me on that bus to perdition, not to mention vertigo was setting in and there was no way I was going to be able to defend myself on that roller coaster bridge.

The helicopter roared overhead, banking, obviously watching Boone Linsenbigler's imminent demise.

At the pinnacle, I gave the bridge one more try to toss my adversary into the chasm. I grasped the rope handrails, lowered my center of gravity, and swung my body back and forth to destabilize the bridge and slow the old man down or shake him off. Alas, I couldn't get that much purchase on the bridge's weight from the end, and though the bridge swayed it was not enough to stop El Pescador from standing and staggering toward me.

So I backed up and let him come.

What was there that I could use, other than his sprained ankle, to my advantage? He was liable to kill me with a well-timed lunge. He was an expert swordsman even if he was older.

Could I make him angry, use his temper to cloud his judgement?

He limped off the bridge breathing hard, but murder

was still in his dusky eyes. I kept my blade pointed at him, we circled each other, and he launched an attack.

Stepping into me, his hilt connected with mine, and he pushed my blade to the ground.

El Pescador elbowed me hard in the side.

I spun and slashed, but he was ready, steel clanging.

Stumbling on a rock or something, I skipped backwards, conscious that the cliff edge was close. I brought myself to a sudden stop and glanced behind me and down all the way to the surging ocean, which was playfully tossing Enrique's mangled body among the rocks.

Captain came at me as I jumped away from the precipice. My sword circled down onto his thrust. His blade was forced into the ground, causing him to stumble, but he staggered back from the edge of the cliff.

The helicopter swooped low overhead and out over the ocean. I didn't have time to think if it was trying to help or hinder the fight. I was just staying focused on saving my hide.

I took advantage of El Pescador's imbalance by swinging my blade high in a downward chop, but he unexpectedly regained his footing and brought his blade upward at my face from below.

The tip of the blade stung my left cheek again as I wheeled back to his left and further away from the brink.

He barked a laugh of impending victory and leapt forward onto his bad ankle, howling with pain. Yet he delivered another unexpected thrust. My blade was already circling down and I again forced his blade into the ground, and pushed away.

There was a lot of pepper left in this old goat – I'd be lucky to outwit him.

Outwit him? But how?

We paused, opposing blades at arm's length, catching our respective breaths.

Hang on – I already <u>had</u> outwitted him! And letting him know as much should make him angry.

I gasped: "You know, old man, you…you didn't really catch those permit."

He squinted, his chest heaving, and I continued.

"I put crab scent on your flies so you could catch a permit. But you already knew that. You must have because you really don't have what it takes to catch a permit on your own, you needed this imposter, me, Boone Linsenbigler to let you think you had."

"Lies!" He growled, brow furrowed and face red just like the first time I mentioned permit over Rob Roys.

"Why do you think I always managed to hold your fly just before you cast? It was because I was smearing them with crab scent."

"Lies!" He roared.

I think I mentioned that haunted permit men get pretty agitated.

"So you don't have a permit and you don't have a grand slam! And even if you kill me you will die never having done it! I tricked you!"

He spat and charged forward.

I darted to his left, my steel meeting his, forcing him to turn on his bad ankle just once more.

He tried to pivot on the ankle and it gave way. In a bid to keep his balance, his sword swung out away from me, leaving his left flank wide open to my blade.

Without hesitation, I spun and brought my sword to bear in an upward thrust.

It didn't penetrate the same way it had with Enrique – I think I was too exhausted to feel anything about it. But in it went, lower, under his rib cage and up into his chest cavity.

Deep.

He faltered away from me, blood staining his side.

Dropping his sword, he fell hard onto his knees by a wooden cross and flowers, blood surging from his nostrils. He toppled onto his side.

The helicopter thundered directly overhead, hovering.

Stepping up to where El Pescador lay gasping, I watched as he convulsed in pain.

It was only then that I noticed the knee-high wooden cross and flowers, and as I looked around at the ornamental flowers and shrubs, I realized this pinnacle of rock was a shrine.

The rope bridge was access to a shrine.

I circled around the dying gangster and read the name on the cross: *Esmerelda.*

El Pescador didn't open his eyes or say anything.

Convulsing again, he shuddered and groaned his last: dead.

Had he really meant to kill me, or had he come out here to die on Esmerelda's grave? I would never know the answer to that.

I may have been relieved that I had managed to ram that blade into a man bent on killing me, but I was not beyond realizing that this particular man could have been much more, had violence not corrupted him. Had not his Esmerelda been murdered and the cycle of retribution, hate and greed begun those many years ago.

Captain had the soul of an angler, a lover and a cocktailer trapped in that of a tortured butcher.

And he in turn forced another man with the soul of an angler, a lover and a cocktailer into a butcher: me.

How many of his people had I killed or maimed? Five? The fact that I wasn't sure was chilling.

On that windswept pinnacle in the bright tropical sun, the aquamarine blue ocean all around, waves crashing below, I wept openly as I stood over El Pescador's body, the helicopter hovering over us like the very wings of Death.

Here's one for you, Dad: *Love the sinner, hate the sin.*

CHAPTER 23

WHERE TO BEGIN WITH HOW IT ENDED?

My first question to my DEA and Mexican Marine liberators was how on earth did the Guatemalan military collude to take down their benefactor El Pescador aka Alberto Ramirez de Ortiz? As it happened, the Guatemalan military didn't know anything about it. It would seem that the electorate of Guatemala had seen fit to recently elect a president on an anti-corruption platform, and this new president was actually – for a change – intent on embracing that mandate. As such, he had met secretly with the U.S. consul and representatives of the DEA to trade intelligence on who and where the drug kingpins were in his country, the ones that were corrupting his country's apparatus with drug money and bribes. The result of the meeting was that this president, through an executive action of debatable legitimacy, suspended sovereignty over several areas of his country so that foreign agencies – notably the Mexican Marines and the DEA – were afforded a one-day opportunity to come into Guatemala and make arrests and extraditions by any means necessary. Said president, in his wisdom, arranged for a Military Appreciation Day, complete with parades, the same day to prevent his own armies from catching wind of what was transpiring until it was too late.

While popular with the electorate, and heavily debated in the conservative and liberal Guatemalan press, this suspension of sovereignty and tipping of the apple cart was not wildly popular with the military. In a gesture of reassurance, *El Presidente* decreed that amnesty was in order for those who had accepted bribes in the past, to include those in the military. Whether this president would be forcibly deposed or mysteriously die in a plane crash had yet to be seen.

El Pescador's little sales meeting and orgy had finally been arranged on that same day precisely because the navy was pulling back and turning a blind eye to the many incursions of their territorial waters by aircraft and boats carrying the 'sales staff.' This fortuitous decision provided the Mexican Marines and DEA with a distracted target and lots of noise to cover their nighttime ascent up the steep hillsides of that island redoubt and thus position themselves for an early-morning attack on the compound.

The invading forces had no idea I was on that island drinking and fishing and fencing and frolicking with Karina. The Mexican Marines had found my phone in that Utopia Lodge flats boat adrift and all concerned assumed the worst. It was damned unlikely that they would have imagined I had been taken into service by El Pescador as a bartender and fishing guide. So when the helicopter was hovering over my sword fight, they thought I looked like Boone Linsenbigler but could not imagine how I could be.

As luck would have it, my wounds were relatively slight. The slash to my leg was fixed with twenty sutures, though I have some numbness there due to nerve damage. A few sutures were also required for the crisscross blade cuts to my left cheek. Along with my rakish mustache, I now had what in the parlance of Otto von Bismarck would henceforth be called my 'dueling scar.' You can imagine how excited my Bismarck homage – shaped like crossed swords – made Terry. As did the helicopter surveillance video of me sword fighting at that rocky pinnacle, proof positive that I was a first-rate swordsman, which in turn had every real (or imagined) swordsman up in arms – literally – challenging me to duels on social media. The media storm surrounding my survival was palpable, if not a little alarming, at least to me.

Second most pressing question on my mind was the fate of the Utopia Lodge captives. Astoundingly, El Pescador actually had the captives released, though regrettably the DEA agent Tom had been savaged by interrogators (while Diego was forced to watch.) Both survived, as did all the others, and I have been credited with saving their lives as it was likely they all would have been killed as a customary yet grisly calling card of Mexican cartels everywhere. That I was able to free them in exchange for my own captivity came as a great relief to me as it made my ordeal with El Pescador in sum total worth it. Imagine if that had not been the case? I would have felt – and been – the complete fool, the jester at court rather than a white knight in waiting.

Third? What had become of Karina? Both she and Paola completely vanished, and without last names, or even likely correct first names, the search was futile. She could have reached out to me – the civilized world knew who I was upon finding that I had escaped with my life yet again. I suppose my fame may have intimidated her, or perhaps sharing the limelight with me would have made plain the fact that she was a courtesan. Then again, what would our relationship have been like transposed from a tropical hideaway with few cares onto the real world and the media breathing down my neck? I'm enough of an adult to know that there is not just one person out there who you can love and have love you back, and that the circumstances of a relationship matter a great deal. It was with a heavy heart that I abandoned efforts to find that lovely girl.

It may have been for the best that I never found Karina, but my heart was going to take some convincing.

Which leads us to another kind of internal damage from what have since been labeled my 'exploits' – or worse – 'adventures.' I had come to understand how our men in uniform who serve and distinguish themselves disdain being called a hero. For them, they are enacting their training and then under dire circumstance do what needs to be done to protect others around them or just save their own skin. That's not bravery to the 'hero', that's just suppressing fear and taking action simply because it needs doing, and I think that's an important distinction. It wasn't as if I girded my loins, raised my sword and rode into a volley of bullets and almost certain demise. Those bastards came after me with swords, I didn't seek them out, and the only reason I'm here at all is because I found the opportunity to run away and try to hide. Look at it! Most of what I did throughout the entire imbroglio was not lead the charge but lead a hasty if unsuccessful retreat. Otherwise, I was pressed into service. Unless I am mistaken, there is nothing brave or heroic about becoming someone's bartender and fishing guide. Yet at the same time, my actions were laudable by benefit of a desirable result. So not so much 'hero' as 'you lucky, crafty bastard!'

Ah, but America and the world love and want a hero, and none more so than Conglomerated Beverages. As such, I determined that the best way to be a hero was to redirect credit to the real heroes – if there are any at all on God's green earth – at the DEA and the Mexican Marines. These are the ones who raise their sword and charge into battle. So if through my own fame I was able to shed light on their accomplishments and sacrifice, so be it. I was on every talk show you can imagine and I made it my business to credit the bravery of professionals and talk down my own deeds.

A month after my return, Terry Orbach and Conglomerated had been pushing my brand so hard that I sensed backlash during some of my interviews – the show hosts sensed ultimately that I was just a shill, a front man, a sharp trying to sell more products. I suppose my hostage video in which I mentioned the 'fine people at Conglomerated' had not sat well over time. The suggestions were subtle at first, like about where my New Jersey accent went, and weren't I just a middling free-lance fly fishing writer in disguise? This perturbed me if for no other reason than it was, in essence, true. As I have previously noted, I resent it when Conglomerated thinks that they own me and can tell me who I am who I am not. At the same time, I have recognized internally all along that my beginnings were humble.

Are we all not a work in progress? How to express this, and to best divest the media's growing notion that I was a fraud, eluded me. That is until a certain interview on a late night talk show, the transcript of which went like this after the pleasantries were dispensed:

Host: "So Boone, can I put you on the spot?"

Me: *"Do your worst."*

Host: *"Who are you, really? We know this is your name, and that you invented your brand of cocktail bitters and were kidnapped and all that, but how is it you are now suddenly some sort of adventurer? Wasn't this all created by Conglomerated to sell products with your name on it?"*

Me: *"I have said all along that I am not a hero. At the same time, I am not who I was, and I dare say none of us are. I'm sure you weren't born a talk show host, and yet here you are!"*

Host: *"Yes, but I'm an entertainer, I'm in show business. Aren't you just acting, trying to be the new Hemmingway or a Man's Man or something?"*

Me: *"One might surmise as much. Yet the truth is that…well, look, we all have the potential to be something more than we are, we learn and grow, and regardless of where you come from or where you've been, there's nothing phony in living up to your potential, of making the most of yourself, or even of reinventing yourself into what you want to be. That seems to me to be the American ideal. As for being a 'man's man' I think that's rather chauvinistic and beside the point. I don't think I'm some sort of template for what it is to be manly as much as a template for someone who lives life large. Nothing exclusive to men in that. Get off the couch and go explore. Put down the video game where you pretend to be sword fighting and go learn how to sword fight. Click off that porno and go find the love of your life. Get off that barstool, invite some friends to your home, and make them your signature cocktail. Go sailing, or scuba diving, or race car driving – but get out there and live life, not virtual reality, but reality reality."*

Host: *"And drink a lot, right?"*

Me: *"In that regard, here is what I admonish: Earn your cocktails! Make your life toast-worthy for you shan't have another. There's only the one life, and you are made keenly aware of that every time you almost lose that one life you have."*

Host: "That's quite a speech, Boone, but not everybody can be famous."

Me: "Good Lord, I would hope not! I can say with all candor that fame means nothing to me and it should be quite plain to anybody who reads the tabloids that it is fool's gold, it isn't what makes anybody happy, usually quite the contrary."

Host: "Then why are you here? Aren't you here because you are famous?"

Me: "I was invited to this show because I have been through a harrowing experience. From that experience, I have learned a great deal that's worth sharing."

Host: "A cocktail recipe?"

Me: "I know you're a comedian and so must make jokes, but I'm being serious when I say that shows like this give me the opportunity to showcase the selfless people who work in law enforcement and are the real heroes. My conviction in that regard comes from having seen it firsthand, and because they saved my bacon and I owe them my life. I've also learned that fame should not be seen as an end unto itself. Don't spend your time trying to be famous and 'go viral' for that alone, it is a hollow accomplishment. If you actually want to be famous, you are barking up the wrong tree. You should want to live life passionately, whether that's about your family and kids or exploring jungles. You should be a famously good human being, a famous husband and father, and live a famously good life. As for cocktails: if you've lived life well and honorably, I'd say you've earned a famously good drink."

Host: [Applauding with the audience.] Well said, Boone. I told you I was going to put you on the spot, and you told me to do my worst!"

Me: "My only other message is that I see the popularity of violent video games and it saddens me as it did not before. As someone who has actually witnessed people being killed, and with these two hands killed people, I can tell you it is not enjoyable, it is an excruciating and inexplicably wretched experience. It frightens *me that anybody could see it as an entertainment as an end unto itself."*

Host: "I've got you now, Boone. It's being reported that Conglomerated is in discussions with a number of gaming developers to sell the rights to your adventure for a video game."

Me: "They can talk to whomever they like, that's their privilege. The fact of the matter is that my contract does not relinquish control of the gaming rights to me or my life. And I can guarantee you and the public that I will not sell those rights to anybody."

Good Lord, who knew Ol' Boonie could be such a bombastic moralist? And yet I meant every word.

So there you have it. I found my soapbox and concretized who I had become in that interview. It all came together for me, and frankly, I think it saved my reputation as well as the credibility of Conglomerated's brand. Though by all accounts, Terry was aghast at my trouncing the idea of selling the gaming rights, and just about had a stroke because I had drifted 'off message.' That said, Conglomerated quickly pounced on a new battle cry for the brand and thereafter printed a million promotional T-shirts imprinted with:

BRIAN M. WIPRUD

EARN YOUR COCKTAILS

EPILOGUE

IT WAS AROUND THANKSGIVING that I was compelled to hang up my overcoat in my new penthouse apartment in Brooklyn and take a cab to LaGuardia for a flight to Nassau. I had been called to testify before the Judiciary of the Bahamas in the case against Carlos Rivera, the Banana Cay Lodge manager who, as a Bahamian national, was subject to prosecution of his crimes as drug smuggler under their flag. (Miguel was charged along with Carlos, but had died from that martini, never awaking from his coma.)

I did not much relish a return to Nassau so soon, and I had vowed to redirect my fishing trips well clear of the Bahamas and Mexico for the foreseeable future. Yet I felt compelled to tie up this loose end, the one that came as close as just about anybody to killing yours truly.

Conglomerated had of course supplied me with the finest counsel money could buy in Nassau to advise me, and he sat next to me in court in robes and a powdered wig like the rest of the magistrates and barristers in the paneled room. Having lived through the ordeal, I didn't much relish retelling it, yet did so in the plodding fashion one comes to expect of judicial systems everywhere. Dull stuff, at least for me, though I was kept entertained by Carlos from across the room. A once-handsome man, the side of his neck and jowl resembled a plate of dried spaghetti marinara. Nerve damage and an infection had rendered him mute, yet that did not prevent him from communicating his feelings toward me through the daggers in his eyes.

After two days, I was released from further obligation to the court on Thanksgiving Day. I returned to my hotel room at the Trident Club, the same fine lodgings where the Japanese girl had done such excellent therapeutic work on me. No, I had not engaged her services. I was there strictly on business and just wanted to jet home, though the prospect of returning home for the holidays held little appeal. My only family is my sister Crocket and we hardly ever saw each other. I was feeling at loose ends, and I still wasn't over Karina to the extent that I felt like being particularly close to anybody else. To be honest, I was a little lonely. Travel is fun, and being a celebrity is exciting to some extent, but I admit at times to a yearning for the creature comforts of an actual home and hearth, Brooklyn penthouse with gas-burning fireplace notwithstanding. Such was the life of this bachelor that holidays were solemn affairs that were tolerated rather than enjoyed.

I went down to the bar and ordered a Manhattan the way I like it. Or used to like it. The taste brought back some bitter memories of El Pescador and Karina.

Pulling myself up by my bootstraps, I called for a car to Café Picasso, my favorite place in Nassau, the one with all the plants. I set myself up with a bottle of Dom Perignon and *cheviche piccante* at a table for two in the corner surrounded once again by the establishment's familiar tropical flora.

Snap out of it, Linsenbigler, you've nothing of which to complain. Drink up, get a good night's sleep and jet back home first thing in the morning.

As I was served my second glass of champagne, I spied a saucy woman with short blonde hair enter the room. She was not dressed for the place, but was instead in fatigue pants and camo T-shirt. This displeased the maître d', and he intercepted her.

By thunder! It was Tanya!

The maître d' was interrogating her as she scanned the room and suddenly saw me.

I smiled and stood.

Her eyes went wide and she shouted angrily: "Get down!"

The command was so forceful that I immediately obeyed and reseated myself – just in time to hear a whoosh over my head and the crash of potted palms on one side.

I jumped away out of my seat, turned and steadied myself on a chair at the neighboring table.

Behind my table in the bushes was the spaghettied and growling countenance of Carlos. He was in a prison jumpsuit holding a big red fire axe, a handcuff dangling from one wrist. He'd escaped.

Axe over his head, he charged from the brush, knocking my table and Dom Perignon onto the floor.

Backed against the neighboring table with nowhere to go, I grasped and raised a little café chair – just in time to meet the fire axe coming down on my head.

Around me, patrons shrieked and scattered away.

As with sword fighting, the dynamic of the situation to me was visceral: the axe was heavy and he was hacking with it and not keeping it in motion as you would a sword. He was wasting time and energy hauling it back, thereby creating opportunities for me to thrust.

I rolled to the side, trying to flank him as would a swordsman, keeping my chair in motion and cuffing him in the flank as he raised the axe for another blow.

He reeled from the impact, knocking over tables, glassware shattering, and silverware clattering about the floor.

He shook off the blow and hauled back for a sweeping chop at my chest.

The axe blade hit the chair and split it in two, leaving me holding the back and two legs.

I spun, swinging the remainder of the chair.

Before Carlos could re-cock his axe, I flanked him and thrust the chair forward.

The chair caught him amidships, one of the legs finding its mark in his sternum with a resounding *thud*.

He tripped backward over a fallen chair into some tables and onto the floor.

Tanya rushed past me, leapt over a table and onto Carlos, a wine bottle raised in one hand.

Nothing like hitting a man square in the face with a wine bottle to put him down.

She stood, panting and before she could say anything police were rushing into the place.

The maître d' was standing behind me, his face in a rictus of horror.

I turned to him and held up a finger: "Check please."

ONCE THINGS WERE SORTED OUT with the police, I grabbed Tanya by the hand and made haste out the back door of Café Picasso to avoid any press. I bee-lined for the balcony of a double-decker bar and restaurant overlooking the cruise ship slips and harbor. Fortunately, there were no cruise ships there at the time – otherwise the place would have been rife with tourists. As it was, we had the balcony almost all to ourselves, a candle in a seashell lamp illuminating our small table.

The preliminaries of how she happened to be at Café Picasso had been dispensed with: Tanya was temporarily still stationed in Nassau as a 'liaison' which meant she did very little except wait for her next assignment from the DEA, probably at their academy in Quantico, Virginia. As a liaison, she was on the Bahamian Royal Police emergency text list and so heard about Carlo's escape from prison transport immediately when it occurred. She also knew from the newspapers that I was in town for my court date to testify against Carlos, and so called my hotel to find out where I was and warn me. When they said I had called a cab to Café Picasso, she jumped in a taxi herself and came down to warn me personally. She saw Carlos coming up behind me with the axe. I must have mentioned to Carlos that I ate at Picasso whenever I came to Nassau and so Carlos bee-lined it there and got lucky. Or not, as the case may be.

Quite the memorable Thanksgiving dinner, I'd say.

Tanya and I had said very little since the preliminaries. I think we were both trying to recover our better graces after the latest in a string of harrowing events on my behalf. I know I did, anyway, I was pretty jacked up and the only words I wanted to speak were to the waitress: "Double Pussers on the rocks, please, with lime."

She ordered the same.

I eyed our surroundings: "You don't suppose there are any other homicidal axe murderers out hunting for Boone Linsenbigler tonight, do you?"

She favored me with a weary ironic smile. "You're pretty much limited to one axe murderer a night around here, so I think you're good, you can relax. You know, you handled yourself pretty well with Carlos. He totally had the drop on you with an axe and you beat him off with that little chair."

I laughed mirthlessly. "Unlike the last time you saw me I've had a crash course in not allowing myself to be sliced up by all sorts of lunatics."

Our drinks came. I raised my glass, and the candlelight danced in her questioning, eyes. She beat me to the oath: "Boone, here's to adventure and survival."

I clinked. "I'll drink to that under protest. I want no part of adventure, certainly not of the kind where my odds of survival are so slim."

She brushed her short blond hair behind one ear, looking at the candle. "I guess you sort of got a taste of what my life has been like."

"I did indeed." I took a deep sip, and let the embers of molasses warm my chilled heart. "You know when you said you needed to focus on whether my name was real in order to stay focused through stressful violent encounter? When Enrique came at me with a sword, I knew I was outmatched, not in swordsmanship but in the force of will it takes to murder someone. My father had a number of nonsensical sayings, so I took one of those and made it my mantra. It worked. Funny, I didn't remember at the time you said to do that, though I imagine it came to me subliminally."

"Maybe it had nothing to do with me – maybe it's just something that happens naturally to let certain people overcome high-stress situations. What was the saying?"

I squinted at my glass by the candlelight, admiring the reddish amber tones of the rum and ice. Then I said with exaggerated import: "When your shorts ride up there's no fixing the tractor."

She began to laugh, those crazy eyes bright, her lovely full lips forming a smile. "No! What does it mean?"

"I didn't know until that moment that it meant you can't let those uncomfortable shorts prevent you from doing what you need to do."

She thumped the end of the table tilted her head back and roared. "That's ridiculous! Insane!"

I laughed some myself, and she cocked her head. "Boone, you OK?"

"I'll be OK, Tanya. Like you, I just took a bit of a bashing in all this. I may have become better at fending for myself, but seeing people die and killing people is just a bit much. The worst part, in some ways, is that after killing Enrique, it was easier to kill El Pescador. I now know how to find the resolve to kill and I'm not sure how I feel about that."

"*Pfft.*" She twirled her drink with a finger, nodding slowly. "Feel? How does it feel to be alive? That's the feeling you should be thinking about. That scar on your cheek should remind you of that feeling every time you look in the mirror. Looks a lot better than the Black Beard braids, for your info."

"How are your scars, Tanya?"

"Still a little bothersome when I sleep, but I'm OK, I take a licking and keep ticking. You know, the only reason I knew which hotel to call to track you down tonight was because I heard you were going to be in town and so I called around."

"Blast, you should have rung me up and we could have gone to dinner. What were you waiting for, girl, an axe murderer? Apparently so! And we could have had dinner someplace else, a nicer place that doesn't have axe murderers lurking in the shrubbery."

She folded her arms, looking at the candle again. "I guess I was a little resentful, deep down. You accomplished what I couldn't, in a way. You arrived, pushed me aside, and then ran off with El Pescador, the top guy himself, and even managed to kill him yourself. I mean, that's just ridiculous."

I leaned in and put my hand on her smooth warm arm. "Tanya, if I had it to do over, I would relinquish the honors in a New York minute."

She put her hand on mine and looked me in the eyes. "Thanks, Boone, I know you weren't seeking glory. But always remember that what you went through had a purpose, that because of what you did bad people met with justice, and that's what counts."

Grinning, I shook my head. "What nonsense, girl! What rot! This is what matters." I leaned in farther, my hand on her cheek, and kissed her gently on those full, cushiony lips, her tongue touching mine gingerly.

When I stopped to look at her, she had tears in her eyes, and was biting her lip. She blinked at me and said: "Well, maybe I don't know as much about what matters as I should."

I smiled gently. "That ship hasn't sailed, Tanya."

"Can you stay?"

I blinked back at her. "Stay?"

"In Nassau. Last time, in the hospital, you said you were footloose. I'm footloose here until January when I have to report to Quantico."

"I am staying in Nassau...oh, you mean longer than...what did you have in mind, dear heart?"

"See, you called me *dear heart*. I don't think anybody has ever called me that." She looked away at the ship terminal, then at anything else she could lay her big eyes on before they came back to me. "Can you stay until Christmas?"

"Christmas?"

"I put a little tree all decorated on the front of my sailboat, the one I live on at the marina. Be nice to share that with someone for a change. Maybe give presents? Isn't that what normal people do? You could give me sword fight lessons on the boat deck around the tree. Or am I being ridiculous? I'm being ridiculous. I'm sorry, I shouldn't have asked... *Pfft*, I should go."

I reached out a hand and placed my index finger over those lovely lips, both to prevent her from standing and to quiet her.

She blinked those violet eyes at me curiously.

With my other hand, I put the glass of rum in her hand.

Then I raised mine:

"Sword lessons around the Christmas tree!" I clinked her glass. "I'll drink to that!"

BEHOLD – THE SEQUELS!

"LINSENBIGLER THE BEAR"

"HAIL, LINSENBIGLER!"

ABOUT THE AUTHOR

Brian M. Wiprud's previous novels have earned starred reviews from Kirkus, Publisher's Weekly and Library Journal. Winner of the 2003 Lefty Award, he has been nominated for Barry, Shamus and Choice awards, and been an Independent Bookseller's and regional bestseller. His books are available variously in large print, audiobook and Russian and Japanese translations, and have been optioned for film. He has also been widely published in fly fishing magazines to include American Angler, Fly Fisherman, Fly Tyer, Massachusetts Wildlife and Saltwater Fly Fishing.

Previous Novels
The Clause
Ringer
Buy Back
Feelers
Tailed
Crooked
Sleep with the Fishes
Stuffed
Pipsqueak

Made in the USA
Middletown, DE
09 August 2020